The PERFECT AFFAIR

Claire Dyer is a published poet. Her collection, *Eleven Rooms*, is published by Two Rivers Press. She lives in Reading.

Also by Claire Dyer

The Moment

The
PERFECT
AFFAIR
CLAIRE DYER

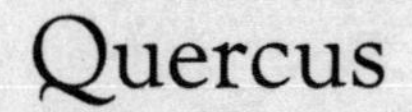
Quercus

First published in Great Britain in the year of 2014 by

Quercus
55 Baker Street
7th Floor, South Block
London W1U 8EW

A CIP catalogue record for this book is available from the British Library

ISBN 978 1 78206 483 1
EBOOK ISBN 978 1 78206 484 8

10 9 8 7 6 5 4 3 2 1

Printed and bound in Great Britain by Clays Ltd, St Ives plc

Typeset by Ellipsis Digital Limited, Glasgow

For my mother
Margaret Eustace
(1933–1970)

Unlike us,
They knew how, and when, to detach themselves
From the love that moves the sun and the other stars.

'Karlsbad Caverns', Ted Hughes

And like music on the waters
Is thy sweet voice to me

'There Be None of Beauty's Daughters',
George Gordon (Lord) Byron

Winter

So, when it happens it is, of course, inevitable, as it had been since that moment their hands touched the summer before.

'Well,' Rose says when the three of them get back from the races, 'I think I'll go upstairs. It's been a long day.'

'Are you sure?' Eve asks, bending down to kiss Rose's cheek. 'Won't you have a hot drink, warm yourself up a bit?'

Eve straightens and looks across at Myles. He's standing by his desk. The late-afternoon sun is falling in layers through the louvred shutters, making a pattern on the floor.

'No thank you, dear. It's been lovely, so lovely, such a wonderful reminder of long ago, but I think I'll go up, settle in for the evening, rest these weary bones.' Rose laughs a little as she says this and turns to go.

The door closes softly behind her and Eve and Myles can

hear her slow footsteps as she climbs up to her flat. The quiet she leaves behind her is astonishing.

'Would you like a coffee, or . . .' there is a pause, 'tea perhaps?' Myles asks, his voice travelling across the room in gulps, 'if you can stay a while, that is. Or do you need to get back?'

Eve looks at her watch. She can stay. Andrew won't be back until much later so she nods; it's a tiny nod, barely perceptible, but Myles must have seen it because he begins to move towards the kitchen. As he passes by her she can smell horses. Even though they'd only visited the paddock a few times, the sweet scent of the animals seems to cling to his clothes and when he's gone she sees the strength of them, the sun glinting on their coats, and it reminds her of summer, the summer before and the light threaded through Myles's hair, the light lodged in his eyes, and she's aware she's not breathing. She gasps.

'You OK?' he asks, switching on the kettle.

She hadn't realised he'd heard her.

'Yes, fine.'

As she waits she touches a few things on his desk; she doesn't move anything, just lets her fingers brush the lid of his laptop, the back of the chair he sits in when he writes. The sun is lower now, the central heating has come on; she cannot hear Rose move around upstairs, and outside, the sound of the traffic in Belle Avenue is sketchy and muffled.

Then she senses him behind her. He leans in and puts the mugs on the desk next to the laptop and a blue folder with the number nine written on it in emphatic black ink. His movements knock a pen which rolls very slightly and she reaches out to stop it, then turns to face him, the edge of the desk pressing into the back of her thighs, and his arms are around her and it feels like this is what perfect is.

His lips, when they kiss her, are warm and dry and the kiss travels through her sternum and into her belly; the space between her legs starts to howl.

'You OK?' he asks again.

She nods. She cannot speak.

This is the inevitable moment, not what will follow, or the fact they're here in his flat on this December afternoon and Rose is upstairs and that she knows. This is the culmination of the emails, texts, calls, the snatched lunches they've had together in anonymous bars and tucked-away pubs, that November evening in the hotel, all the times they'd told themselves they were nothing more than good friends but when her skin had hummed at the nearness of him.

It's getting dark in the room now as he cups her face in his hands. She loves the shape of him, everything about him; hadn't thought she would ever feel anything like this again. But it's here, it's like instinct and, in this particular place at this particular time, it is totally and irretrievably right.

And there's no guilt. Not yet.

The mugs stay on the desk, the streetlamp flickers on and the light in the room becomes like old gold. He leads her to the bed and afterwards she will remember his mouth on her breasts, the smooth length of him inside her, the rise and fall of him and the rhythm and release of him, the warmth of his skin on hers. She will remember the fist unfurling inside her when she comes and that she heard the sound of the sea.

This is perfect, she thinks later as she watches his face on the pillow next to her. His eyes are closed and his breathing is steady. For now she really believes they will be good at this; that this will be something good.

The summer before

1

Eve is puzzled. At the top of the staircase she had been happy. But, by the time she reaches the hallway, she is filled with a kind of fury, her teeth feel too large for her mouth and all she wants to do is run.

But instead she says, 'Oh,' as she steps into the kaleidoscope of colours streaming through the stained-glass panels in the front door of Rose's house. 'Oh,' she says again, as she opens the door and the solid heat of this July day presses up against her.

The man on the other side of the door moves back a fraction. They look at one another and, for a second, time slows to a crawl. 'You must be . . .' Eve says.

'Yes,' he replies, holding up a carton of milk and a banana as if by way of explanation. 'Myles,' he says, 'new tenant, downstairs flat.'

'The writer?' Eve asks.

Rose had said he would be moving his stuff in and then going on holiday with his family for a couple of weeks. 'He writes those DCI Pletheroe stories,' she'd said, 'and he's going to do his writing here, said he wanted it to be like having a job, you know, like going out to work, that he couldn't concentrate at home, what with his children, the dog.' She'd hesitated, then added, 'Suits me just fine,' and had smiled at Eve, her eyes shining. Eve had stooped down to kiss her on the cheek and said, 'Oh, if you're sure, then I'm sure it'll be fine too.'

'Yes,' the man who is the writer of the DCI Pletheroe mysteries and whose name is Myles now says to Eve, 'the writer. For my sins!' and he laughs.

Eve likes his laugh and his smile; likes the way his hair is unruly and tumbles on to his forehead and how the sun lights up the glints of gold in his stubble. He has the most amazing eyes, she thinks. She is, she realises, no longer angry and the swiftness of this change back to happy makes her dizzy.

'I'm Eve.'

There is a pause, and in this pause Myles looks at the milk and banana and says, 'Refreshments! For later.'

They swap places as Eve steps out of the door. Myles is still smiling.

It's two o'clock and the sun is at its most savage. Eve should be getting back to work and is actually running a little late, but it'd been so lovely sitting on the veranda at the back of Rose's first-floor flat; the shade cast by the house had been gentle and kind. She and Rose had eaten the sandwiches Eve had brought and drunk Rose's lemonade: made from real lemons, it was tart and cold on their tongues and Eve had been content. At that time all had been well.

The veranda and the set of steps leading down into Rose's garden are made of metal and are painted black. There's a small platform between the seventh and eighth steps on which Rose keeps fuchsias in pots; their heavy flower heads bright red against the ironwork. They had trembled as Eve had moved the chairs and positioned the low table so she and Rose could sit down to eat, and had watched Eve carefully as she'd laid the table with small plates made of porcelain so delicate it was almost see-through. As she'd sat down, the ice in the jug of lemonade had cracked and popped and it was as though the fuchsia blooms were listening to this and nodding their heads in approval.

Now, it's as though it was hours, not minutes, since Eve and Rose had chatted companionably as they'd had their lunch and, standing on the path with this man's shape dark in the doorway, Eve can't remember what they'd said, only that the small patch of sky above Rose's house had been blue like cobalt is blue and the air had smelled petrolly, thick with fumes and summer, and that the bird-song had been insistent.

'Ah, refreshments,' Eve says to Myles, laughing a little. She has no idea why, but it seems the best thing she can do. 'I must be getting back to work, I guess.' As if I have any other choice, she thinks.

'Me, too,' Myles replies, reaching out the hand that's not holding the milk and banana.

He makes to close the door.

At the self-same moment Eve reaches out her hand, the one that's not holding the bag she'd brought the sand-wiches in, and pulls the door to. Their fingers touch.

'Oh,' they both say together.

It's only a fleeting touch, no more than a hover of skin on skin, but they both snatch their hands away as if the wood of the door is on fire.

Then Myles closes the door and Eve walks down the path to the gate and Belle Avenue. She doesn't look back, but imagines him standing on the other side of the door looking through the coloured glass panels as she fades from view. The gate-handle creaks as she lifts it. She steps on to the pavement. Her car is parked a little way down the road and the space outside Rose's house has now been taken by a light green Mercedes sports car; an old one, by the look of it. Eve says the word 'vintage' under her breath as she unlocks the door of her battered Polo which her daughter, Jodie, says is the colour a cheap purple felt pen would make on bright yellow card, but which had been known simply as 'Blue' when Andrew had bought it for them back in 1997, when Jodie had been three.

Eve drives back to work without knowing that Rose had been watching from the upstairs window. The house is Edwardian, semi-detached and was where Rose's parents had once lived, was where Rose had grown up, and Eve also doesn't know that Rose had seen her meet Myles on the doorstep, seen the carton of milk and the banana he'd been carrying and how their hands had touched.

Eve doesn't turn the radio on and doesn't notice this either.

Later, in the kitchen of her own house in Byron Road, Eve pauses as she slices carrots into matchsticks for a stir fry. She's already prepared the chicken and cut up the peppers, has picked out the seeds, which kept sticking to her vegetable knife. She is hot and tired. The meal seemed an easy choice, but it isn't. It's fiddly and time-consuming. The day outside the window is exhausted and seems to have collapsed on to the tinder-dry grass. The children next door are playing swing ball and she can hear their laughter; in fact she envies them the lightness of it. Somewhere a dog is barking and a siren is wailing limply in the distance. She has consciously not thought about meeting

Rose's tenant all afternoon. She didn't think of it when she was at work, taking the minutes in the departmental team meeting, or when she chatted to Stella from Accounts at the coffee point, and she didn't think of it when she pulled up on the drive, walked into her hall and stopped to listen to the house's silence which, it seemed, had the weight of the day's heat stored up in it.

But, she is thinking of it now and she's remembering his eyes and how that touch, that briefest of touches, had felt and she's puzzled again, this time by how much it meant, how furious she'd suddenly been and then how differently his touch had made her feel, just for that specific moment, just as their fingers had touched one another rather than the door. She does not understand this. It shouldn't make her feel different, should it? There should be no surprises left, not now, not after all these years of being married, being a mother, living here in this house with its garden and windows and wooden garage door. She's here and this is what's real: this kitchen, the table where she, Andrew and Jodie sit to have their meals, the rosemary bush growing just outside the back door. She takes sprigs from it when she's cooking a joint of lamb. 'You're being ridiculous,' she tells herself and reapplies herself with vigour to the carrot in front of her.

Then she hears Jodie say, 'Mum?' and she turns to face her daughter, wonders how long she's been standing there and whether what she'd just said had been loud enough to hear.

'Oh, hello, love,' Eve says. 'Sorry, I was in a world of my own there. When did you get back? I didn't hear you come in.'

'Only a minute or two ago,' Jodie says, leaning against the wall.

Eve glances at her impossibly beautiful daughter, at her smooth long legs, at her hair which is thick and dark and reaches to her waist, and she marvels anew at how she and Andrew could have produced something this wonderful. Her own height has always been something to which she has never quite become reconciled. She's never been able to sashay or drape her long thin arms and legs in the way a supermodel would and which, at five foot eleven, she really could and should be able to. Nor has she ever got used to the size of her hands and feet; they too seem to have lives of their own. Her only saving graces, or so Eve believes, are her hair, which like Jodie's is thick, dark and meaningfully long, and her eyes, which in a rare moment of lyricism Andrew once described as the colour of thick-cut marmalade.

'And how was your day?' she now asks her daughter.

'Oh, fine. It was so hot in the shop, though, and the heat makes everything sticky.'

Jodie is doing volunteer work in a charity shop in town

while she waits for her A-level results. She's taken five of them and had, by the end, worked herself to a standstill. This beautiful, amazing daughter of hers is now on the cusp of something momentous. Only a few more weeks of waiting and then they'll both know what's going to happen next.

'I'm doing us a stir fry,' Eve says now as she tips handfuls of the carrots into the wok.

'Oh, didn't I say I won't be in for dinner tonight?' Jodie says, whipping her phone out of her shirt pocket and staring at the screen. 'We're going down to the river, me, Tash and that lot. Someone's ordering pizza and one of the boys is bringing his guitar. Thought I'd told you.'

'No, don't think so, but it doesn't matter. Your dad'll be home soon, anyway. Keep in touch, won't you, though, and take some insect stuff; you'll be bitten to blazes otherwise.'

'Yeah, oh, all right,' Jodie says, tapping the keys on her phone, a smile playing at the corner of her mouth that has nothing to do with anything her mother has just said. Eve knows her daughter isn't listening to her, that she doesn't really need to any more.

Jodie leaves in a car with music pumping out of its open windows and Eve stares at the courgettes. She's yet to tackle the onion, knows that slicing it will make her eyes water. Taking a break, she stands at the back door in the hope of catching a bit of breeze, but the air is still thick and solid. Next door's children have given up on their game and it's quiet for a moment, so quiet that Eve can imagine hearing the pull and push of waves, the hushing sound they make as they draw sand up and then release it. She's always wanted to live near the sea, sometimes resents being here, so far from the coast. And she thinks of sewing, of how she's always wanted to sew too. She sees herself sitting in a cottage, looking out on to a headland, a bank of low clouds lit from beneath by an amber sun so heavy and bright that it makes the sky purple and churn in a rhythm like the sea. In this scene, there's a bolt of fabric on her lap, the cold metal of a needle in the palm of her hand and the puck, puck sound it makes as she hems.

Eve is so busy with the sewing and the sea that she's surprised to hear Andrew's van trundle on to the drive, but she hears the handbrake ratchet as he pulls it up into position and the driver's door slam shut. He's whistling. Andrew always whistles. She returns to her chopping board, picks up the courgettes to run them under the tap.

'Hi,' he says jauntily as he strides up to her. She's heard his keys clatter on the table in the hall and the sound of him slipping his shoes into the cupboard under the stairs. These are sounds he makes every evening and she knows he will have paint freckles in his hair and on his arms, knows he will have left his overalls in the van and will have changed out of his work boots and that the skin on the back of his neck and shoulders will be conker brown from working outside in this heat. He is a tall man, strong from a lifetime of labour, and he is broad and safe and she's known him most of her life.

'Hi,' she replies. 'Dinner'll be ready in about half an hour.'

'Oh, sorry,' he says, 'didn't I tell you? We've got a gig tonight. At the Crown. Thought I'd said. I think I told Jodie. Didn't she say anything? I won't have time to eat anything just now, maybe later. Could you plate something up for me?'

And he's whistling again and she has to speak loudly so that he can hear her over the noise of it.

'No,' she says, knowing her mouth has thinned to a line and that she's tugging her hair behind her ears in an angry jagged way. The day, which was just about surviving, shudders and cracks. It is still, she realises, such a fragile line between chaos and calm. 'No, you didn't tell me, I would have remembered. Why do you think I'm here in this bloody kitchen, doing all this when it's so hot outside?' She scoops up the blanket of hair that's hanging down her back and holds it in her hands to release some of the heat that's built up on her neck.

'Oh, I'm sorry, I really am. It's just we can't turn them down, the gigs, that is. Not now. Not when we've been asked to play. We're being paid, you know, and it's money, not beer this time, honest!' He pauses and laughs good-naturedly and then takes off his T-shirt and wipes his chest and back with it. His skin is glistening. 'I'll just hop in the shower and change, grab my guitar and go. I am sorry, really I am.'

Eve doesn't want to listen any more. She clatters the plates as she gets them out of the cupboard to show him how he's made her feel, but he's gone, bounding up the stairs two at a time, and he's whistling. Another evening in on her own, then. Of course she'll cook him a meal, of course she'll tidy the kitchen and put the dishwasher on, but for now she grabs a bottle of wine from the fridge and pours herself a large glass. Maybe she'll eat something later, maybe not. If she'd known neither he nor Jodie would be in, she'd have just made herself something simple, like a salad. But anyway, she's not hungry now. She's just tired; sad and tired.

'I won't be late,' he says as he picks up his keys again from the hall table a little while later. 'Jodie not in either, I presume?' He doesn't wait for a reply but says, 'You'll have a nice quiet evening to yourself, then. Wish us luck, my love.'

Yet again, he hasn't asked if just this once she'd like to go with him and sit in the pub garden with a long cool drink and listen to the band playing inside. He hasn't asked her to do this for so long now that she's almost given up hoping that one day he might.

And then he's gone too. He's back in his van with his paint-spattered overalls folded neatly on the passenger seat and his pots of paints and his brushes, which he will have already washed at whoever's house he's working at now and which he'll have wrapped in newspaper, and he will have secured the back door of the van with a padlock the size of a dinosaur's foot.

In the space that yawns open in his wake, Eve is conscious of the vegetables waiting in the pan, the noodles and sauce in packets on the side, the chicken she's cut into strips. She takes a mouthful of wine and purposefully doesn't think of the man on Rose's doorstep, how the sun lodged diamonds in his eyes and wove his beard with threads that were thin and the colour of gold.

She cooks the stir fry, puts a lid on the wok and turns off the heat. She was right; the onions did make her eyes water, at least that's what she told herself at the time. She did not cry, definitely did not cry, and she takes her half-drunk wine to the lounge and sits on the sofa under the open windows. The air is softer in here than in the kitchen; it ruffles her hair very slightly. The day's exhaustion is more measured and composed, the crack in the day seems to be slowly mending itself and the birdsong falls like liquid from the trees. She bends forward and opens the drawer of the coffee table and takes out a DVD. Then she texts Debs: 'Season 5, Episode 11, The One with All the

Resolutions,' and puts the DVD into the player, watches yet another episode of *Friends* while she finishes her wine and the dinner that no one will eat sits expectantly on the hob.

2

After Eve leaves, Myles is also puzzled. He takes a sip of the tea he's made with the milk he was carrying when he met her on the doorstep and he lets himself remember her astonishing hair and her topaz-coloured eyes. Inside his chest his heart is hammering; all the certainties of his life seem to have shifted. He'd been OK when he'd left home earlier but now he mostly feels unsettled, as though a fault line has positioned itself under his feet and he knows it's there and it knows it's there too.

However, he has to work, so he tries to forget the woman on the doorstep, how she'd stood there and smiled shyly at him. And so he stretches his arms high above his head and then lets them drop so his fingers are hovering over the keyboard of his laptop. Where should the body be found this time? Book Nine in the DCI Pleth-eroe series; the last of another three-book deal with the publisher he's been with since the start. Not many can say that these days, and then there's Tom, his agent, who is beginning to mutter about adaptations for TV and is talking to people whose job it is to wonder who could bring Myles's rumpled and unlovable detective, Derek Pletheroe, to the screen. But what all this means now, though, is that Myles can afford to rent this small flat in this house in Belle Avenue and have the space and silence away from Celeste, the boys and Benjy the dog he tells himself he needs.

His desk is positioned in front of the downstairs bay window at the front of the house. The white-painted shutters are folded back like a concertina. He imagines how the light would fall through the louvres were they to be closed against the afternoon sun, how it would stripe the floor. The hedge outside is baking in the heat and, through a gap in the curled metalwork of the gate he can see a glimpse of the Thistle Green sheen of his Mercedes. He is inordinately proud of his car. It is his one extravagance, the one thing he has that isn't about being a home-owner, married or a father.

Behind him, with its back to the wall between the room he's in and the hallway, is an old leather sofa, and next to the fireplace is a small flat-screen TV he hasn't even turned on since he moved his stuff across from the cramped box-room Celeste used to allow him to work in at home.

The back room of the flat leads off from the front room, separated by a pair of open French doors. In it there's a bed which he's covered with a duvet from the store of spare duvets Celeste keeps in her frighteningly efficient way in the loft of their house on the other side of town. He's bought himself a new cover for it, though; a kind of burnt sienna colour which goes well, he thinks, with the brown carpet and the cream curtains hanging at the bedroom window. The rest of the furniture is dark and heavy, has been here for years and speaks to him of the thirties and the war and of a time when men wore hats. There are no pictures on the walls and no mirror. Even he thinks there should be some of either, if not both.

If there's one thing about his old writing room he does miss it's the view; there's a difference between looking out on to the tops of trees and seeing the sky, and looking out of a ground-floor window on to a hedge, tantalising glimpses of road and the heads of people walking by. But, he tells himself, it's a sacrifice worth making for the peace and quiet of here, where the only disturbances are the small sounds Rose makes as she busies herself upstairs, the occasional peal of her laughter at something she's listening to on the radio and the burble of water in the pipes when she does her dishes. Moreover, it's also a sacrifice worth making to have a little bit of distance between him and the house he lives in with his wife and sons. He loves his sons, of course he does, but he's finding it harder and harder these days to love his small, preoccupied wife.

At the back of Myles's flat is a tiny kitchen with a shower room behind it. A back door leads off the kitchen into Rose's garden. Her flowers seem to press up against the house; they are definitely more important to her than he is. He seems to know this without having been told it.

So, he thinks again, where should the body be found? It will obviously have to be morning, a dog-walking find most likely and on sand dunes maybe; he hasn't used sand dunes before or started a book at the very far reaches of Pletheroe's patch where the land meets the sea. There's been sea before; sea that features halfway through books; journeys made by boat, things like that, but never dunes. Yes, he thinks, we'll have sand dunes this time and it will be cold, let's say January, and the wind will be whipping up the sand and bending the grasses back; it will be the kind of wind that can take your talking away. Myles smiles when he thinks this. It's something one of his sons said once about the noise made by Underground trains. He types:

'Morning, sir!'

'Morning, what we got?'

'Doesn't look pretty, sir.'

'They rarely do.' DCI Pletheroe stamps his feet and blows

into his hands. 'Bloody cold this morning, eh? Who's got the coffee? Someone better have coffee . . .'

Myles pauses, runs his fingers through his hair, thinks, yes, the body will have been there for a day or so, enough time for the sand to bank against it, making a kind of shallow grave. Maybe this murder will have been committed by someone savvy about ancient Egypt, who will have surrounded the man's body with gifts and relics to take to the afterlife, like they did in the pyramids, and that these gifts and relics could be clues (with the obligatory red herring ones, naturally) as to the identity of the murderer and his motive.

But, hang on; he pauses and takes another sip of tea. Why does he think this victim is a man? Wouldn't it be better for it to be a woman, someone who could remind his DCI of a lost love, give him yet more demons to face as he sets about putting the fragments of this person's life back together, gently, piece by piece?

Yes, DCI Derek Pletheroe would, as ever, carefully and skilfully reconstruct his victim's life until it led him back here, to this place and this cold, dark morning when the wind is whipping up the sand and bending the grasses back and he is standing on the other side of the incident tape, itching to cross over it, his hands stuffed into his mac pockets, his collar turned up.

Oh God, thinks Myles, this is all so clichéd. Why, when he'd started writing over twenty years ago in time spare from the corporate job he'd once been so proud of, and from Louisa, before she did what she did to him, had he not foreseen this would all be done so many times and so much better by others? But, also how could he have known that his character would, in his turn, become an unlikely hero too, a hero who had a loyal following of fans, a surprising number of whom are in China, apparently? Maybe he should have given birth to a completely different kind of hero; like James Bond maybe with a wardrobe of sharp suits and an Aston Martin on the drive or, alternatively, he could have had a quiet man with indistinct watery eyes; one who lives at the end of the cul-de-sac and who buys potting compost from the allotment society shop at weekends, but who is really a secret agent and has a garage fitted with false walls and an underground cellar where he keeps an arsenal of terrifyingly savage weapons which would, naturally, only ever be used to facilitate the triumph of good over evil?

There have been times of late when Myles has wanted, like Conan Doyle wanted, to kill off his character, but having him tumble over the edge of a waterfall would be too obvious. But if he did this, like Conan Doyle did with Holmes, he could pave the way for his DCI's return one day maybe. Perhaps the end could be Pletheroe gasping for air as the waters swirl around him, his body carried by the rapids until it comes to rest in the tangle of tree roots, or something like that. The very last scene of the book could show his DCI with his eyes closed, a bruise darkening on his temple, the shallows lapping around him . . .

Stop, Myles tells himself now and, taking a deep breath, starts to type, fills in the details about the sand dunes, the grey dawn unfolding across the sky, the luminous white of this latest victim's skin, the dark glint of an ancient goblet resting against her cheek and about the man who found the body, how the wind parts the fur on his dog's back, how the dog whimpers at the sound of the sirens and how men are shouting into phones and someone somewhere is saying, *'We have an ID, sir. Her name is . . .'*

And so Myles doesn't allow himself to think of the woman he met on the doorstep, or how he wishes he could write about love and the small beautiful things that matter in people's lives; that moment, for example, when a man finds himself falling in love and feels he could grow wings and fly. Why, Myles asks himself again, do I spend my time investigating the dark underbelly of it all instead? But he does, and he writes about the body on the beach, her head angled so that a slither of her neck is showing. It is the softest, most vulnerable part of her neck and, as he bends down to scrutinise it, it reminds DCI Derek Pleth-eroe of the one love who'd got away from him, how he used to touch that part of her neck and think he'd found the answer to everything.

And when Myles finishes for the day, reads back over what he's written and saves it on a memory stick and into his Dropbox for safe-keeping, that thought of that touch of finger on skin reminds him of the tall woman with the astonishing hair and eyes the colour of topaz and he realises something remarkable. He thinks that he'd really like to have the chance talk to her in full sentences someday.

Later, Myles eats his banana, does his stretches and puts on his Asics trainers. The heat, when he steps outside the front door, is punishing, but he runs anyway. He plugs in his headphones and selects his running playlist. He starts with Linkin Park, runs through the tired hot air of this July day to the rhythm of 'The Catalyst'. As the cars thrum their way home, once again he puts off the time when he'll do the same and face the strict regimes of meals and no dust his small, fierce wife and her massive job have imposed on him and their sons. The track circles in his mind as he runs. He hears the singer's plea to be lifted up and let go and tries to imagine that he could fly away if he really wanted to.

3

When Myles has gone, the house settles around Rose and she stands in the kitchen of her upstairs flat and allows it to do so. She's washed up the plates and glasses she and Eve used earlier and has put them away and wiped down the draining board and she's waited for Myles to leave, and for the house to be hers again. And he has and it is.

She has, she tells herself as she lifts Father's work coat off its peg on the back of the kitchen door, arranged her affairs quite perfectly. She harrumphs with quiet satisfaction as she starts to shrug her shoulders into the coat. It's like the one worn by Ronnie Barker in *Open All Hours*; it's brown, experienced, fraying at the edges, and although Father died years ago, she's kept the coat, has darned and patched it and keeps it as a kind of talisman; it links her, helps her. But a button, she notices, is coming loose. She should sew it back on before it falls off altogether and so she hurries into her sitting room, takes off the coat and drapes it over the arm of a chair. She bends down to pick up her sewing basket from its place under the sideboard. Her back creaks and she has to stand up slowly. It hurts sometimes, this getting old business, she thinks, not for the first time.

Her decision to split the house into two had taken years to make but once made, she'd embarked on the refurbishment with gusto. She'd employed an architect and a builder and obviously Eve had helped and Eve's husband Andrew had decorated those bits which needed painting afterwards and she'd loved the way the workmen had walked around the house with their loud voices, tools and large feet. For the months when the work was being done, it had made the whole place seem so much more alive, so much less of a shrine. And she'd made innumerable cups of tea and bought biscuits by the barrow load home from Mohsin's shop on the Wokingham Road. And she'd loved the tinny sound the builders' radio made and took a strange delight in seeing the dust they made eddy in the air as they knocked things down and built things up. It was like starting again, she'd thought.

When it was finished she moved into what had been her parents' bedroom at the front of the house. What had once been her childhood bedroom had been made into a sitting room, and the third bedroom split into a bathroom and small kitchen. She'd had a door put in the back wall of the house and they'd built her the small veranda she'd sat on earlier with Eve and given her a set of steps leading down into the garden. And they'd left the garden untouched, because she'd asked them to and because that's the one place where Rose can still find them all; her father, mother and sometimes when she lets herself, Henry too.

She'd known for a long time she would have to do something. Living here again after everything: the house off the Talgarth Road and the room she'd rented in its attic; the Tube journeys to and from work; Father's death; after she'd told her one secret to Eve's grandmother and, she pauses as she selects a needle from the case, after Henry, had been so hard. And then, looking after Mother and always waiting for something, but she didn't know what, to happen had, for a while, threatened to derail her. But here she is, aged eighty-one next birthday and, she thinks again as she threads her needle, it's like she's starting all over again and it is marvellous.

There had been too many times when, in the low light of a late spring evening, or in the sharp square light of a cold November morning, she'd found herself stepping around the ghosts who lived with her; Father, Henry, and then Mother, and she'd taken to talking to them, the odd sentence here and there, like 'Tea bags, mustn't forget tea bags,' or, more alarmingly, asking them the do-you-remember questions which played in her head with the insistency of music. Of course, they never replied. For their different reasons, they'd each run out of answers years ago.

But now is different. Eve is in her life and is like the sun, and Rose will remain forever grateful for the twist of fate that brought Eve to her in the end, and now is also different because she has Myles downstairs. She can watch him come and go, hear his footsteps in the hallway and his now-and-then cough, the rumble of his voice when he's talking to someone on the phone or the distant beat of the music he plays sometimes when he writes, and she loves the familiar shape his car makes in the road outside the house; there is something about it which reminds her of Henry. He'd had a car a little bit like it once.

Such small similarities, she thinks as she turns in the chair to face the light coming in from the back window and casts on to start refastening the button are, like Father's coat, what links now to then. They help her to make sense of it all. And then, out of nowhere a memory crashes into her and she has to stop mid-stitch and catch her breath. It's odd when this happens; part of her relishes these moments, another part of her, the one that's mourned losing Henry for so long, sometimes fights hard against them, almost pleads with them to go away. It all hurts so much still; so much more than she ever thought it would, even now after all this time.

This particular memory is of the day when she'd sewn a button back on to Henry's jacket; the day of the board meeting which had decided the purchase of the *Ajax Star*, the ship which eventually was to launch from the port at Piraeus: the event that was to change everything.

'Good afternoon, all. Miss Reynolds? Coffee, I think, and get me Lucas on the telephone,' Mr Georgiadis said as he strode into the office, smelling of sharp cologne and ouzo after a lunch with a financier in the City. He took off his hat and coat and passed them to her with his air of studied insouciance, the one he'd perfected since coming to England from Greece when he'd been nineteen and penniless. For a small man, Mr Georgiadis took up a lot of space. Henry, as ever, followed in his wake with the paperwork and the intricate knowledge of what would and would not actually work, what was and was not actually legal. He tipped his hat at Rose and smiled.

She can still remember smiling back.

'Of course, Mr Georgiadis,' she'd said, standing and pushing her chair back and straightening her skirt. She'd finish typing this batch of letters later; they would still catch the evening post. She dialled Lucas's number and put the call through to Mr Georgiadis's office, then, picking up the meeting file, her shorthand notebook and three 2B pencils, she made her way across the thick carpet and pushed open the heavy door of the boardroom.

Weak winter sun limped through the windows overlooking Welbeck Street and bathed the broad sweep of the oval table and Mr Georgiadis's chair under the massive oil painting of a bull's face. He'd bought it after reading *The Sun Also Rises*, or so he'd told Rose when he'd first interviewed her for the job as his secretary the year before.

As she started to prepare the tray with cups and saucers, she could hear the rumble of buses outside, the shouts of the boy on the corner selling the *Standard*. It was a normal day, much like any other. The remaining directors would arrive soon, but for now it was just Mr Georgiadis and Henry. A china cup chinked as she placed it on a saucer. Mr Georgiadis was speaking loudly into the telephone in his office and she could feel a presence behind her.

Turning round, she saw it was Henry. Tall, a little stooped, with his thinning fair hair and his eyes the colour of forget-me-nots, he was, she knew, an unlikely hero. However, since the moment she'd met him it had been like there'd been a pale but unbreakable thread connecting her to him, something she couldn't explain. It was his scent – lemony, zesty – and the warmth of him; the fact that she felt she could reach out and put her arm on the sleeve of his jacket and that it would feel right somehow. These thoughts brought her no comfort, however. Instead they were like a pain she carried around with her and which tucked itself just under her ribs.

'Oh, Rose,' he said. 'Look.'

The button on his suit jacket was coming loose.

'I'll fix that for you,' she said. 'I have a needle and thread in the drawer of my desk.'

'I knew you would.' He laughed gently as he slipped his jacket off. She'd never seen him in his shirtsleeves before and it was strangely intimate. It was also odd how she'd never noticed the freckles on the bridge of his nose until now but, as he looked at her that afternoon as if he were seeing her for the very first time, she did.

Of course he was married. He was married to a woman called Penelope and they had no children, none whatsoever, and Penelope spoke loudly, wore tweeds, had money. She kept horses at her parents' house in the country, or so the office girl had once told Rose. Rose couldn't remember why or how this conversation had arisen. But the fact of his marriage was a solid thing and it stood between them as he handed her his jacket and her heart beat a shade faster at the knowledge of it.

Rose was nearly twenty-six years old then and had not yet been in love; not real, breath-taking love, the kind she read about in novels or saw in films at the pictures. She was a small woman and, back in 1959, her hair was short, brown and curly. It's now white but still thick and her skin is still good, her eyes still the Elizabeth Taylor eyes she'd once been told they were. But she's never been conventionally beautiful; her face has always been one of those which is better when mobile. She was and is someone who has never looked good in photographs.

Later, amid the bustle of the other directors' arrivals, Mr Georgiadis's characteristic impatience and the aroma of the bitter coffee he liked to drink, Rose handed Henry's jacket back to him, the button neatly sewn on. Briefly, in this exchange, their hands touched. It was only a fleeting touch, no more than a hover of skin on skin, but they both snatched their hands away as if the fabric of the jacket was burning.

Now, as Rose casts off after mending Father's work coat, she remembers that touch and how she'd watched Eve and Myles as they'd stood on her doorstep that afternoon. She hadn't realised it at the time, but did now, that the stirring she'd felt then had been the same as that long-ago day when she'd been faced with the choice of not falling in love or of falling in love; a choice that had actually been no choice at all.

She puts on the work coat and makes her way to the back door. Gingerly, she goes down the steps into the garden; even in the heat of summer the metal treads seem slippery. She holds on to the rail tightly and remembers something Eve once said to her about Andrew. 'It's always been so safe,' she'd said. 'Like we're in a landscape which is totally featureless and you can see for ever. There are no mountains, no cliffs, no surprises. It's always been enough for him. But I . . .' She'd not finished the sentence because something must have happened, the kettle boiled or the phone rang perhaps, but, as Rose plucks a pair of secateurs from the shelf in what used to be her father's garden shed, what Eve said comes back to her like an echo, a kind of threat. Rose had wanted such a life of mountains and surprises for herself once. But it hadn't worked out that way, not that way at all.

It's dusk, and this late July day sighs as she snips the dead heads off her Gertrude Jekyll roses. Some she catches and puts in the pocket of Father's coat, others seem to dissolve in her fingers and spin to the ground like dust does.

4

Eve is in bed when Jodie comes home. Jodie's light footsteps trip up the stairs and Eve hears her daughter's bedroom door close softly. After a few minutes it opens again and Eve holds her breath, hoping Jodie will tap her fingernails on her door and ask to come in like she used to do when she was younger, when she'd told her mostly everything. But she doesn't, not tonight. Tonight Jodie uses the bathroom and creeps back down the landing. Eve feels like crying, but the darkness is pressing down on her eyelids and she can't.

It doesn't seem possible that the years of having her daughter's hot body curled up against hers during story time or after nightmares are passed. Nor does it seem possible that this self-possessed girl is the same person who had been handed to her moments after she'd been born and had stared up at Eve, a look of bewilderment on her face as if to say, 'What am I doing here?'

But, Eve argues, as the house quietens once more, this is how it's supposed to be, isn't it? When Jodie leaves to go to university, it will be more the start of one thing and less the end of another and she'll not be far away: a train journey or car ride and they'll be in the same time zone. She will still be near. This is what Eve tells herself as she adjusts her head on the pillow and waits for Andrew to come home.

It's shortly after twelve when his van rumbles back on to the drive and he locks up downstairs. She didn't eat anything in the end, wonders if he had anything at the pub. The sounds he makes are so familiar as to be almost like breathing but, as he approaches their bedroom, for a second she feels a kind of fear she hasn't felt since that Bonfire Night when she'd been a child. Then the whole road had joined together and built a huge fire on a piece of wasteland at the back of their house and she'd been convinced her garden, her house and herself would be consumed by the flames. She hadn't known then that her father had a hose at the ready, that even he'd known the risks involved and had made plans to protect her.

Her father hadn't turned out to be much of a parent but he'd been a bit of one, for a while at least. Later she'd tried so hard to do it differently from her parents, maybe too hard, that perhaps being this other type of parent has taken up too much of her energy and has left her scared of what she and her husband may or may not say to one another as he gets into bed beside her. Have they forgotten, she wonders, how to be people as well as parents?

'Hey,' he whispers as he takes off his jeans, folds them and puts them on the back of a chair. 'You asleep?'

'No,' she says quietly. The light from the landing has made the room yellowy and she follows Andrew's shadow as he moves around it; one moment it's vast, like a giant, the next it's shrunk to the size of a child. 'How was it?' she asks.

'Yeah, it was good,' is all he says.

Long gone are the days when she'd go with him and sit on a stool at the bar and watch the band play or, after Jodie was born, he'd come home and tell her everything; about every chord change, what it had felt like to bask in the applause, how happy it had made him feel. Long gone too are the days when he'd ask her about her day. She wanted to tell him about Rose, about sitting on Rose's veranda that afternoon and how the air had smelled of heat and fuel and that her heart had beaten just a shade faster but she hadn't known why. She wanted to tell him about her day at work and how, tomorrow, she was going to plan this year's conference and how the thought of this worried her. But, for some reason, she can't tell him these things or that today she met Rose's tenant for the first time.

It should be easy to say these things, but it isn't; it is

incredibly hard and so, instead, as he closes the door and makes his way over to the bed, pulls back the covers and slides into it beside her, she wonders again when it was that they'd stopped appearing in detail to one another. Rather than forming an intricate pattern in one another's lives, they are now more just like shapes, a smudge of colour and presence, the memory of words and promises rather than the actuality of them. Having said that, these shapes and colours and presence are good things; they are things that bring comfort – mostly, anyway – and she can't imagine a different life than this, really she can't, and so she tells herself that the reason she won't tell Andrew about the man she met in Rose's hallway is because it's not important that she does.

She closes her eyes and wishes that her husband would sometimes turn to her and hold her face in his hands and search her eyes, ask to count the flecks of amber in them, and that he would make love to her like he used to do when they were younger. She does not want to lie in the dark, too afraid to ask him to do these things. His breathing soon steadies. The pub smells still linger around him.

When Eve's house was built in the thirties it had cost £500 with an extra £50 for a garage. Eve had been told this by an elderly neighbour who had long since disappeared, taken away by well-meaning relatives to a home for the elderly nearby. A young man had moved into her house and had come and gone and they'd nodded to one another over the fence, but he'd worked abroad quite a lot and there were times when Eve missed the old woman and her stories and wished she'd had more time to stop and listen to them when Jodie had been small.

Now their house fits around her like a skin. It had been wonderful moving in and making it theirs; it had seemed vast at the time. Even now that Andrew's life is filled with it, the smell of paint always takes her back to those days when they'd decorated it; it had been a fresh start, the start of something good, something full of promise.

She'd never minded that she didn't know who'd lived in it before. Her neighbour had been vague about this, had said something about a couple with two blond-haired boys and, after them, the couple Eve and Andrew had bought it from who'd moved to the Isle of Man, but who'd sent Christmas cards each year for the last twenty with unfailing regularity. Those first boys must be old men by now, Eve has often thought and sometimes she can feel the presence of the others who have lived there, but this is a good feeling too, like there's a sense of joined-upness from her life to theirs. These ghosts are friendly, benevolent. She always makes them welcome when she senses them near.

But, as she lies there in the dark, she wonders when her own life changed from being enough to not being enough, and then Andrew says, 'Well, night then. See you in the morning,' and pats her lightly on the shoulder. He turns away from her and soon, he's gently snoring.

Eventually, she sleeps and dreams a series of fitful dreams, like flashbacks in films, and there is a kind of musical score to them and somewhere in the background, hiding in the shadows of a building that is at once familiar and unfamiliar, is a man. She's sure she knows who he is but, each time the beam of light from a nearby lighthouse illuminates him, she blinks, the burst of light disappears and the man is hidden once more.

The next morning Eve waits for the alarm to ring. It's six thirty and already the patch of sky she can see through the gap in the curtains is kingfisher blue. It's frilled by the vapour trails of the first planes out of Heathrow and she lifts her hand and traces them with her finger, wondering where they are going, who is on board them, why their journeys are important.

Andrew is sleeping soundly with his back to her. The strip of sunlight falls on it and makes it golden. The bird-song is like crystal this morning. She's always loved the hairline on the back of his neck, remembers gazing at it when she sat behind him in History lessons at school. Even then and without really knowing why or what it would lead to, she'd wanted to touch it. He grunts and turns over, blinks just once at her and then falls back to sleep. He still smells faintly of beer. Ah, those History lessons! And she remembers how, after them, she'd gone to his house for tea and, when no one laughed at her for doing so, she went again and again. His mother never liked her, though; it always seemed that Eve would, in time, disappoint her.

But, then there'd been kissing him and being kissed by him and the hardness inside his jeans and the damp in her knickers and, when they were sixteen and did it for the first time, how everything fell into place. She's never been with anyone else. They did their A-levels and it was, as her own mother said before she and her father moved to America, 'Like you can't get a cigarette paper between you two!' and then Eve went to college to do a secretarial course and Andrew was apprenticed to a painter/decorator, believing that the band would make it big and he could give up working for him in time.

Of course, this never happened, but she and Andrew got married and moved into the house in Byron Road and his mother still didn't like her. Even when his father retired and they moved out towards Basingstoke, his father telling them, 'You get more bang for your buck over there,' she'd take Jodie over to stay with them occasionally and she would feel as though she were leaving her daughter on the moon. She'd never actually been alone with her in-laws; Andrew and Jodie had always been like a filter between them and the whole system seemed to work just fine.

Now she waits for Andrew to wake and, as she waits,

she studies the contours her body makes under the thin summer duvet and the white nightgown she's wearing. She studies her long thin arms, narrow hips, the space between her legs and she's filled with a huge longing; like an emptiness it fills her. Oh, how she wishes he would wake and turn to her, brush his fingers over her breasts, kiss her on her mouth. This would make her feel better, more connected – to him, to herself. She's afraid she's starting to forget who she is in all this. It's been a while, she thinks, since they last made love, in fact she can't remember when they did. Morning has changed nothing; it seems that there's still a kind of wall between them that they are both too hesitant to mention, far too scared to scale and see what remains on the other side.

The alarm rings.

'Morning,' Andrew mumbles, stretches, rolls over and swings his legs out of the bed. He doesn't look back at her as he sits on the edge of it and flexes his toes, runs his fingers through his hair.

'Hi,' she says and watches him walk out of the room, can hear him whistling, a quiet almost-whistle as he pads towards the bathroom. Then she hears the shower run.

Jodie gets up shortly after and the three of them perform their customary routine; making way for one another, knowing without asking who is going to do what next. It's like dancing, but without the music and without the words of the song, Eve thinks as she brushes out her hair, scans the hangers in her wardrobe for something to wear to work.

By eight o'clock the house is silent, its windows are closed and the day will happen around it. Andrew made his sandwiches but didn't touch the stir fry she'd left for him the previous evening. Eve wipes up the crumbs he's left on the bread board, scrapes the contents of the wok into the bin and puts it in the dishwasher. She tries very hard not to mind, is hungry but can't face eating anything; not yet.

She drives to work and the sun is beating on the roof of her car. At the roundabout at the bottom of their road she sees a flash of metallic green and, for a second, is reminded of the man in Rose's downstairs flat and his car and the way his eyes crinkled at the corners when he smiled. She turns the radio to Radio 4 and shakes her head, telling herself not to be so stupid.

Instead she thinks about the day ahead. Andrew hadn't asked her what she would be doing during it, what small triumphs and fears would punctuate it. This is because he didn't need to, doesn't need to; she's been working at Woodward Electronics for years; it too is a comfortable fit. Being the Head of Design's PA is a good gig, Max is a good man and it's a nice place to work. The offices are shiny and air-conditioned, there are big plants in the corridors and the lift doors always open and close with an elegant sigh. Even the mirrors on the lift walls seem to have the ability to make Eve look less gawky than she feels.

Yes, she's lucky and she knows it as she drives on to the business park, her Polo one in a line of cars snaking alongside the river. She's always reminded of worker ants when she's in this queue and looks out of the window at the silver gleam of the Thames. A pair of swans is skimming the surface, their wings moving almost in slow motion. Eve can see their reflections in the water and wishes she could hear the sound the air makes as it travels through their feathers; a sound that reminds her of the scans she had when she was expecting Jodie and of hearing the whoosh-whoosh of her baby's tiny heart. Even though Jodie's heart had been small, the noise it made had filled the entire room.

Eve nods to Sarah the receptionist as she makes her way to the lifts and then presses the button for Floor 3. Sarah raises a customary aloof hand in acknowledgement. It's cool in here and momentarily Eve thinks of Andrew and of the heat stored in wood and bricks and how the breeze will ruffle his hair when he's high on the ladder painting the eaves of someone else's house.

'Watcha,' says Debs as Eve passes her desk on the way to where she and Max have their office. 'Penny for them.'

Eve wishes she could tell Debs at least some of what she

felt last night and this morning, but the office is already busy; phones are ringing, designers are hunched over their Macs, there's a steady hum of activity which stretches to the other end of the floor to where the Accounts Department sit with their tidy files and spreadsheets. She leans on the waist-high partition in front of Debs's desk and says, 'They're not worth that,' and adds before Debs can interject, 'Anyway, could you let me have those contact details for the hotel in Surrey we talked about at the last management meeting? I'm going to start pricing up for the conference today and Max has suggested we look at that one too.'

'Yeah, sure,' Debs replies, her fingers flashing across her keyboard. 'There, have sent it. We'll talk later, I guess? Lunch maybe?'

'I'll see how the day goes but yes, hopefully,' Eve replies, stepping back and turning slightly. She waves to Debs as she walks away and, as usual, Debs smiles her wonderful smile at her. Even though they haven't said anything of consequence, Eve feels better for this encounter. She always does after being with Debs.

Like Eve, Debs is tall and willowy but unlike Eve, Debs's flaxen hair is very straight and cut in a tidy bob. Also unlike Eve, she moves neatly and precisely; her nails and make-up are always faultless and her hazel eyes, although just slightly too far apart to be really beautiful, are packed with wit, intelligence and heart.

If Eve were asked to sum up her friend in one word, however, that word would be 'considered'. Debs is a considered person who makes wise decisions and who rarely rushes. Eve wishes on an almost daily basis that she could be more like her.

Debs is also tidily divorced from Simon, to whom she'd been married for five incident-free years but whom, she'd told Eve, she'd decided with all seriousness and with almost no regret to leave after they'd got up one Wednesday morning, looked at each other over their cereal bowls and realised they were no longer in love. 'It was almost as though neither of us had known it until that moment,' she'd said to Eve on the phone after they'd been to see their solicitor to draw up the papers. 'He just put the milk back in the fridge, turned to me and there was just nothing there. Absolute zilch. Made me wonder if there ever had been, but in the end, it was just such a relief, for both of us. The solicitor's just said he's never known such an easy divorce.' And Debs has never uttered a bitter word about Simon, or even one which could have undertones, about how she felt when they sold the house and divided up the furniture. And even when Simon starting dating a twenty-two-year-old beautician called Sandy, Debs stayed resolutely cheerful, totally convinced that they'd done the right thing. No one had been disappointed that the marriage had ended, not even Debs's mother, who'd invested in Chanel for the wedding. Instead, Debs goes on about one date a month, always makes it plain afterwards that there'll be no second date and so there are no 'Can I call you?' conversations. She lives in a two-bedroomed, well-apportioned flat in a development near the station, drives her Pepper White Mini Cooper S to work every day, goes to her Pilates class twice a week and, like Eve does, watches old episodes of *Friends* to bridge the gap between getting in from work and making herself something to eat.

'Do you think it would be different if you'd had children?' Eve had asked her at the time.

'Quite possibly,' Debs replied. 'But it's kind of pointless thinking that. We didn't have children and it's fine, really it is.'

And Eve believed her then and believes her still and that's part of the reason she always takes heart from Debs's wide smile and why she relishes the emotional umbrella her friend seems to hold over the less contented life Eve is living at the moment, one which, as she makes her way to her desk outside Max's office, seems to have crept up on her when she wasn't looking. When did it change? she asks herself again, putting her bag down on the floor next to her chair and switching on her computer. When did she start minding about things she didn't mind about before, about Andrew, about what they do and don't say to one another, about how there's this ball of fury constantly lodged between her breasts? Surely it wasn't only as recently as yesterday? Surely it isn't just since meeting that man on the doorstep of Rose's house that her mind has starting thinking these things?

She remembers being angry at the foot of Rose's stairs and then this anger evaporating as she talked to Myles. Then she was angry again at home later after Andrew had come and gone out again and, as the icons appear on her screen, she tries to remember how she'd felt the day before yesterday, but somehow it's a blank, like white noise, as if she's been momentarily blinded by the sun.

Max arrives shortly afterwards and the day settles into its routine of emails from and to him and calls she makes on his behalf and going to Reception to greet the people who have come to meet him, and talking to the hotel in Surrey Debs sent her the details of, and the one in Hertfordshire Max went to once with his wife and thought was 'quite classy, not very, but quite', about twenty-four-hour delegate rates and A/V equipment costs. The heat is pressing up against the windows and bouncing off the next-door building. No sounds come in from outside; it's like being in a cocoon, Eve thinks as she and Debs make their way to the restaurant for lunch, or in a bubble, or that they're actors in *The Truman Show*. They talk about inconsequential things as they eat their paninis and drink Diet Cokes and when she leaves work that evening, she can't remember much about the last eight hours. They have passed, it's been another day and now it's time to go home.

As she gets into her car she notices that the air is beginning to thicken as though a storm is brewing. A bank of sulphurous grey cloud is hanging over the horizon and over Caversham Park, where the BBC do their listening. The wind is starting to whip itself up and whirlpools of dust are eddying across the hot tarmac. As she drives home, huge drops of rain hit the windscreen, making patterns like flower blooms across it. She switches on her wipers and has to squint to see properly until the glass clears. Without really knowing why, she takes a detour on the way home, just to check Rose is OK, she tells herself, as she pulls up outside the house in Belle Avenue. The wipers speed back and forwards, the engine is humming and the tyres of the other cars on the road are making slick, wet sounds; they fill her head until there's no room for anything else. She's never done this before; never come unannounced, and refuses to let herself wonder why she's doing so today. But when she realises the green Mercedes is not there she knows she won't go in, tells herself that, after all, she's sure Rose is fine, she'll go for lunch again next time as planned, and so she pulls out, turns right on to the Wokingham Road and waits at the lights. A number 17 bus is rattling away in front of her indicating right and someone is battling with an umbrella outside The Three Tuns pub. The lights change. She's almost home.

Later, when Andrew is showering, Jodie's checking Facebook and watching music clips on MTV in her room and the lasagne Eve made when she got in from work is warming in the oven, she settles herself on the sofa. The storm's passed and it's like the air's been washed clean. It has a sharp edge to it which is both oddly comforting and unsettling. Like after the storms when she'd been very young and had gone back out in the garden to play, this day could be something totally new and untried, filled with a different way of doing things. She texts Debs: 'Series 6, Episode 14, The One Where Chandler Can't Cry.'

5

A week or so has gone by and it's early August. The intense heat of before has gone; day after day the sky's now peppered with clouds which move with an energy more fitting spring than summer. How is it, Myles thinks as he sits at his desk and looks out of the window, that August always promises so much and always disappoints and yet, we don't expect much from September or October, and sometimes, just sometimes, the weather can be glorious and undemanding, like a late gift which we'd almost given up hope of receiving? Today he's watching the clouds and is making shapes out of them like he's done with one or other of the boys on occasion. He can see a ram's head; it's huge and menacing, although when it's gone it's replaced by a shape that's like a kitten asleep on its back. He can see its paws, the curl of its tail. 'The correct word for what you're doing is "nephelococcygia",' he tells himself in a tone of voice much like Celeste would use. Of course, she'd know the right term for this; was probably born knowing it, he thinks, a little unfairly, as he switches on his laptop.

The proofs for Book Eight had arrived last week and have been distracting him, but he's promised himself a morning with his new story, is comforted by that familiar buzz in his chest which tells him it's going be OK; today the words will come. The icons settle into place on his screen and he tells himself he'll check his emails later and, if the morning's gone well, he'll go for a run and hopefully get home early. Maybe he'll see the boys before Anka puts them to bed; maybe he'll even see his wife tonight, eat a meal with her. Surely she'll be home tonight? She needs to pack as she's going to New York tomorrow, or so he remembers her telling him last weekend. He thinks it's tomorrow, anyway.

Myles scans forward to this evening, sees his wife's glistening black BMW on the drive, hears the tip-tap of her heels on woodblock around the house, the inflexion of her voice as she talks into her phone about situations he knows nothing about and cares about even less. All she ever seems to do these days is mouth across the room at him, 'Sorry, may be a while. Got a bit of a "situation" going on . . .' It's as though she puts the quotation marks around the word herself. He stopped trying to understand her job years ago and sometimes wonders if actually he understands who she is any more either, whether if he passed her unexpectedly in the street he would be able to recognise her.

Ah well, he says to himself and closes his eyes momentarily. He sees a room etched on the back of his eyelids. The room's in a flat overlooking a tree-lined road. Outside, cars are parked along both sides of the street and the houses are a mishmash of old and new; some are Edwardian like Rose's, others are Victorian, a little gothic (Why not! he thinks) and there are a couple of new box-like houses built in the gaps left by bombs during the war. Clusters of people are standing on the pavements watching; a man is climbing out of a blue Transit with the words 'Sharp's Aerials' on it and there's a woman pushing a double buggy; one of the children is asleep, the other is whimpering quietly. The mother looks exhausted, has smudges of tiredness under her eyes. There are seagulls wheeling and cawing. Of course, there are always seagulls in a scene like this.

Directly outside the flat are three police vans; the scene-of-crime guys are packing away their stuff, there's the ubiquitous incident tape, a flurry of journalists and DCI Pletheroe is walking up the path.

Once inside the room that Myles can see etched on to the back of his eyelids, his DCI stands completely still and breathes in and out, slowly, very deliberately. He is trying to visualise the victim here, see her going about her daily routines. He imagines the kettle boiling and a TV newsreader saying in a tone of voice usually saved for the bereaved, and as though she's slightly surprised by the fact, that apparently the country could be heading for a triple-dip recession. And, as he stands there, Pletheroe feels the familiar blade of frustration just under his ribs because he doesn't yet understand why the body of the owner of this flat was left where it was left, or why it was surrounded by the articles which have all now been photographed in situ, out of situ, dusted for fingerprints, bagged and stored back at the nick.

DCI Derek Pletheroe lets out a long sigh and gets to work, going around the room methodically, carefully. He picks things up and puts them down, puzzled by the fact that, as yet, he hasn't found a single photograph of anyone who could pass as a relative, friend or lover of the dead woman. His hands are hot inside the police-issue gloves he'd snapped on earlier like a surgeon about to perform an operation.

Just as Myles is typing this, there's a knock at the door of his flat. 'Bugger,' he says under his breath. 'Damn and bugger.' He saves what he's written and answers the door.

'Oh, hello,' Rose says. 'I'm so sorry to have disturbed you.'

Myles finds himself saying, 'It's no problem, no problem at all.'

'It's just I was wondering if you could do me a totally wonderful favour?' Rose asks.

She is, he notices, tiny; much smaller than she sounds when she's moving around upstairs. But, in the jewelled light of the hallway he notices the intense blue, almost violet of her eyes, thinks they remind him of someone's, but doesn't know whose.

'Sure,' he says. 'It will be a pleasure.'

It will be a pleasure, Myles knows this. All his dealings with his landlady so far have been pleasant. He's where he wants to be, doing what he wants to be doing, and it's kind of thanks to Rose that he is.

'I need a box lifted down from the top of my wardrobe,' she says now, turning and starting to make her way back up the stairs. 'If you're really sure you don't mind. It's daft of me, I know. I should wait, could wait until Eve comes next, but . . .' Her voice trails away.

Myles follows, his heart racing stupidly and inexplicably at the mention of Eve's name. He has absolutely no idea why this should be.

Despite having the same floor plan as his, Rose's flat seems much smaller. It's crowded with substantial pieces of furniture and Myles feels a bit like Gulliver in Lilliput as he enters it. It's also like there are other people here too. He can't put a finger on it, but there are presences and he can't distinguish one from the other and he can't find Eve amongst them. He follows Rose into the bedroom overlooking Belle Avenue. Rose is hurrying and he's puzzled by this until she says, 'I shouldn't be taking you away from your work. I'm sorry, perhaps I shouldn't have asked.'

'It's no trouble, really it's not.'

And then comes the question he dreads. 'How's the book going?'

What can he say, other than, 'Oh, it's fine'? Trying to define how he feels when he writes, the constant fear he lives with that the next sentence won't come, is like trying to catch a butterfly without the use of a net. And anyway, he's learned the wisdom of superstition. It's much better not to say much, if anything, to anyone. Celeste seems to understand this. At least, she never asks him about his books any more and for this he's bizarrely grateful. She occasionally acknowledges the money they bring in; it is after all just a drop in the ocean compared to what she earns. He has, over a number of years, tried very hard not to feel reduced by this.

'Ah, that's good then, oh and here we are.' Rose is standing in front of a mighty double-fronted wardrobe. Myles doesn't know what wood it's made from but it could be oak. She opens it up.

Inside, to the left of her other clothes, is a row of dresses from what look to be the fifties; they're colour co-ordinated from yellows at one end, through greens and into blues.

On the far left-hand side is one black dress and one red dress. Myles once had a fifties storyline in one of his books and had studied Opie's *1950s Scrapbook* so he recognises them, or thinks he does.

Rose laughs self-consciously. 'Oh, I should really get rid of them. The dresses, that is. No occasion to wear them now. And they wouldn't fit. But even so . . .' She lifts the fabric of one of them and rubs it gently between her fingers. Then she looks up at Myles. Her violet eyes seem bottomless for a second. 'It's up there,' she says, pointing to a box about eighteen inches by eighteen inches. It too is made from wood, a lighter, less dense wood than the wardrobe. Pine, maybe. It's plain save for the initials 'GR' on its lid. 'Father made it,' she says by way of explanation. He holds it for her and she traces the letters and smiles somewhat sadly. Her hands are wrinkled and dotted with age spots. She's wearing no jewellery.

'Here, let me carry it into the other room for you.'

'Thank you,' she pauses, then adds, 'my dear.'

He likes being called this. It reminds him of his own grandmother, his mother's mother who'd died when he'd been a boy and hadn't yet come to realise how necessary the things and people are which join the past to now.

He takes the box into the lounge.

'Put it down here,' Rose says, pointing to a coffee table in front of a chintz-covered armchair, says again, 'I know

I should have waited, could have waited, but just sometimes . . .'

Again, she doesn't finish what's she saying and Myles doesn't mind. It's not his business anyway. He looks around the room. On the mantelpiece is a black-and-white photograph of a couple. They're standing outside the gate of the house on Belle Avenue. The man's in a jacket and tie, the woman is holding on to his arm but doesn't seem to be touching it, her hand's hovering over it instead.

'Mother and Father,' Rose says. 'They were,' she stops, looks from the box on the table, at Myles and then at the window, 'very proper people.' There's another pause. Then after what seems like five minutes, but is probably only about thirty seconds, she asks, 'Can I make you a cup of tea?'

He doesn't want tea, hasn't really got time for it. He should be back at his desk by now.

'That would be lovely,' he says.

And she bustles off to the kitchen, calling over her shoulder, 'Sit down, my dear. Make yourself at home.' She laughs when she says this and he likes the sound of her laughter.

He sits in the chintz-covered armchair and looks at the box, curious suddenly as to what it contains. He doesn't look in it, obviously he doesn't. He chuckles at the thought that of course his DCI would, but then, in many ways he and his DCI are very different men. In many ways they are also very similar. He studies the room further. Apart from the photograph of the couple he'd seen earlier, there's only one other. This time it's of a man with thinning fair hair and pale, very clear eyes. For all this, he looks unremarkable. It's only a head shot, something done in a studio maybe, the type of picture kept on a shelf in a boardroom. The man looks kind, a bit cautious maybe, but kind. Why, he thinks, are there no pictures of Eve?

Rose carries the tea tray in; tiny cups and saucers, a teapot, hot water, milk jug and sugar bowl, a plate of digestive biscuits.

'It's lovely to have guests,' she says, her breath a little short and gasping.

'Here, let me.' Myles springs up and takes the tray from her, putting it on the table next to the box.

'Thank you,' she says and sits down opposite him. 'Shall I be mother?' She laughs some more when she says this.

As she hands him his cup, from nowhere, comes the word 'Eve?' It's the end of a sentence he'd been saying to himself, something along the lines of 'Why are there no photos of Eve?' and instantly he feels foolish, a schoolboy again. He drinks his tea. It is gone in two mouthfuls.

'Oh, Eve's not . . .'

'Related?' he chips in. He doesn't have a clue what he's doing, or why.

'No, sadly,' Rose says. 'It's a long story, perhaps one for another day? More tea, dear? A biscuit?'

So that's that, Myles thinks; a long story and one for another day. Not here, not now. 'Yes, that would be lovely, thank you.' He holds out his cup and saucer, picks up a biscuit and takes a bite, trying not to drop any crumbs.

'Tell me about your family,' Rose says, with emphasis on the *your*. 'I remember you saying you have children, right?'

'Yes, three boys.' He laughs self-consciously. 'Bruno's eleven, just about to go to secondary school, next month actually, and Orlando's eight and Garth's just four.' He thinks hard as he says this, knows he knows his sons instinctively but can't, as with Celeste earlier and just for that second, remember exactly what they look like.

'Your wife must have her hands full,' Rose adds, passing him back his cup.

'Well, my wife –' Myles stops, has no idea how to define his wife. 'She works, rather a lot, actually. We have a nanny, her name's Anka. She's Polish. Her name means favour, or grace. We rely on her very heavily.'

'It must be hard,' Rose says, but she doesn't say what must be hard. Myles seems to understand, though, and finds himself telling Rose about the ten years he spent with Louisa, how badly they ended, about meeting Celeste at work and how it was in the early days, about his writing and how now isn't really how he expected it to be. He only talks for a minute or two but these minutes seem to be his life encapsulated, his life speeded up and, when he finishes speaking, he's overcome with an overwhelming sense of despair about where it's headed next.

After he leaves Rose with her saying, 'Well, thank you, my dear. For the box, for letting me disturb you and everything,' and him saying, 'It was fine and thank you, for the tea and the chat,' Myles stares at his laptop screen with something akin to hopelessness. He knows that Rose's request, Rose's tea and biscuits, the things he's told her, all mean that he won't be able to write any more today. He has been too diluted by these things; has lost focus. So, he leaves Pletheroe gazing forlornly around the victim's flat, saves what he's done so far and decides to go for a run.

The weather's still unseasonable; the sky overcast and there's a chill in the air. It promises rain. Perfect conditions for running, Myles thinks, as the Proclaimers' 'I'm Gonna Be' blasts out of his earphones. He nods his head in time to the music as he sets out along Belle Avenue, turns left into Whiteknights Road, then right on to Wilderness. He'll run round the university, up Pepper Lane, along the Shinfield Road and back round to Whiteknights. It's one of his favourite routes, probably something to do with the university, the feeling that whatever else is happening, the university goes on; students come, learn and go. The place gives the town a sense of vigour and purpose. Myles likes this, hopes his sons will one day go to a university somewhere, learn things he doesn't know.

The pavements are hard under his feet, it's like the concrete is some form of punishment and Myles likes this too. As he runs he wishes hard for other things; he doesn't rightly know what these other things would be, but he wishes for them anyway and, as he jogs back up Belle Avenue and turns into the gate of Rose's house, he scans the road for the sight of an oddly coloured blue car, is disappointed when he can't see it and shakes his head at his own stupidity.

Later, he goes home. The drive across town is sticky because it's rush hour. He crawls along London Road, round to the Oracle and on to the ring road. Caversham Bridge is jammed and he taps the steering wheel impatiently, wanting his arrival to be over. He's impatient to know what will greet him when he gets there. Outside the house he points the remote control at the electric gates and they slowly open. The drive sweeps round to the right and the house is partially screened by laurel bushes. All this has been carefully designed by his wife. Her car is not there and he lets out a snort. Why had he expected it to be? Of course she'll still be at work. New York'll be in full flow right now. He used to mind the time difference, how it shaped their lives. Now he's kind of resigned to it, knows how he feels about it won't change a thing.

He lets himself in and stands in the hallway listening. There are sounds in its heart and he's comforted by this.

The door to the playroom opens and Orlando rushes out of it and crashes into Myles's legs. 'Daddy,' he pants, 'come and see!'

Their dog follows him, his claws making a *pink, pink* sound on the wooden flooring. He's wagging his tail madly and is smiling widely at Myles.

'Hello, Orlando,' Myles said. 'And hello, Benjy Dog.'

Orlando doesn't take his father's hand but instead expects him to follow them back into the playroom, which of course he does.

'Look!' Once inside the room, Orlando skips over to the corner by the window and crouches down on his haunches. Myles can see the back of his son's head and marvels anew at the seriousness of it, how it bends forward, how delicate his neck is, how heavy his head, how perfectly his hair curls over the collar of his pyjamas.

'Hey, that's great, my man,' Myles says, squatting down next to the Brio train track his son has constructed.

'Here's the sidings, the sheds, platforms one, two, three,' Orlando points and then picks up an engine, turns it over and gazes at its wheels adoringly. 'This is the train to London,' he says. 'Like the one Mummy goes on sometimes.'

'Ah, there you are. Time for teeth cleaning,' Anka says from the doorway.

'Do I have to?' Orlando whines.

'Yes, you know you do.' Her voice is kind, full of patience. She nods in Myles's direction. 'Hello, Myles,' she says, her voice accented, somewhat guttural.

'Hi there,' he says. 'Have you had a good day?'

'Yes, thank you.'

Anka is big-boned and strong. She has capable arms and legs and stands no nonsense. She is only twenty but already has a maturity which Myles cannot comprehend. It's almost as though she was born older than her years. He's rarely heard her raise her voice to his children, has sometimes heard her sing as she goes about his house and is often saddened by the thought that she is the person his sons will run to if they hurt themselves or need an arbiter to solve an 'It's my turn, No it isn't' kind of argument.

'Go on, go with Anka,' he says now to Orlando.

'Promise you won't touch my trains,' he says.

'Of course I won't. Look, I'll come upstairs with you. Is Garth in bed?' he asks Anka.

She nods as she leads Orlando out of the playroom. Myles and the dog follow. Myles is concentrating. It shouldn't be like this, he tells himself. I shouldn't need to try so hard with them.

Upstairs, he finds a drowsy Garth curled up under his Thomas the Tank Engine duvet.

'Night, Daddy,' Garth says, turning his face to the wall, his body bunched up and tiny. How is it, Myles wonders not for the first time, that these children seem so all-consuming when they are awake, so huge and powerful, yet when they are asleep they are so small and vulnerable?

Myles has often been surprised by how fatherhood came to him, like it was preordained by his wife; a kind of 'Fuck me now' sort of thing. Did she really say, 'I'm ovulating and if it works I can have the baby before the next set of sales figures come in,' as though it was some kind of performance metric? Even so, Myles had fucked his wife and three times it had worked as she'd wished, but there are times when Myles has trouble remembering the details of the pregnancies and the births and he doesn't know why. After all, shouldn't they be permanently engraved on to his heart? Aren't they the most important things in his life? After what happened with Louisa, aren't these the occasions that should define him?

He creeps out of Garth's room and taps lightly on Bruno's door.

There's a grunt from inside. He ventures in.

'Hi,' he says. 'I'm home.'

'So I see.'

Bruno stopped talking to him about six months ago, about the time when the shape of his face changed from that of the boy Myles had always known to that of an almost-adolescent who is an almost-stranger. His son's limbs seem to lengthen daily and there are times when his voice drops a register and Myles gets a glimpse of the man his son will become. Already, this boy who is sitting in front of a TV screen, an Xbox controller clamped firmly in his hands, is moving away from him as all children move away from their parents with barely a backward glance and with, obviously, no idea how much this puzzles and hurts them, as it's now puzzling and hurting Myles.

'Good day?' he asks tentatively.

'Uh-huh,' his son replies, his thumbs a blur as the sounds of swords crashing and men's voices shouting fill the room.

'Great. I'll see you later, then.'

'OK.'

It's as much as he could have hoped for, much, much less than he would have wanted and, as Myles pulls his son's door to, he hears his wife's heels on the parquet flooring in the hallway. Benjy Dog stays close to him on the landing. He doesn't bound down the stairs to greet her. Neither of them does. Instead, Myles takes a deep breath and makes his way to the top of the staircase from where he can see the top of Celeste's head and follows her brisk movements as she puts her briefcase down, takes off her jacket and folds it over the newel post.

'Hi there,' he says.

6

In Belle Avenue, Rose washes up the tea things slowly and carefully; it's like she's playing a game with herself. She puts the crockery away in the kitchen cupboard, the teapot in the sideboard in the lounge, the leftover biscuits in Mother's tin with the picture of Windsor Castle on it. The house is quiet around her. It's mid-afternoon and she can't remember having had any lunch so cuts herself a piece of Madeira cake and carries it out to the veranda where she sits, wrapped in a shawl, and very deliberately eats it piece by tiny piece with a small silver fork, and all the time she is aware of the box on the table by her chair in the other room.

There is, she thinks, probably no point her having asked Myles to get it down for her; after all she knows its contents by heart. But still, there are times when actually to hold them is as necessary as breathing. It's been so long, far too long.

She'd asked Eve to put it on the top shelf of her wardrobe to avoid temptation; there's no way she can get it down by herself and, yes, she could wait until the next time Eve comes to visit, but when she'd heard Myles downstairs earlier, the idea came to her and it grew in her head, and it grew until it filled all the available space. And he'd seen her dresses but hadn't commented, and for this she is grateful. How would she have been able to explain? Even though it was years ago, she still feels a slight sting of shame about what happened, though it's only very slight now, like the merest whisper of it, and it's long been swamped by, covered over with the joy of it, the grief at its going.

She looks out over the garden as she finishes the slice of cake. The leaves are heavy with summer, the sky overcast, and for a second she feels claustrophobic, like her garden is pressing in on her on both sides. She must get out there and do some trimming back; there's always so much to do.

But, for now, she carries her plate back into the kitchen and puts it down by the sink and then moves with a feeling of inevitability towards the box, taking off her shawl as she does so. She's known all along she would look in the box and, when she picks it up and its weight is square and tactile, it's like she's in the thrall of a drug; the thrill of the anticipation, the high of it, the inevitable low that will follow when she has to put it away again. But for now she traces her fingers over Father's initials and is reminded once again that he never actually met Henry, nor had Mother, not really. The two of them had talked about him briefly, obliquely, when the news came, but Rose had thought at the time and still does that should she ever try and tell anyone else about it, it would dilute it. And anyway, how could anyone else understand? They'd say that what she'd done had been wrong; they'd make what was a hundred shades of grey and as ephemeral as mist into something black-and-white and tangible, something that could be defined as dishonourable, but she knows, as everyone should know, that the truth is never as clear cut as this. There is never a right or wrong way to love someone you shouldn't. Eve's grandmother, Verity, had understood this, had been the only person Rose had ever told, was probably the only one who could ever understand. Even Rose and Henry had found it difficult to know what was happening to them at times; they too had struggled to make sense of it.

Rose opens the box and picks out a piece of paper from the top of the pile of its contents. The paper is folded in half, is brittle and yellow with age and, as she unfolds it, her hands tremble very slightly.

It reads, 'Deconomus/Rose ~STOP~ launch Ajax Star, Piraeus, Oct '63 ~STOP~ Fix ~STOP~'

*

In late 1959 Mr Georgiadis had gone to Athens to see the family. Rose had booked him a BOAC flight and he'd been gone for two months when the telegram came. In his absence, the office had settled into a routine of calm under Henry's stewardship, but Rose knew that over the oceans, Mr Georgiadis would be busy doing deals, cementing relationships with his brothers, cousins and in-laws, oiling the machinery of his newly built shipping empire.

The Suez Crisis had changed things; there was now increased demand for large-tonnage ships, tax laws were tighter but oil was like liquid gold; money was flowing through the Aegean and despite his flamboyance and unpredictability, Mr Georgiadis was a shrewd businessman. He might not be in the office on a daily basis, but his presence could be felt everywhere. By none more so than Henry, who, as he showed the telegram to Rose, said, 'Deconomus? Do you know what that means?' A smile played at the corners of his mouth. He leant over Rose's desk and she caught a scent of his cologne. It was sharp and lemony.

'No,' she said. 'I don't.' She carried on typing to try to distract herself. Since the episode with the button, she'd found herself thinking more and more about Henry, especially at night in her room in the top of Verity's tall, narrow house off the Talgarth Road when she'd lie under her eiderdown and draw her knees up to her chest and marvel at how much loving Henry silently and secretly like she did could hurt.

'It's an ancient Greek word. It means manager, housekeeper, treasurer, that sort of thing,' Henry said. 'It's nice to see he's not lost his sense of humour.'

Rose wondered at the time and still doesn't quite know for sure what Henry really thought of Mr Georgiadis. It wasn't something that got talked about in those days. Henry came into the office at nine each morning and left again at five; he was mild-mannered and thorough and very, very private and Rose watched him come and go, constantly wanting him to rest his head on her breasts and for her to be able to hold him as she would a child. For a seemingly self-sufficient man, she had the feeling that, deep down, he was also a very lonely man. She waited for him to say something more; after all, it wasn't her place to speak.

It was a Tuesday. She remembers this now as she studies the telegram in her hands. It was late morning, just before lunch. The office boy had just carried in the second post together with the telegram and one of the copy typists from the pool had left a pile of letters on her desk to check. They had to be so careful; paper was still in short supply. Mistakes could be costly. Henry took the telegram over to the window. A bus must have pulled up at the stop just outside; Rose could hear the throaty pump of its engine.

What happened next surprised her. It still does. It was,

after all, really the beginning of everything that was to follow.

'Shall we . . .' Henry said, still looking out of the window. Rose presumed he was talking to her – the office boy and the copy typist had gone – the office was just the two of them. 'Shall we,' he said again, 'go and get some lunch and talk about the launch as per this?' He held up the telegram like it was a flag and waved it around self-consciously in the air.

'We?' Rose asked, her voice desperately quiet. She was terrified he didn't mean him and her; she was terrified that he did.

'Yes,' Henry said. 'Us.'

It's odd, although Rose can remember so much about that day, she can't recall what the weather was doing when they stepped on to Welbeck Street and Henry hailed a cab and said, 'Simpson's-in-the-Strand', but she does remember how worried she was about leaving her desk. What would happen should Mr Georgiadis telephone, or a client, or, and worse than anything, a ship was to hole, their worst nightmare . . . but she does remember being relieved she'd worn her navy blue, and her Joyce shoes and that her gloves had recently been laundered. She sat in the taxi cab, her handbag on her lap, her hands resting on top of it, and stared resolutely out of the window. Henry sat next to her and did not say a word. She was puzzled by how he thought going out for lunch would make their discussions about the launch any easier.

The streets flashed by them; women pushing prams, men tipping their hats, strong boys unloading deliveries from lorries stopped on the kerb. They passed greengrocers and newsagents, art galleries and clothes shops, but the legacy of rationing, even though it had ended five years before, meant there wasn't what you would call plenty. There was, however, the customary buzz around Shaftesbury Avenue, its newly reopened Queen's Theatre and John Gielgud's name in lights.

Henry turned to her and said, '*Rebecca* was playing there when the bomb hit in 1940.'

'Oh,' she replied, not knowing what else to say.

The cab pulled up outside Simpson's and the driver opened the door for her while Henry paid the fare. Then he rested his hand on the small of her back as he steered her under the glass canopy and left it there as the maître d' welcomed him like an old friend. Rose remembers shimmying her body slightly so that Henry's hand fell away, but once it had gone, she realised she missed its gentle pressure.

A waiter took their hats and coats away while the maître d' steered them into the Grand Divan, where he seated them at a table for two.

'What would you like?' Henry asked her as they studied the menu.

'Oh, I really don't know,' she replied. She had never been anywhere like this before. Her mother's kitchen produced bacon and kidneys with sprouts and potatoes from her father's garden; sometimes there were poached eggs or rabbit stew or a little grated onion and Bovril added to a tin of soup, followed by custard and stewed dates. When Rose went home at the weekend, Mother was often to be found shaking her head over the stewing pot and saying, 'Best end of neck, one shilling and ninepence. Look, there's hardly anything to it.' But here was elegance and weighty cutlery and linen napkins.

'Shall I choose for you?' Henry asked.

'Oh, would you? That would be kind,' she said in reply.

'We'll both have the fish to start, then the chicken,' Henry said to the waiter who had appeared as if by magic. 'Oh, and a bottle of the 1950 Bordeaux.' Henry looked across the table at Rose and added almost apologetically, 'My wife. She . . .'

But he did not finish saying what his wife was because the waiter was back again, pouring water from a jug into their glasses and snapping out their napkins and laying them with a flourish on their laps. Around them was the gentle hum of conversation. The maître d' had slipped away. Henry and Rose smiled awkwardly at one another.

'So,' Rose ventured, 'the launch. Should we discuss the launch?'

'Yes, maybe, but later, perhaps.' Henry shifted in his seat, played with the inch of cuff showing underneath his jacket sleeve.

At this time Henry was only forty but to Rose he seemed much older, much wiser, wiser than her father, than Mr Georgiadis actually. His pale blue eyes blinked at her and she found, as she looked at him across the table, that his outer edges seemed to blur until he became more a shape than a person, more and more familiar, more necessary to her as each second ticked by. This, she felt, was where she was always destined to be.

But, over his shoulder she could see and feel the presence of his wife; could imagine him returning home after a day at the office and leaving his briefcase in the hallway of his house and his wife putting down the book she's reading, *The Bell* by Iris Murdoch perhaps, and calling out in a firm and confident voice, 'Hello there, Henry, am in the drawing room.'

The waiters in Simpson's brought their food and they ate, mostly in silence, just the odd, 'This is delicious, Henry,' from her and 'Are you sure you're enjoying it?' from him.

Then, over their main courses, he said apropos of nothing much at all, 'It's not just about the launch, why I suggested lunch.'

'Oh,' she said, 'I see.'

'I wanted to talk to you, I mean, really talk. We see each

other every day. We say “Hello” and “How are you?” and we’re always, “Fine, thank you, really well.” But, there’s more, isn’t there? There must be more?’

‘Oh,’ she said again. ‘I suppose there must.’

‘I mean,’ he continued, spearing a piece of carrot but not raising it to his mouth, ‘there just has to be more.’

There was a silence then. He ate the carrot, she took a sip of the wine; it made her tongue sing. She had tasted nothing quite like it before.

‘I was ten,’ he said suddenly into the silence, ‘shopping in Harrods with an aunt. It was the summer holidays, my last year at Honeywells. Mother was in the country, Father had stayed in town for work. This aunt, the one I’d been fobbed off to for the day, was my mother’s brother’s wife and she’d just bought nylons and I remember feeling outraged at being made to witness the purchase. She didn’t have any children of her own, so maybe she didn’t understand.’ He laughed a little when he said this. Rose stayed quiet, fearing that any interruption from her would break the spell. This was obviously something he needed to say, maybe not specifically to her, maybe just to anyone, but it needed saying anyway.

Henry continued. ‘We’d just come out on to the Brompton Road when I saw him. Father, that is. He was with a woman. Tiny she was, very well dressed, a fox fur around her shoulders. I remember thinking she must have the smallest feet I'd ever seen on a grown-up. And she was holding on to Father's arm and smiling up at him and he had a look on his face I'd never seen before. I spent years afterwards trying to find a word for that look and finally, when you handed me my jacket recently, you know, the one you'd sewn the button back on?' She nodded. 'Well,' he continued, 'the word came to me. It was the look on your face. It was suffused with something and there was the word, suffused. That's what Father's face was like that day. I'd never seen it before and never saw it again. That was 1929, you see. It all changed after that. The stock-market crash took him out and he . . .'

Here Henry picked up his wine glass, took a mouthful, rolling the wine around on his tongue. He blinked once, twice, as he held out his right hand and covered Rose's left hand with it. She dared not move, felt the skin on the back of hers tingle at his touch.

'He,' Henry said, after he'd swallowed the wine, 'killed himself shortly afterwards, had lost a packet, you see. So it was a shotgun, in the library, brains all over a complete set of Dickens that was rather valuable, apparently. Mother never forgave him, either for killing himself, or for the Dickens, and of course, simply everything changed after that. Mother knew Penelope's people and the deal was done when I was eighteen. She also knew Mr Georgiadis, got me the position with him, and so it's taken twenty years of marriage to Penelope and learning the shipping business from Mr Georgiadis and him fixing it for me to be reserved during the war, what with shipping being so fundamental and everything, he was awarded a Liberty ship, you know, and us all surviving Korea when it had seemed a matter of when, not if, and anyway, now I'm here and it's twenty years later and I've never felt suffused.' He paused to take a breath, then continued, 'That's it, Rose, although I hated Father for a long time for what he did, there have been times recently when I've envied him the look on his face that day with the woman who's name I never knew, who wasn't even able to be at his funeral.'

Rose carefully puts down the telegram she's been holding and studies her hand, remembers how, when Henry had finished talking, she'd slowly turned it over and wound her fingers through his, had sworn to herself that he would one day look at her and his face would be suffused with joy. It would be her perfect gift to him; it would be her perfect gift to herself.

It's evening and Rose is wearing Father's work coat and is tying back the clematis with garden twine. It's a most satisfactory activity and Rose is humming quietly to herself as she works. The sky has lifted a little now that dusk is approaching and the birds are chorusing, shouting at one another from the trees. Next door's cat slinks through the undergrowth, passing close by Rose, and both she and he nod in greeting as he stops to stare at her for a while. Then he lifts his head as if to smell the air and saunters away.

There's been something nudging at the edges of Rose's mind all day, ever since she put the telegram back in the box and closed the lid of it firmly and pushed it to the far end of the table so it wouldn't be directly in her line of sight when she sat in her chair. She will ask Eve to put it back for her next time she comes round and now, as she stretches a little to lean into the fence to find a slat around which to tie the twine, she realises what it is. It's that there is something Henry-ish about Myles. Talking to him, or rather listening to him earlier, had reminded her so much of Henry; not just the way he tilts his head, or looks at her as if she has the answers, but in the fact that, like Henry, he too seems trapped in a situation over which he has no control. There is an innate sadness in the hearts of both of these men, she thinks, as she lifts a clematis shoot and gently wraps the string around it.

Then she lets herself think of that evening, after the lunch at Simpson's when she'd got in from work and Verity had said, 'Hello, Rose dear. Good day?'

'It's been a different day,' Rose said, pausing at the bottom of the stairs and looking down the long narrow corridor to where Verity and Meredith had their rooms. Verity was standing in the kitchen doorway, wiping her hands on a towel. 'Henry took me to Simpson's-in-the-Strand for lunch. Said he wanted to talk about the launch of a ship Mr Georgiadis is planning, but we didn't talk about the ship, or the launch or Mr Georgiadis.' Rose smiled hesitantly at Verity. She could, she remembers, still taste the wine on her tongue and the cloves in the apple pie Henry had ordered them for dessert.

'Oh, did he?' said Verity. 'Would this be Henry, the married Henry?'

'Yes, but there was nothing in it, it was just lunch, we just talked.'

Verity came out of the kitchen and along the hallway towards Rose and looked carefully at her in the gloom cast by the weak electric bulb in the ceiling. She wore a printed cotton dress, a cardigan she'd knitted herself and a pinny with flowers on it. 'Be careful, Rose dear. Men aren't always what they seem.'

At this time Verity was forty-three and had been a widow since D-Day. Her daughter, Meredith, had been conceived on Ray's last leave and had been born in January 1941 when there was snow on the ground and the Blitz all around and now Meredith was eighteen and stepping out with a nice young man who worked in a bank. All this, of course, was before Meredith ditched the nice young man who worked in a bank and, in 1970, met Roddy, the aged hippy Roddy who, after they'd had Eve and tried the whole dull suburban thing in a terraced house to the west of Reading, had upped and moved to California, leaving Verity to die in the Royal Berkshire Hospital with only the newly pregnant twenty-five-year-old Eve, and Andrew, of course, by her side.

But all this was in the future, Rose is jumping ahead. For now she's back in the house off the Talgarth Road smiling at Verity, pleased to have her wisdom at close hand, pleased she could say things to Verity she could not tell her own parents, pleased she has a room in the eaves of this house, pleased she has her wash basin, gas ring, meter and the bathroom and separate lav she shares with the other girl on the top floor, pleased that outside the skylight each morning she can see her very own slice of London sky.

And Verity was more than Rose's landlady, she was, Rose now realises as she wipes away a stray and unwelcome tear that's become caught in the creases in the skin on her cheek, the older sister she never had. That's why meeting Eve again at Verity's funeral, having Eve as her friend now means so much; it links the past to now, it's an indirect link, but a link nonetheless back to then, back to Henry. It proves that once he had been real.

But, she thinks, as she looks up at the darkening sky, that's all a story for another day as well. Today has been full enough as is it. In the gap between her house and next door she can see that the streetlamp in Belle Avenue has come on and so she puts the twine and garden scissors away and slowly climbs the steps back up the house. She holds on to the railing tightly, her knees creak complainingly. Suddenly she is very tired.

7

It's Wednesday, a couple of weeks later; Jodie's results are due tomorrow and Eve feels jittery. More so than Jodie, it would appear. She'd got up and gone to work as usual that morning with only the slightest incline of her head to acknowledge she'd heard Eve say, 'One more day then, my darling.' And now, as Eve puts the key in the lock of Rose's front door, she has to stop and breathe slowly; in, out, in, out.

It's been one of those August days of no weather. It could have been beautiful if it had decided to but, even now, at just before one o'clock, it hasn't committed itself either way. Eve has a bit over the hour for lunch today as Max is out at a meeting and doesn't need her back. She can always work a bit later this evening; it will help take her mind off tomorrow.

She steps into the hall and walks quietly past Myles's

door. She knows he's there; his car is parked outside and right now she doesn't want to question too closely why her heart missed a beat when she saw it. Probably to do with the results, she tells herself as she listens briefly for sounds coming from inside the room. She can hear the faint tapping of fingers on a keyboard. The rest of the house is in silence.

'Hi there,' she calls as she lets herself into Rose's flat.

There is no reply.

'Rose? It's me. I've brought bagels. Salmon and cream cheese.'

Still no reply.

Eve puts the bag containing the bagels down on the floor and goes into Rose's bedroom. All is as it should be. The bed's made, the curtains are drawn back, Rose's silver-backed hair brush is positioned neatly on her dressing table. Eve rushes into the kitchen. Again, there is nothing out of place, but neither is there a note by the kettle saying 'Popped out for milk. Back in five minutes' as Eve would have expected. She unlocks the back door and peers down the steps. 'Rose?' she calls. 'You in the garden?' Of course she isn't. The back door wouldn't have been locked if she were.

She's met there by yet more silence, only distant bird-song and the hum of traffic, but no Rose calling out, 'I'm here, dead-heading again!' so Eve bounds down the steps and into the garden. The full, flat summer leaves are rustling quietly and a blackbird sets up an alarm call at Eve's intrusion. She turns and climbs the steps back up into the flat, doesn't wait to think, she can't; she doesn't know that it will all really start from now, but finds herself outside Myles's door. 'Myles!' she shouts, hammering on it. 'Myles!'

From inside is the sound of his chair being pushed back and his footsteps hurrying across the floor. He opens the door.

'What? What's wrong?' he asks, looking at Eve, rubbing his stubble with his hand, his eyes dark with alarm.

'Rose isn't home. I'd arranged to bring her lunch. I'm worried. She's never not here. She hasn't left me a message or anything. Do you know where she is?'

Myles leans up against the doorframe. He looks weary. 'She went out,' he says, 'about an hour or so ago. Turned left out of the gate. I presumed she was popping to the shops, or something. Didn't she tell you she was going out?'

'No!' Eve's anger is refreshing.

'Look, come in. Wait for her here?' Myles looks over his shoulder into the room behind him.

'Oh no, I couldn't. You're working.'

'It doesn't matter. I could do with a break anyway. My detective's at the path lab, just about to be told the contents of the victim's stomach. I think I need to steel myself for it, so really, a break would do me good.'

He smiles at her as he says this and the bizarreness of the conversation calms her. Path labs? Victim? Stomach contents? He takes a step back into the room and she follows, saying, 'I'll ring her mobile, just in case. She never has the bloody thing switched on, though. And,' she pauses, looking at the sparse but solid furniture, the absence of pictures on the walls, 'perhaps we could leave your door open, so I can catch her if she comes back?'

'Of course,' Myles says. 'Shall I put the kettle on? Looks like you could do with a coffee.'

'Oh, yes. That would be lovely.'

And before she knows what she's doing, Eve is sitting on the battered brown leather sofa in Myles's flat, listening to him in the kitchen. Outside the window, the sun decides to make its first tentative steps into the day.

Eve rings Rose's phone. It is, as she predicted, turned off.

Myles comes back carrying two mugs. He puts one down on his desk and walks over to where she's sitting with the other. He looms over her and she can feel the heat of him. As her breath catches in her throat, she tells herself not to be so stupid. When he holds out the mug, he turns it so that the handle is facing her. For this she is grateful. She doesn't have to touch any part of his hand this way.

He sits at his desk, swivels his chair a bit and leans back

in it. She holds on to the coffee as though it's a lifeline. There is an awkward silence.

'I'm sure Rose'll be back soon,' he says.

'Yes,' she replies. 'Just wish I knew where she'd gone, that's all.'

'She looked jaunty enough. When she left, I mean,' he adds, taking a sip of his coffee. He glances across at his laptop screen, leans over and presses a key on the keyboard.

'Sorry, I'm disturbing you.'

'No, as I said, I could do with a break. Just saving the document, that's all.'

'It must be wonderful.'

'What must?'

He looks at her and all at once he seems so utterly familiar to her and yet so new. A kind of pain flashes across her chest; it takes her completely by surprise, it leaves her breathless. She doesn't answer his question immediately but instead thinks how odd it is that she's met so many men throughout her life – Max, others at work, the members of Andrew's band, the window cleaner, people in shops, at garages, men crossing the road who look fleetingly at her as they do so, and not once has she ever felt this: this feeling of being suspended, this kind of floating, this thought that only his voice could ever ground her. Not even in the early days with Andrew had she experienced this. That had been more of a gradual thing, not this sudden inexplicable fist of something which seems to have bunched up and settled somewhere at the base of her throat. It's obviously wrong that she should feel this way, but it's instinctive, like he's calling to her and she's answering him. And that's OK, isn't it, because it's harmless, at a distance, a fiction; it's something she's made up, not part of her real life? After all, this man is someone else's husband, no doubt. She is someone else's wife, and yet, and yet . . . She shakes her head. Tells herself to stop.

'What is?' he asks again.

'Oh,' she looks down into her coffee cup. 'Being able to create something out of nothing, with your writing, I mean; you know people, places, other people's stories which complete strangers want to lose themselves in. I'm not,' she pauses, looks out of the window, wishes she hadn't started this, 'I'm not expressing myself very well, am I?'

'I know exactly what you mean.' His voice is kind and deep and his eyes are shining as he continues. 'Most people,' he says, 'ask how the book's going. But it's not ever really a question of that; it's more like every time I sit here, there's a kind of miracle that lets the words out. That's what I want to tell people about. It's hardly a conscious thing and yes, you're right, it is amazing, this act of creation. I guess it's the same for all artists: writers, potters, sculptors, poets, people like that. They must feel the same way.'

Eve shifts position on the sofa, stretches her legs out a bit further. She is beginning to relax a little. This is a nice place to be, she thinks. She hopes Rose comes back soon and she hopes she doesn't. It would be good to stay here a while longer and lose herself in this particular place which is so different from anything she has ever known, so far away from the routines of her normal life. She can be a new person here and she likes the thought of being new, she likes this very much.

'So,' he continues, 'what are your favourite books?'

'I don't actually get much time to read.' She's ashamed when she says this.

'Oh,' he says. 'You should. I could recommend some titles to you if you like. On email, or text, maybe?'

'Oh, that would be kind.'

'Here, write your details on this.' He passes her a used envelope. The address is facing downwards. She turns the envelope over. It says Mr M. Stephens and there's an address in Caversham.

'Oh, you live in Caversham then?' she asks.

'Yes.' He doesn't say anything more. She wishes he would, is glad he hasn't.

She writes down her work email and her mobile number. 'It's probably good to have each other's mobile numbers anyway, you know, just in case, about Rose.'

'Yes.' He smiles as he says this and the pain is back in

her chest, like ice, like fire. It takes her by surprise again. 'I'll send you mine.'

And he does. He picks his phone out of his jeans pocket and a moment later her phone buzzes in her bag at her feet.

'There,' he says. 'That's done that.'

'Yes,' she says and it felt that something indeed had been done, something irrevocable, something wonderful. She is now finding it even more difficult to breathe.

She starts to stand up. 'I guess I'd better be going. Shall I put your cup in the kitchen?'

'Aren't you going to wait for Rose?' he asks.

'I'd love to, but time's getting on and . . .' She stops by the doorway to the kitchen and looks back into the room at him.

'I can text you when she gets back if you like.' He sounds eager.

'OK, or I can leave her a note and get her to phone me.'

'We could do both!' He laughs as he says this and there's a glint of mischief in his eyes.

She likes this; the air in the room tingles with it, the skin on the back of her neck tingles with it. He'd said 'we' and just for a second it had sounded right somehow.

Neither of them hear the gate latch lift or Rose's footsteps on the path and, when the front door closes behind her, it makes them jump; they look at one another across the room like school children caught out doing something they shouldn't. There is no need for this; they have done nothing wrong, Eve tells herself, as she hurries to Myles's open door and pops her head out and says, 'Rose! Where *have* you been?'

If Rose is surprised to see Eve in Myles's flat, she doesn't show it. Instead, she puts down her shopping bag and looks up at Eve.

'Oh, sorry. I must have lost track of time,' she says. 'I popped out for a few things, met Adele Evans outside the Post Office and you know how she can talk!'

Eve doesn't know. She doesn't know who Adele Evans is. Rose has never mentioned her before.

'I was worried,' she says now.

'But Myles looked after you?' Rose asks. She doesn't wait for a reply. 'That was kind of him.'

Eve watches as Rose glances at Myles. Rose's face is inscrutable and Eve has no idea what she's really thinking and, for the first time in a long time, she wonders about the secrets which are lodged deep in Rose's heart, about what's in the wooden box she asks Eve to lift down for her now and again and what really happened with the man in the photograph; the man with the sad smile.

The potted history Rose has shared with Eve is tidy and harmless; something about Greeks and ships, this house, Rose's parents and an office in Welbeck Street in London.

There have been facts but not much else. Rose has always been more interested in Eve's stories and they've filled the years they've known one another with them and so now, as they are standing in the hallway of the house in Belle Avenue, Eve is struck by the thought that perhaps she doesn't know Rose as well as she should; there is more to find out.

'Yes, I did,' Myles says now. 'Well, I tried at least. I gave her coffee. Told her not to worry.'

Again, he's smiling and everything seems possible. This man has a gift, Eve thinks, a gift of strength and certainty which is refreshing. She believes she could believe in him; that he would be good for her; that he could fill the spaces which seem to have appeared in her life recently. And this would be OK, wouldn't it? They'd just be friends. They'd talk about books and Rose and current affairs and one day they might exchange news about their families like ordinary friends would. She could be this new person to him; she could make it up as she went along and she could keep that fizz in her chest, this fizz which is something light and colourful, like a firework, not a pain after all.

Yes, knowing this man could be a good thing, she tells herself as she looks back over at Myles, says, smiling at him, 'He did. Thank you.' It will be nice to know him and be known by him and these new feelings are nice too; they are refreshing and she will stay safe. This is a situation she will be able to control.

And, on her way back to work Eve tries to sort out the sequence of events in her head. There was arriving at the house, Rose not being there, knocking on Myles's door, but the rest is a jumble. She can't remember exactly what was said, knows she left the bagels with Rose, said she'd grab something from the canteen at work instead, that she'd see Rose again soon and that there'd been this other presence surrounding her; someone warm and good and not dangerous at all.

After she parks her car, she looks at her phone. The sun is hot through the windscreen. Briefly, she thinks that this evening will be a beautiful one after all. Someone's sent her a text and, for a second, she can't think who it could be from, doesn't remember receiving it and then she does and it's like she's falling. She saves the number as 'Myles Stephens', telling herself that using his surname makes it OK. It's what she would do with any other number, any other acquaintance, isn't it?

8

The path lab is cold and its stainless-steel surfaces glint somewhat cruelly. DCI Pletheroe is standing behind a screen and the disembodied voice of the pathologist is coming out of a speaker behind his head. The actual pathologist is next to a trolley and on the trolley is a body covered in a green cloth, but the pathologist and the amplified voice seem to have nothing whatsoever to do with one another. Derek Pletheroe knows that the victim's organs have been scrutinised, weighed and tidied away and the body stitched back up; he knows the contents of the woman's stomach will have been catalogued.

'Well?' he shouts. He doesn't need to shout. His colleagues are always telling him this.

'Curry,' says the voice from the speaker behind his head. 'Chicken, Balti by the look of it. Mushroom rice, naan bread.'

'And?'

'About two hours before death. She'd been dead for thirty-six hours when found.'

'Anything else?'

'She'd had a child. About ten years ago. Caesarean section.'

Myles stops typing. He can't concentrate because Eve is still in the room. She's been gone for two hours, yet she's still there; the faintest trace of her perfume, the warmth of her body on the sofa. He tells himself it's because he's had so few visitors here that her presence lingers. All is quiet upstairs. He assumes Rose is resting. He pushes back his chair, goes into the kitchen and lifts up the mug Eve used. He tips the dregs into the sink and fills the bowl with hot soapy water. He washes it and then his own and leaves them to dry on the draining board. They are close up to one another, almost touching. He feels better for having done this and goes back to his desk.

'In the briefing room, Pletheroe barks, 'Curry houses and hospitals!' A sea of faces stares at him and a huge sadness wells up in his chest. He has been here so many times before.

Myles stops typing again. This time he goes out in the garden and stands listening to the traffic and birdsong. He touches the soft blue petals of an agapanthus and tries, he really tries, not to think of Eve.

But he'd said he'd recommend some books to her, hadn't he? That would be an OK thing to do; it's the sort of thing that a friend would do. He tries to remember her face, but can't; it's more an impression of movement and shade and the way her hair rested against her shoulders. He finds he's lifting his hand from the petals as if to touch a strand of it.

Back in the flat, he clears his throat and opens his emails. He'll leave his DCI alone for a bit with the sea of faces suspended in front of him. Pletheroe's colleagues are bored – they don't care about the victim, not really. They want to get this next bit done so they can go down the Feathers and gossip about the new girl in Vice. There's an email from Celeste. It was sent at 8.03 a.m. Myles's heart sinks.

Its title is 'Tasks' and he imagines her fingers flying across the keyboard of her iPad; they make no sound on it. He sees her sitting at her desk, bunched, already a little cross and someone is probably waiting to speak to her. She will be impeccably dressed.

The email has no salutation, it is just a list:

1. Increase standing order to gardener by £20 pcm
2. Arrange gutter clearance
3. Fill in and return PTA form for B's new school

There is no 'Love, Celeste,' or even, 'Thanks.' The email just ends and there is white space to the bottom of the screen.

Myles wonders if the tasks are for him or whether they're an aide-memoire for her. He suspects it's the former and highlights the message as unread to remind himself that he has to do these things. He tries not to bristle with annoyance, but he's vexed and not just about this particular email, but about everything; all the mundaneness of their relationship. It really shouldn't be like this.

He starts an email to Eve; the title is 'Book recommendations' but then he stalls. There are millions to choose from. How can he possibly recommend two or three? He closes his eyes and takes a mental walk past his bookshelves at home. Celeste had allowed these shelves to be built in what's known as the 'den'. It's a room with a large black sofa in it, a huge TV screen, a white rug. There is a Mondrian print on one wall. There is nothing relaxing about this room and he rarely goes in it, although Anka sometimes spends her evenings in there rather than her own room and he visits it occasionally to look at the shelves either side of the fireplace and lift out a book and flick through the pages. The books he has written are in amongst them; under S, where they should be, apparently.

'Hi,' he types. He should be good at this. He's good with words, isn't he?

'Have been thinking about some books you might like to read. How about *Rebecca* by Daphne du Maurier, or *The Guernsey Literary & Potato Peel Pie Society* (Mary Ann Schaffer & Annie Barrows), or *Pride & Prejudice* by Jane Austen? All very different, but . . .'

He tails off, doesn't quite know why he's doing this. How can he possibly know what she'd like? He barely knows her at all. She's lived a whole life without him, has all sorts of private thoughts and relationships he knows nothing about. What's her favourite colour, favourite food? Where did she grow up? What does she think of global warming? The fact he doesn't know these things seems insurmountable. Where could he start? He'd given her a cup of coffee; had assumed she took it as he did, with milk, no sugar. But maybe he'd got it wrong? He hadn't even asked her. And yet, and yet, he feels drawn in by her, by something in her that is like a flare being sent into the night sky, seeking help, asking for company. He saves the email to Drafts. It wouldn't be good to send it too soon and anyway, he needs to decide how to finish it, how to sign his name at the end.

Typing the link for BBC news into the browser bar, the screen flashes at him and in the second headline down he sees the name 'Louisa'; something about an appeal in the High Court. He doesn't read any further because he's thinking back to his conversation with Rose about the Louisa he knew, about his IT job in the City, and his motorbike, the smell of his leathers, about weaving in and out of the traffic and the alleged freedom of those days.

He and Louisa had lived in a flat in Wapping. They'd met at work. She was twenty-one, he was twenty-seven. It didn't seem that big an age gap when they'd started dating and she'd accepted his offer that they should live together nice and quickly and with barely a backward glance at the boyfriend she'd had at university, or at her parents who lived in one of the nicer houses on the run into Watford from the M25. Louisa was easy on the eye, very easy. She was tall, slender, had short dark hair. Her eyes were the colour of mink. She worked in Accounts after joining the company straight from university where she'd studied Business with Marketing. In the early days Myles hadn't met Louisa's ambition, but he soon came to know it very well.

Louisa's ambition was hard and bright and sometimes when they fucked, their limbs against the satin sheets they'd bought to be ironic (or so Louisa had said at the time), he got the feeling that he was not much more than a notch in her bedpost but then, in the morning, he'd find her in the kitchen making coffee wearing one of his shirts, and her skin would be dusky and she would smile at him over her shoulder and he would tell himself not to be silly, this was the best place they both could be.

But he wasn't like Louisa; his ambition was transitory

and a bit devil-may-care. He'd kind of fallen into IT after doing a course at the local college after his A-levels. Then came a few years doing mobile work, turning the PCs of harassed home-workers on and off again and reconfiguring their modems and sometimes getting rid of viruses and he was bored, mostly bored. Then he saw the advert for City Microsolutions, who had offices just by St Paul's, and he'd applied, got the job and liked being the guy who could fix things for the guys who worked there; sorting out security issues, monitoring emails for undue amounts of flesh tones, that sort of thing. And, of course, he'd bought his motorbike, started to fancy himself as a writer, met Louisa and had thought himself a player, sorted.

And time had had a habit of seeping on, quietly, unobtrusively. Their routines were simple and agreeable: Monday to Friday he and Louisa would work, go out with friends in the evenings, sometimes to the cinema or the theatre, sometimes together, sometimes not; Saturdays they would exercise at the local gym and watch a DVD and Sundays they would make love, read the papers, go to a market, buy stuff and he would write in odd oasis-like moments. But also, and imperceptibly, during this time Louisa steadily moved up the rankings at work until she was number two to the CFO and the Monday-to-Friday working thing took precedence, there was less sex and Myles started exercising more, writing more. And more and more often he'd pass a woman in the street pushing a buggy, or see a man holding on to a child's hand and wish family life for himself.

Who knows where it might have ended up had Louisa not gone away for a few days just before Myles's thirty-seventh birthday and the maintenance company who looked after their block of flats not had a question about the drains so he'd needed to contact Louisa and, when he couldn't get through to her on her mobile, he'd asked her PA, who'd been cagey and embarrassed about where Louisa had gone. And so this is what happened when Louisa came back. The scene is still playing in a loop inside Myles's head, even now; even all these years later.

It was a Wednesday night. Myles was in the flat watching TV when he heard her key in the door.

'Oh, you're home,' he said. He tried not to sound narky, but in his head were flashing images of her with some other bloke; her wearing nothing but a pair of lacy knickers, the man's mouth around one of her nipples, her lips open, her head thrown back.

'Yes.' She sounded tired. She put the case she'd been carrying down by the door.

'May I ask where you've been?'

It seemed to take hours for her to walk across to where he was sitting. He told himself not to move. He crossed his legs and put one arm along the back of the sofa and looked up at her.

'Oh Myles,' she said. And then she cried. Huge, hot tears; her shoulders shook. She sank to the floor and drew her knees up to her chin. The tears fell on to them.

In the ten years they'd been together, she'd rarely, if ever, cried. If she had, it would be a sort of dry sob, one slightly damp eye. Not this.

'Oh my God,' he said, sliding off the sofa and sitting down next to her on the floor. He tried to hold her but she shook him off.

It was then he thought she must be ill, dying most likely, and he'd have to nurse her and he wouldn't know how to do it and he'd do it all wrong. 'What it is? What's wrong?' he asked.

Even now he doesn't know whether it would have been harder for him to cope if she had told him she was ill. He still doesn't really know how he feels, so he writes about dead women instead, women who've had Caesarean sections, who have children somewhere out there in the world his DCI has to find.

There'd been a baby, fourteen weeks' worth of baby. Later he'd found out it would have been three and a half inches long and would have weighed one ounce, but she'd had a termination because she wanted to be CFO more than she wanted to be a mother, and because she was only thirty-one and there'd be time later and just then, when she told him this, he started to hate her and the hate drew back in on itself and grew in the dark spaces in his head, gathering strength over the next few weeks until he could barely look at her for making this decision without him, for going through it without him, for not letting him have the chance to know his child.

Now he is a father Myles is sure he would have wanted Louisa to have the baby; he's utterly convinced of this and he's never reconciled himself to her betrayal, although there is some small part of him that is still uncertain whether he minded more about the fact that she'd made the decision without him or that she'd made it at all. Would it, he wonders even now, be easier to accept if he'd been able to go with her, hold her hand afterwards? Whatever the case, what is certain is that he moved out shortly afterwards and within six months had met Celeste who, he believed, was someone totally different, that he'd get it right with her.

This is what he'd told Rose in the two minutes after he'd carried her box into the lounge upstairs. He'd reduced ten years and his heartbreak to a few short sentences and now he looks at his email screen, sees Celeste's message highlighted, sees the number one in brackets in the Drafts folder and is filled with something akin to despair that he'll ever actually get it right. He rather thinks he won't.

He writes for another hour, fuelled by some kind of fury and a need for vengeance, is pleased with his progress, is pleased with his DCI who has ordered an analysis of the victim's phone records and bank accounts. He's even got a specialist from the British Museum to scrutinise the chalice. A picture is starting to emerge; like the pieces of a puzzle, each fragment is slotting into place. For the present, DCI Pletheroe is in control.

So Myles decides to go for a run. This is a day for The Boss if ever there were one. He selects 'Born in the U.S.A.' on his iPod and sets off, turning left out of Belle Avenue and down the Wokingham Road, runs past the shops, the primary school, the United Reformed Church, until he gets to Palmer Park. The track's finished now, the playlist on shuffle and he regulates his breathing to the beat of the music and his footsteps on the path. He sets off around the park. It's a circular track one mile long. He will, he thinks, do five laps. This will be a good number to do.

And as he runs, he thinks of circles, of his life with Celeste and about his books and how he always seems to meet himself coming back from where he thinks he's got to. He desperately hopes it won't be the same for his boys. His love for them is both linear and circular; it is the best thing about him, it has to be. But then he thinks of his own parents and has to stop running for a moment. He rests his hands on a tree trunk and catches his breath. He hasn't thought about his mother in a long time, but here she is; her disembodied face is floating in his line of sight, and she is radiant, she is smiling.

Myles doesn't remember much about his childhood, it's more a cluster of images: ice cream melting in a blue plastic bowl, the smell of shoe polish, being an only child with a cat called Shadow who disappeared one day and never came back and, on the periphery, is his mother; somehow she is always twirling, always laughing. And then he gets sent away to boarding school – his father's idea, no doubt – and the memories change to hard mattresses, steamed puddings the consistency of cement and sitting in Latin lessons gazing out at the cricket green. But mostly it's the day his father came and Myles is sent for, is standing in the headmaster's office and his father has his back to him and there is something hunched about him, something already remote and untouchable. His mother is dead; she died on the operating table from a rare reaction to the anaesthetic during a routine hysterectomy.

One day she is there, twirling in the distance, laughing, and the next she's totally gone and how he felt about this became the start of this thing he has about pregnancy, why what Louisa did was so unforgivable. Myles wasn't actually told about the hysterectomy at the time but found this out for himself years later; it had been the kind of closure he'd needed at the time. All his father tells him that day in the headmaster's office is that his mother has died, that it is sad but that Myles, aged nine, needs to be a man about it. Myles, now aged fifty-two, is still unmanned by it.

And his father leaves, not just the school, but the country; he moves to Australia where he rides the dot-com wave, makes a fortune, remarries a girl half his age called Amber, has four children with her and doesn't contact Myles again, has never contacted Myles again. And whereas Myles has not forgotten his mother, he cannot remember his father, does not need to. It would not matter if he never heard from him, heard of him, spoke to him or saw him again. So Celeste's parents are the only grandparents his sons know and although they are more present, they too are at a distance and not entirely satisfactory. But, he argues, you can never miss what you've never known. Can you?

Myles starts running again. There's a pain in his chest. He's on lap three, thinks of his three sons, can't imagine ever not being close to them. It would break the heart that's now beating painfully under his ribs if he were ever estranged from them permanently. 'Estranged', such a tidy word, but one so packed with bitterness.

'Fuck it,' he says, as his playlist goes back to The Boss and 'Born to Run', and he swerves off the path he's so faithfully been following and heads diagonally across the park to the exit. En route he passes a group of students who've obviously stayed down during the summer to work, smoke weed, have uncomplicated sex. They're playing Frisbee, are all legs and torn jeans. They're obviously stoned.

'Hey, man,' they call to Myles as he runs by them.

Myles raises a hand and smiles, at least he thinks it's a smile; his face has contorted and, as he gets back to the Wokingham Road, he realises his eyes are watering but he's not crying – no, certainly not crying.

Back at the flat, he showers, changes, puts his running gear in the washing machine and turns it on. The sound of water and the whirring of the drum are oddly comforting. He goes back to his laptop, pulls up the draft email to Eve.

He's written, 'All very different, but . . .' and he sits and stares at the screen for a long time until his breathing steadies. Finally, he adds, 'I do hope you like them. Perhaps we can compare notes sometime?'

It's an invitation, a daring and possibly wrong one but, right at this moment with his skin stinging from the shower, his muscles sore from the run and his heart even sorer, he doesn't care. He believes he needs the chink of light Eve seems to have brought into his life so that one day maybe he'll be able to see the end of the tunnel he seems to be running through.

He signs the email, 'Best, Myles,' and presses Send. He doesn't let himself wonder what the best thing is he's offering her, all he knows is, as he switches off the laptop, takes his washing, which has somehow completed its cycle in the time it's taken him to finish the email, out of the machine and hangs it on the rack in the bathroom, that for the first time in he doesn't know how long he's feeling good.

9

The next day Eve sews. It's not so much an act of creation as an act of survival. Jodie had checked the UCAS website first thing and said, 'Nah, can't get on. Must be overloaded with everyone trying. I'll check later when I get back from school.'

And Andrew had gone to work.

'Surely, you're not going today?' Eve asked him as he got dressed.

He glanced over his shoulder at Eve and there was a look in his eyes she didn't recognise.

'Oh, Jodie'll call me. I know everything's going to be OK,' he said.

Jodie has chosen Durham as her first choice and UCL as her second. She wants to do Law, and every time Eve thinks about it a breath catches in the back of her throat and she has to hold on to something to steady her. The thought of Jodie being anywhere other than at home leaves her bereft but, she tells herself, with both places she'll only be a car journey away, there are phones and emails and this is what they've worked for; she should be proud of her daughter, and she is. And neither place is on the other side of the world, after all, is it?

However, as she threads the sewing machine and picks out some material from her remnants box on the landing, Eve is filled by a kind of bizarre anger and has to concentrate on smoothing the cloth, matching her breathing to the rhythm of the machine, focusing on the needle.

She'd decided to take the day off to spend with Jodie but, as soon as Andrew had left and Jodie's friends had come to call for her, she realised that this had been a foolish thing to do. Neither of them needed her today. The need came from her instead; she'd wanted to be wanted, for her daughter's day to have had her at its centre but, as she snipped the thread through the cutter at the back of the machine and studied the stitches, tutted at the way she'd obviously snagged them when her foot had pressed too hard on the pedal, she had to admit to herself that today will be a day when she moves closer to the edge of her daughter's life than she is already. Perhaps she should go and see Rose later instead? She doesn't wonder why she is drawn there today of all days, doesn't let herself think of Myles, his number on her phone, the fact he now has her work email and that they are already connected, very tenuously, but they are connected.

Her mobile rings and her heart jumps. No, she tells herself, it can't be him and it isn't. It's Jodie. Of course it's Jodie. Eve is stung with guilt.

'Three A stars, two As,' Jodie says breathlessly. In the background there is shouting, cheers and the sound of people running.

'That's fantastic, darling; so it's Durham, then?'

There is a pause, yet more whooping at the other end of the line.

'Well, no, Mum, actually I'm not going, not this year anyway. Dad'll explain. I've got to go. Sorry, Mum, talk later, yeah? Love you!'

And the line is silent. Eve stares at the screen and tries to breathe. Not going this year? Andrew knows something she doesn't? What's going on? The already shaky foundations of the day start to rock. Eve looks at her sewing machine, then out of the dining-room window. Cars are trundling past as usual, there are people on the pavement, somewhere up high an aircraft will be taking off from Heathrow and far, far away there will be the sea and it being there will be wonderful. But here, with this swatch of fabric on her lap, Eve is rootless, purposeless. Her daughter has got amazing A-level results but nothing is as it was when she'd woken that morning. No amount of imagination could have prepared Eve for this.

She switches off the sewing machine, grabs her keys and hurries out of the house. Andrew is working in Darell Road in Caversham. It's a short road, only twelve houses or so, it shouldn't be hard to find him, and she drives through the early morning traffic, occasionally glancing in the rear-view mirror, catching sight of her eyes, shocked to find she doesn't recognise who they might belong to.

The journey takes about twenty minutes; there is congestion on London Road outside the hospital but eventually she clears it, swings by the Oracle and up on to the IDR. Caversham Bridge is sticky too but then she's halfway up St Peter's Hill and waiting at the corner to turn into Darell Road. She sees Andrew's van parked by the side of the road and about halfway down it.

He's standing on the driveway of a large house, Edwardian by the look of it. He's been working here for a few days already and has undercoated the eaves. He has his back to her and he's looking up at the house. Andrew is a patient man, he always has been, and he has a wisdom Eve has depended upon in the past, but now, now she is full of a nameless anger, is furious with his patience and wisdom, wants him to be someone completely other than he is.

'Andrew,' she calls.

He turns and starts to smile. 'You've heard, then?' he asks. He doesn't seem surprised to see her there.

'The results? Oh yes, they're amazing, but . . .'

He is walking towards her. She wants him to hold her, to let her rest her head on his chest. He will smell of paint and of their school days, of the first time and the day Jodie was born. But he doesn't hold her. Instead he stands in front of her and looks at her. The sun is behind him and she can't see his features too well.

'Ah, what did she say?'

'That she's not going this year. What's it about, Andrew? What's happening?'

'She wants to defer, go next year. She's got a job teaching English to kids in Thailand. It's called Project Trust. She did all the research herself, you know. She did want to talk to you about it, but didn't want you to worry until it was definite. It all depended on the results, you see. If she didn't get into Durham, she probably would have retaken her exams, but now, well, now it's all sorted. It's wonderful, isn't it?'

He takes a step towards her, reaches out to hold one of her hands. She keeps both of them firmly by her side.

'Why, though? Why not involve me in this? Don't you see? It's massive and both of you have shut me out. It hurts, Andrew, it really hurts.'

'We didn't want you to worry, that's all. There's nothing sinister in it.'

But to Eve there is. There are all the times when it's been Andrew and Jodie on one side of the table and her on the other: Andrew taking Jodie to football practice when she was nine, them laughing over *Family Guy* on the TV. Eve has never understood the programme, hates the shrillness and stupidity of it. And then there's the music which binds her husband and her daughter; the constant swapping of texts saying, 'You heard the latest from . . .' and the emails with links to YouTube, the laughter afterwards, the quiet hallway conversations between a father and his daughter.

'But you just didn't think of me, did you?'

Eve recognises she's more vulnerable than usual this morning; it is a huge day, a crossroads day and this wound she's suffered is massive, it changes things. It is the kind of thing that won't easily be forgotten.

Just at that moment a car noses its way out of the gated driveway opposite, the driver in it sounds his horn and both Andrew and Eve look up. The car is a Thistle Green vintage Mercedes, the driver is Myles. Eve lifts a hand.

'Who's that?' Andrew asks.

'I don't know,' she says, looking down at her feet. 'Perhaps they think we're someone else.'

It is the first lie.

Later that day Eve is at home, Andrew is still working in Darell Road, Jodie is out with her friends. She has been home briefly, hugged Eve, let Eve cry on her shoulder, said,

'It'll be OK, Mum, it's not for ever. I'll be back before you know it,' and didn't realise that Eve was not only crying because her daughter will be going to a place on the other side of the world, will live in a different time zone, have her days when Eve is sleeping, her nights when Eve is awake, but that neither her husband nor her daughter had thought to involve her in this monumental decision and that she would be the one left behind, the one most hurt by this unconscious but platinum betrayal. And so, in the quiet of this Thursday afternoon when the August sun is huge in the sky, when the grass is suddenly summer brown as if it hasn't rained for weeks and the leaves are dry and languid and inviting autumn to arrive, Eve logs on to her work emails via the remote access link on her laptop. This, she thinks, is something I can do. There's the conference, changes to Max's diary for next week, next quarter's figures to assemble for the management meeting; all these things are to do with the future and she will look forward to them.

In amongst the emails is one from Myles Stephens. She stares at the name, her heart is racing. She hovers the cursor over it and clicks to open it.

10

Weekends have always been hard for Rose. When she was working and living in Verity's house off the Talgarth Road, her weekends were filled with mundane things like washing her clothes, buying food for one, occasionally visiting Kew Gardens or the Natural History Museum and afterwards treating herself a toasted teacake and watching the rain skitter down the café's windows, or sitting in Verity's kitchen and drinking tea and trying not to think of Henry in his house and of the sturdiness of Penelope's shoes.

Then there was after Henry, when it was just her and Mother and she'd busied herself in the garden, doing the dusting, pressing her mother's sheets and mending the worn ones sides to middle, and helping Mother with the flowers at church. On Saturdays they'd do weddings and the flower room next to the vestry would be littered with chrysanthemum leaves and stray sprigs of gypsophila and the air had been damp and filled with green and Rose had found it difficult to watch the bride arrive and witness the promise of it all. On Sundays they'd do christenings and these were even harder; she'd falter at the sight of the mother holding her child and imagine she could hear the soft snuffle of its breath, see the tiny bubbles it would blow from its perfect lips.

And now, well, weekends are still hard. Myles doesn't tend to come over at weekends and Eve has always been busy with her chores and helping to run Jodie's social life of birthday parties, Guide camps, that sort of thing, and Rose doesn't do the flowers at the church any more, not after Mother died; it was one of the things she had to let go of. At the time she'd thought it would liberate her.

So it's Saturday afternoon and she's in the garden. It's late August and she's weeding around her dahlias. She'd popped to the shops this morning and bought herself a tin of ham and picked out some potatoes from the sack outside the shop and Mohsin had said 'Good morning' as he'd wiped the road dust from the massive pile of water melons he'd put next to a box of okra and the glow of nearby pomegranates.

'Hello,' she'd said. 'Another lovely day.'

'Yes, but oh we need the rain, indeed we do.'

His phone rang and he spoke quickly into it in a language she had no way of understanding, but he'd lifted his eyes to hers and smiled, shrugging complicity at her. She smiled back, loving the mix of it here; the mounds of Golden Delicious apples, the mangoes, the box of dangerous-looking chillies and the scent of spices that hung in the air next to the Dunkin' Donuts display; sugar and spice and all things nice, she'd said to herself at the time and she'd swung her shopping bag just a little on the walk home.

The earth on her fingers is warm as she picks out the more stubborn of the weeds. She's kneeling on the low folding thingy Eve had ordered for her from the internet; a Hozelock 4190 Garden Kneeler Seat it is apparently and it's mighty useful. Rose finds it more and more difficult these days to move around her garden and even the simplest tasks take her longer than they used to do, but every day there is something to do. This is where the life is, in amongst these trees Father had pruned and the path he had laid. Here is where continuity is.

She drops the weeds into the trug by her side and thinks about the word continuity. The package from the solicitor had arrived that morning and she'd wanted to put it in the box which Eve had put back on the top shelf of her wardrobe but obviously hadn't been able to reach, so had had to be content to put it in the drawer of her dressing table instead. When the time comes Eve will find it there, of this she has no doubt. Rose also knows herself well enough by now to know the other reason she didn't want to look too closely in the wardrobe today is because of the dresses. She also knows why she still keeps them when they wouldn't fit her and would be wildly out of fashion for anyone other than gamine art students in London maybe.

The sun is hot on the back of her neck and she wishes she'd brought a drink down with her. She bends forward to tackle another weed as next door's cat slinks by her, looking at her with his clear auburn eyes; his fur gives off heat, and he walks like Sidney Poitier.

'Hey, boy,' she says.

He stops and lifts his head very slightly for her to stroke him. He purrs and pushes himself against her hand. It's a conversation of sorts.

'Busy day?' she asks.

Then he hears a rustle in the hedge and turns sharply towards it. The moment is gone and with a flick of his whiskers he's gone too, to become nothing but a shadow in the leaves.

For some reason the way he skitters off reminds Rose of horses.

Wednesday 1 June 1960 had dawned softly, the slice of sky Rose could see through her attic window glowed pink. Derby Day. Mr Georgiadis's big day.

Six weeks ago invitations had gone out to government ministers (albeit junior ones), financiers from the City and a few high-society couples whose names had been given to the office by Henry's wife. She'd sent a letter to Mr Georgiadis with her and Henry's address embossed across the top of the page in startling black lettering. Her writing had been surprisingly small. Rose had expected flourishes, dramatic loops and artistic capitals, but instead the letter was businesslike, terse, merely a list of names and addresses. Rose had typed up the invitation letters and Mr Georgiadis had signed them. The replies started to trickle in.

'An important occasion, I feel,' Mr Georgiadis said in the last week of May as he ran his finger down the list of those who had accepted. 'We must be on our best behaviour. You will come, Miss Reynolds, to make sure all is how it should be.'

It wasn't a request.

'Yes, Mr Georgiadis,' she said, and in her head was the thought: Henry will be there. Henry.

There'd been no more lunches since the one at Simpson's but that had been enough; they were connected now. She was on dangerous ground and it was wonderful; awful but wonderful. It seemed there was no turning back, even if she had wanted to.

'But what should I wear?' she asked the office girl later that morning. From this distance, she can't remember the girl's name and is disappointed by this when so many other details of that time are pinpoint sharp. 'How formal do you think it will be?'

The girl shrugged and continued to put stamps on today's envelopes. 'I'm sorry, I don't know, I'm afraid, Miss Reynolds,' she said. 'You could look in a magazine or something.'

And so Rose did. She studied hard, looked at patterns in the Army & Navy store, spoke despairingly to Verity about it.

'I could make you something if you get a pattern and some fabric. We haven't got long, but it's possible, isn't it? You have shoes, hat, bag and gloves, don't you? We can work around them, surely,' Verity had said the next morning when Rose was getting ready to leave for work.

'I suppose so,' Rose replied, glancing at her reflection in the hall mirror. 'Oh,' she then said, turning to look at Verity, 'I am grateful, really I am. It's just such a shock; I really wasn't expecting to have to go.'

'I know, dear. I know.'

And then a day later, or maybe it was two, Rose can't quite remember this either, she came back from work and it was raining. She shook out her umbrella on the doorstep and hung her coat on the stand in the hall. Verity was frying bacon in the kitchen; the scent of it hit Rose with surprising force.

'Oh Rose,' she said, hurrying down the hallway. 'A package arrived for you today. I have it here. A boy delivered it. He was wearing some kind of uniform. I didn't recognise it. I tipped him sixpence even so.'

Rose followed Verity, followed the smell of bacon cooking. Her shoes were wet, her hair coiled damply on her neck. She was tired; the weather had been unseasonably cold that day. The package was on the kitchen table, wrapped in brown paper.

'Will you open it here?' Verity asked. 'I'm agog to know what it is.' She smiled as she went back to the cooker, flipped the bacon, turned down the heat.

'I should give you the sixpence.' Rose rummaged in her handbag and found her purse. Somehow she knew what was in the box was going to change things yet further, and she wanted to delay the moment of discovery for as long as possible.

The sound of the paper tearing was huge in Rose's ears; the room was quiet now Verity had stopped cooking. In the distance, car tyres made a shushing noise on the damp road and someone was walking around upstairs. Water was running in one of the bathrooms.

Of course it was a dress. It was blue, green, it reminded Rose of the sea. It had shirred sleeves and a tucked bodice, the skirt was pleated, would fall just to her knees. It was made of shot silk. It was beautiful.

The women looked at one another as Rose held it up to the light. The tissue paper it had been packed in fell on to the floor. 'Oh my goodness,' Rose said. 'What should I do?'

'I presume this is Henry's doing?' It was hard to know if Verity was angry or pleased at this possibility. She went back to the cooker. Rose's heart beat loudly in her chest.

'There's a card,' she said.

Of course the dress was from Henry. The card simply said 'With my compliments. For Derby Day. Henry'.

'I should hang it up, away from the damp and the cooking smells,' Rose said, 'shouldn't I?' but the question wasn't just about the dress, Rose was asking for Verity's approval, her permission to accept the gift and all its implications.

'Yes,' Verity said, breaking an egg into the frying pan, turning the heat back up. The egg sizzled. 'You should. Now you'd better go so I can get Meredith's tea on the table.'

Rose folded the dress carefully and put it back in the box. She picked the tissue paper up from the floor and placed a sixpence next to Verity's knife and fork. As she walked upstairs, the thinness of the white tissue paper in her hand reminded her of a wedding veil.

It was awful waiting for Henry to arrive the next morning. All night Rose had practised what she should say:

'I can't possibly accept your kind gift' was, she'd decided, the most sensible response. But, when she'd changed out of her damp clothes and tried on the dress in her small room at the top of the house off the Talgarth Road, the feeling of the silk on her skin had been like a kiss. It was as though Henry was in the room with her, was standing in front of her, his hands on her and the heat of him had been everywhere.

So when he came in, took off his hat and coat and walked by her desk through to his office, she'd said, 'Thank you. Thank you for the dress.'

He stopped but did not look at her, seemed to take a breath and said as he gazed into the middle distance, 'It is a pleasure, Miss Reynolds, really it is.'

When he got to his office, he closed the door almost angrily and all Rose could do was stare at her typewriter keys as if they held the answer.

So, on Wednesday 1 June 1960 Rose wore the blue-green dress which was the colour of the sea. Mr Georgiadis had arranged for a car to pick her up early so she could be in the private room at Epsom racecourse to greet his guests when they arrived. And all day, as Rose oversaw the waiting staff, answered questions about parking and directions to the cloakrooms, helped clear the plates after lunch, she was aware that across the room was Henry in a dark suit, his clear eyes grave with something unspoken. She wanted to touch his hand so much it was like her own skin was burning.

'Weighed in, weighed in,' the announcer's crisp voice informed them through the public address system.

Mr Georgiadis strutted around the room. He charmed, smoothed, made jokes. He was good at this. He was a small, solid man; he made flamboyant gestures, spoke loudly, laughed even more loudly. It was as though he had created an orbit and the guests that day were trapped inside it; he was like the sun.

'Let me put a bet on for you,' Henry said to Rose. 'Lester Piggott's riding St Paddy. He's got a chance, I think. I could put a couple of bob on for you if you like.'

They were standing looking out on to the course. The crowds below them bustled happily, the sun shone. Betting slips littered the ground around the bookies' stalls and the bookies waved to one another in the way that bookies do, the room behind Henry and Rose was full of cigarette smoke and the sweet smell of warm champagne.

Rose had drunk two glasses and it was like she was melting. She knew she shouldn't have had either of them.

'Yes,' she said, looking up at Henry. 'Yes please.'

'Come down to the paddock and the track with me? If Mr Georgiadis can spare you, that is.'

Mr Georgiadis had himself just left, flanked by Mr

Wilson from Lloyds of London and Sir Reginald Cuthbert Smythe who had something to do with making steel. The ladies of the party were nicely settled in chairs around a small table, their conversation a constant hum. Penelope, Henry's wife, was with the horses. She would be down with the horses all day, so Rose understood.

'OK,' Rose said, picking up her bag and pulling on her gloves. She was hot in her hat but the silk of the dress was cool and it made a sound like water when she walked.

Down by the track Henry and Rose stood at the railings, the earth was baked brown, the air hummed with expectation. Rose held the betting slip in her hand, her arm was pressed against Henry's; for that moment the world was just the two of them. They did not speak.

The ground throbbed with the sound of the horses' hooves getting ever nearer, it was like thunder. They flashed past in a blur of flesh and heat, their nostrils flaring, the jockeys' muscles straining, the eyes of both animals and men blazing forwards. It was something like sex might be, Rose thought: that build, that rush, that silence afterwards.

As the horse crossed the finish line Henry turned to Rose and put his hands around her waist. 'We won, Rose. We won!' He lifted her up and kissed her on the mouth. His lips were dry and tasted of champagne. It took a second, it lasted a lifetime. When he put her down he tried to smile at her, but didn't quite succeed.

'Miss Reynolds, I'm so sorry,' he said.

'Don't be,' she replied. 'Don't be.'

His arms hung down by his sides, he didn't look at her.

'I'd better collect our winnings,' he said at last. 'Shall I walk you back to the box first?'

'No, it's fine. You go off. I'll find my way.'

Rose needed time to compose herself and, as Henry disappeared into the crowd, she felt that tug, that connection again. It was building; building since she'd sewn on his button, since the lunch at Simpson's. But she also felt that somewhere in the throng of people, in the noise of them, and in amongst the sweat beaded on the horses' flanks, Penelope's eyes were fixed on her, were seeing through her, that Henry's wife knew that not only the horse Rose and Henry had backed had crossed a line that afternoon.

Henry drove Rose home afterwards. It had been Mr Georgiadis's suggestion.

'You,' he'd said, pointing at Henry, 'you should take Miss Reynolds home.'

'Yes, Mr Georgiadis,' Henry said. 'It would be my pleasure. But how will you get back?'

'Miss Reynolds has organised a car for me. Isn't that right?' Rose nodded. 'And anyway, I shall be going back to town with a few of my guests,' he continued. 'We have some celebrating to do!' He waved a fistful of five-pounds notes at Henry and Rose as he said this and smiled broadly at them. Mr Georgiadis was a very happy man that day.

Henry's car was a light green 1956 Ford Zodiac and, when he opened the door for Rose, the leather inside smelled hot.

They drove mostly in silence. Once, as they approached Ewell on the A24, she asked, 'How will your wife get home?'

'She will go with her friends and their horses. I'll see her later.'

It was at that moment that it started to rain; thin, see-through rain that damped the road. Henry switched on the wipers, the glass smeared and Rose was filled with an unaccountable rage at all the unknowing. There was so much she didn't know about this man: what his house was like, what he said to his wife each night in bed, what he dreamt about, and yet, here she was in his car, with the rain on the windscreen, wearing a dress he had bought for her and he had kissed her. He had put his hands around her waist, had lifted her up and he had kissed her.

And then from nowhere the words came.

'What shall we do?' she said. She looked down at her lap, at her hands in their white gloves, at her fingers knotted together around the strap of her handbag. She wanted to stay here for ever. She didn't want to be here at all.

'I don't know.' His voice was quiet, almost a whisper. 'I really don't know.'

More miles. More silence.

Then he said, 'I know what I want, though.'

'Do you?'

'Yes. And it's not this, not like this. It's more like Hardy. I want it to be more like Hardy. Like Gabriel Oak and Bathsheba. Do you know it? The bit in *Far from the Madding Crowd*?'

'Yes, I know it,' Rose said. And from when she was younger and had read the book and had believed that dreams could sometimes come true, she said, '"And at home by the fire, whenever you look up there I shall be – and whenever I look up, there will be you."'

'Oh Rose,' he said. 'Oh Rose.'

Of course the journey ended. They arrived outside Rose's digs at just gone seven. It had stopped raining but the air was still humid with it.

'I shall see you tomorrow. In the office, no doubt?' he said as he climbed out of the driver's seat.

She waited for him to walk round the car and open her door. The seconds stretched.

'Until tomorrow, then?' he said again as he held her hand to help her out.

'Yes, tomorrow,' she said. 'And thank you, for the lift home, the dress.' And in her head she said, 'And for kissing me, for putting your hands on me, for what you said in the car.'

'It was my pleasure, my absolute pleasure.'

'And for the tip,' she added, 'for the winnings!'

'Oh yes,' he said. 'The race. I'd forgotten about the race.'

She didn't watch him go, she couldn't. He got back into the car and switched on the engine. He would drive home, wait for Penelope and they would have supper together maybe and Rose would lie on her bed in her blue-green dress the colour of the sea and would hold the fabric of it in her hands and think of him.

And this is what she did, half torn with the wonder of the day, half torn by the fact that it was over, that when he put her down after kissing her, his face had been many things but it had not been suffused. She had not given him the perfect gift, not yet.

In the garden of her house in Belle Avenue, the cat's return startles Rose. 'Oh,' she says, 'you again.'

Slack in his jaws is the body of a mouse; it's tiny, obviously dead. The cat looks at Rose as if to say, 'Yes, I know. I am magnificent.' He doesn't stop this time but saunters off, his back swaying, the sun bouncing off his fur. Rose stands up, very slowly, very painfully. She has sat too long on her stool, the untilled earth around her dahlias is reproachful, but she actually wouldn't have it any other way. These memories are what she lives for; they are most of what she has left.

11

Eve closes her copy of *Rebecca* and puts it on the floor next to the bed. It's the end of August; what Eve always thinks of as Diana Days. Diana was Eve's Kennedy and Elvis and the outbreak of war. Everyone of a certain age remembers what they were doing the day Diana died, don't they? She turns off the light and punches the pillow to make it more comfortable. Andrew is out at a gig again, some Hall of Sound in some local village. It's an acoustic set and it would be fun, she's sure. However, yet again Andrew didn't ask her to go and she didn't suggest it. Jodie is staying over at a friend's house, has left her room littered with the things she's gathering together for her trip to Thailand. Every time Eve walks past her daughter's bedroom and the door is open, she has to close it. She can't bear to look.

Stretching out in bed, Eve lets her mind wander. She has, she admits, rather a crush on Maximilian de Winter, can understand how the nameless narrator's head has been turned, but has no idea yet if there will be a happy ending, rather fears there won't.

It had taken a couple of days to pluck up the courage to answer Myles's email, but she had and now they've agreed to meet for lunch next week, on a date that's only five days away. She will have to ring Rose in the morning and tell her she won't be able to go round as usual and there will be a good reason for this, something to do with work and it will be another lie. Eve has lost count of the lies she's told since that first one when Myles waved at her and Andrew as he drove past the house in Darell Road. They are mostly tiny; are lies by omission. She hasn't told Andrew how she feels about Jodie going or about how they kept the decision from her, or about Rose's tenant and the fact he recommended the book she's reading at the moment and Andrew hasn't asked either. Eve feels these things like weights in her chest; all the words are there but she just can't get them in the right order, doesn't know how they will ever get out of her mouth.

She calls Rose from work the next day.

'Hi, there,' she says.

'Hello, stranger,' Rose replies.

'How are you?'

'I'm fine. I made the mistake of watching a bit of day-time TV this morning though. Won't do that again!'

Rose laughs and Eve can visualise her sitting in her chair and the light is coming through the windows and downstairs Myles might be writing or he might be looking out on to the street. She has no idea what he might be thinking about.

'Urgh!' Eve laughs too. 'What else are you up to?'

'Oh, you know. The usual. Just pottering.' There is a pause. 'How is it at home?'

Of course Eve has told Rose about Jodie going. There are four days to the lunch with Myles, six days until Jodie goes and both these events are huge in Eve's head.

'Organised chaos!' Eve says in reply. 'Jodie's skittering around getting her stuff ready, won't let me help much though.'

'You must be very proud of her.'

Rose's voice is firm when she says this and it helps. Yes, Eve is proud. It is a wonderful thing her daughter is doing but it is also terrifying; the house will be unbearably quiet without her and, when she thinks of Jodie over there, Eve is overwhelmed by a weird sort of grief. Because her own mother has been so elusive, so always far away, she doesn't really know how she should be behaving, there is no precedent, so she's just living on instinct and her instinct is telling her to grieve and to be afraid that her daughter's departure will cause a further rift in the fabric of her life with Andrew. But, as there's already so much she hasn't told him, it seems very unlikely that she'll be able to tell him any of this either.

'Yes, of course I am,' she tells Rose now as Max pops his head around his office door and beckons to her. 'Oh, looks like I'm going to have to go, Max is after me for something,' she says, stung briefly by the fact that her boss has the same name as the character in *Rebecca*. Small world, she says to herself.

'Oh, OK dear, thanks for calling, but before you go, did you want anything in particular?'

'Well.' Eve starts to stand, she grips the phone receiver to her ear; her legs, she realises, are shaking. This is when she will have to tell it, another lie. 'Well, I just wanted to let you know that I won't be able to come round next week as planned. There's something on at work, a meeting that I have to go to, I did try and change it so was wondering if we could we change our day instead?' This, she has said, without taking a breath. She takes one now, it catches in her throat and she coughs.

'You OK?' Rose asks, then says, 'It's no problem, you know. Just come when you can. I know you're busy, with work and Jodie going and everything. Just come when you can. Really, it's OK. I'm quite capable of looking after myself!'

But in Eve's head all she hears is the 'everything' Rose has referred to. This 'everything' is Myles and the fact that she, Eve, has agreed to meet him for lunch on the day she should be visiting Rose. It had seemed easier than batting dates back and forth with him; a simple 'Can you meet?' and 'Yes, that's fine,' is something substantially less significant than, 'I'm free on these dates, how are you fixed?' and then choices have to be made as to which date would be best, different scenarios will need to be imagined about the leaving, the getting there and the getting back again afterwards. This way it's simple, clean cut, innocent. It is a lunch between two people who want to talk about Daphne du Maurier and *Rebecca*. So why can't Eve tell Rose this? Why doesn't she?

'I know you can. Look after yourself, I mean!' Eve says, 'But hey, I really should go. Max is waving a bit more wildly at me now! I'll check my diary and ring you later to arrange another date. Is that OK?'

'Sure. Now go. Go do your work, and give my love to Jodie and,' again Rose pauses, 'Andrew,' she says, 'and have some for yourself.'

'You too. Take care, speak soon. Bye now.'

'Bye, Eve.'

And Eve puts down the phone and walks into Max's office where she talks about work and deadlines and budgets and Max's forthcoming trip to Birmingham, should he drive or take the train? and Eve tries to forget she has just lied to Rose, that she is lying most of the time these days and perhaps she always has been.

*

The four days pass. It is early September, Jodie will leave the day after tomorrow and, as she drives to the pub Myles has suggested, Eve tries to drown out her thoughts by turning the radio up. Each song it seems is about loss, about summer ending, about regret.

The pub is on the outskirts of Henley. It's small, ivy-clad, the car park is almost full. Eve parks and gets out of her car, smooths down her skirt, flexes her shoulders inside her shirt. It's hot, she feels ungainly, her shoes are too shiny for here.

She has just over an hour before she's due back at work; it doesn't seem long enough but, as she opens the door of the pub and bends her head, the gloom startles her, sucks her in, makes her feel like time is slowing, that the minutes she will spend there will last longer than they would anywhere else.

Myles is already seated at a table in a corner by the fireplace. He stands and lifts a hand in greeting. It looks like a gesture of surrender.

'Hi,' he says.

'Hi.'

'You made it, then?'

'Yes.'

'How was work?'

'It was good. Thank you. How was your morning?'

'Also good. My DCI's making progress despite the best efforts of others!'

'That's nice.'

It's a stupid conversation. They're obviously not good at this. Why am I here? Eve wonders.

Then he says, 'Sit down, let me get you a drink. Something to eat. I have a menu.'

He passes her the menu, she sits, the chair legs make a scraping sound on the slate floor. The outside of the pub may be quaint and 'olde worlde' but inside it's uncompromising – all angles and abstract paintings on the wall and there's no music, just the hum of other people's conversations. She feels like she's in a Damien Hirst installation. The menu is similarly avant-garde, she hardly recognises a thing on it, the words bounce off her eyes. She looks across at Myles.

'I'll order for us, shall I?' he suggests.

'Thank you. Yes, that's probably best. I'll have a Coke to drink if that's OK?' she says. It's like being a teenager again, the not-good bits of being a teenager. Being with Andrew had always protected her; after all, she'd been part of a couple since she was fifteen. Being here like this with Myles is, she realises, uncharted territory. It's not like it was in his flat when they were waiting for Rose. Here she is exposed, uncertain; there is no fizz, just fear.

But then he's back, carrying a Coke for her and a pint for him. 'I ordered us chicken fajitas to share,' he says. 'That way we can have what we like, you know, pick and mix, and if we don't recognise it, we don't eat it! Right?'

'Right,' she says lifting up her glass. Her hands are trembling just a little but already she's feeling better. Being with him is nice, he is nice. She likes the shape of him, the faded denim of his shirt, the tuft of chest hair she can see in its open neck, his pale chinos, the tan shoes he's wearing. All is perfectly as it should be; he seems perfect, and his eyes are shining across the table at her. He runs his hand over his stubble and sighs deeply before picking up his drink and taking a mouthful.

'Ah,' he says, 'that's good. I needed that!'

She laughs and the despair she felt a moment ago starts to uncoil, to straighten itself out into something less threatening.

'So,' he adds, 'what do you think of the book?'

She had forgotten they were here to talk about this and momentarily is disappointed. Instead of talking about Manderley, she wants to talk about him and about her and about the 'themness' of being there. 'I'm loving it,' she says. 'It's a lot more sinister than I was expecting, though, and that Mrs Danvers – well!'

'I know, she's spooky, isn't she? Wouldn't want to come across her on a dark night! Although . . .'

'Yes?' she asks. She finds she is interested in what he's going to say.

'It's only the fierceness of her love for Rebecca that makes her that way. When you really love someone, it can change things . . .'

He looks at her, then looks down at the table. There is an awkward silence and then thankfully the food comes.

'Ah, good!' he says and the tension lifts. He rubs his hands.

They are nice hands, Eve thinks.

One waitress brings the wraps and sauces and two plates. Another follows close behind her with the dish of chicken. It is sizzling loudly. Other people in the pub look up from their conversations to check out the noise. The sound and the attention seem momentarily dangerous. Eve's heart quickens.

The drama is soon over, the other people look away and Eve and Myles eat and talk and it is normal and nice. Occasionally she reaches across with her spoon, scoops up some peppers and he does the same and their hands brush against one another again. She likes this. She likes being there with him and the minutes go at just the right speed and, as he pays and she says, 'My treat next time, then!' she knows that something is starting that perhaps she ought to stop but that she has no power or desire to.

'Yes,' he says. 'Your treat next time!'

He walks her to her car and holds the door open for her as she gets in. Andrew has never done this for me, she thinks. Never. And then Myles bends down and kisses her briefly on the cheek. His lips are warm and dry. He smells of fajita spices and beer. When she drives away she consciously does not look back in her mirror for fear that he may not be watching her go and for fear that he might.

'Good lunch?' Debs asks as Eve passes by her desk on her way to her own office. The cool air in the building is like balm on Eve's skin.

'Yes thank you.'

'Go anywhere nice?'

'Just out for a sandwich. Fancied a breath of fresh air, that's all.'

'Not a Rose day, then?'

'No, not a Rose day.'

And so the lies pile up. Eve logs back on to her computer, dares not look across the office to where Debs is sitting. Just like earlier with Myles, she doesn't want to know if her friend is looking at her for fear she wouldn't be able to meet her eyes.

When Eve gets home Andrew is already there. This is a surprise.

'Everything OK?' she calls out as she puts her keys down in the hall.

Her husband comes out of the lounge; he has changed out of his work clothes. He is smiling at her.

'Yes, everything's fine. It's just we're all out this evening. You too. You've got half an hour to get changed. We're meeting Jodie there.'

'Where? Where are we going? What's going on?'

'It's a surprise. For you. To say sorry for not including you in the decision and also to see Jodie off. Her friends will be there too. Go on, run along. See you back down here in a jiffy.'

And Andrew turns and walks back into the lounge. He is whistling. Of course he is whistling, Eve says to herself as she makes her way slowly up the stairs.

She doesn't want to go out. There are so many reasons why she doesn't want to go.

Later, she is sitting in another pub. Andrew's band is playing and Jodie and her friends are at the bar. The air is filled with the smell of beer and hot bodies. Then Jodie is on the stage. Her legs and hair impossibly long, her sweet face is smiling out at the crowd and she sings. She sings and her voice is clear and bright and beautiful and her father is watching her and Eve can't bear it, any of it. Her heart and her head are too full.

She checks her phone. There is a text. 'Lovely to see you. Take care. See you soon. M.'

The thought of him is like a shield. The person she is

when she's with Myles is, she tells herself, someone who is not here, not now. That person and Myles himself are the people who will protect her from this, this losing of her daughter and the fact she's afraid she may not be in love with Andrew, not in the right way, not any more.

And now Jodie is speaking into the microphone, 'And here's a song written by my friend, Alex Chalk!' There is a ripple of applause and then she's singing again and the words of the chorus are, 'I swear to you I'll always stay too young to know what being young is all about,' and Eve can't watch, can't listen any more. It is too hard. Being here like this is too hard.

So she thinks about Jodie's birth, the miracle of it and the pain and the weight of her baby's head as she cradled it and the honey scent of her, the incredible softness of her skin and then the exhaustion of the early days and the tantrums when Jodie was two and the lengthening of her bones, the way her face changed, how she grew away and away and now how she will be gone the day after tomorrow and that every minute of every day will be another loss. She had only ever borrowed her daughter. She puts her phone back in her bag. Nothing, it seems, is ever for keeps.

12

Myles takes a break from writing. He's done a thousand words so far today, which isn't great but isn't a shabby performance either. He leaves DCI Derek Pletheroe studying the incident board. Photographs of the artefacts found with the body have been posted up there together with full descriptions of what they are, where they come from, what their history and provenance might be. But nowhere is an explanation of why they're there; what they mean, who left them next to the body. And, in his hand he's holding a folder. Inside is the name of the child his victim had given up for adoption. The boy is eleven now, is as old as Myles's own son; his adoptive parents have never told him about his real mother and most likely would absolutely refuse to now, especially if they knew of the circumstances surrounding her death.

Myles cracks his knuckles to ease the tension in his

hands and looks out of the window. The year has turned. It's October, the sky is low and the colour of slate. It rained earlier and the leaves on the path are sodden; their oranges and browns muted, ugly almost. He logs on to his emails knowing that there will be one from Eve because this is what they do. They send small updates; have casual chats about what's on TV, the weather, her work, his writing, the cost of petrol. But never do they discuss the big things like how she's coping now Jodie has gone or whether he and Celeste have smiled at one another recently (he can't actually remember the last time they did). Once Eve mentioned her hankering to live by the sea and her love of sewing but it was a throwaway comment, just one of many and sometimes, very occasionally, he lets himself say something tender, like 'Take care' or 'Thinking of you', but he doesn't often, it leaves him exhausted and vulnerable each time he does.

He's right. There's an email from her.

They've started using different addresses; he's set one up using the name Pletheroe, she has one as 'Monica'. Neither of them has admitted why they've done this, it just seems simpler, that's all.

'Hi there,' it says, 'OMG, what is Mr Darcy like? I guess you probably don't see it from my point of view but he's a nightmare! What a snob!'

He replies. 'Wait and see,' he types, 'Not all men are as they appear, you know.'

He presses Send and immediately wishes he could call it back. Does it sound too needy, like he has a hidden agenda, that he's actually talking about himself? Well, there is, he is and he knows it.

Since that first lunch when he'd kissed her as she got into her car, he's been in turmoil. He really had no idea how swiftly and completely he would want the things he tells himself he can't have. He wants to hold her, feel her breath on his neck, run his fingers over the contours of her bones, let her sleep in his arms and yet, and yet how can he reconcile wanting all this with what he feels for his sons, what he should feel for his wife?

It's like there are two of him these days. One is the man who sends Eve texts and meets her for quick lunches when they're both always checking the time, working out how long they've had, how long there is to go. This is the one who sends her emails about films and sometimes sends music clips and thinks he knows her but knows he doesn't really. And, each time he checks his phone for texts and his email for responses from her, he experiences a longing that's deep-seated and very real and he feels a fraud because there is the other him; the man who is a husband and father, the one who tells himself almost daily when he looks at himself in the mirror as he shaves that this isn't an affair, it's a friendship, that's all, and it's perfect as it is and no one need get hurt.

However, he still likes to think of her at work, the coil of her hair, how it swings heavily when she wears it down, the way her eyes glimmer like topaz, and he imagines her in her house, stirring something on the hob, tapping her foot to a track on the radio, taking a sip of wine. But then the front door opens and her husband walks in and Myles has to switch off the image and force himself to think about something else instead.

He never expected it to be like this.

The cursor is blinking at him as he waits for a reply. One doesn't come, not immediately. She'll be in touch later, no doubt, so he decides to go for a run.

The roads are shiny with leftover rain. 'Chasing Cars' by Snow Patrol is blaring out of his headphones. He matches the beat to his footsteps. It's three o'clock and the kids are coming out of the local primary school. He crosses the road to avoid them. His heart feels unaccountably heavy in his chest.

Eve still hasn't replied when he gets back to his desk so he showers, gets changed, puts his running gear in the washing machine, his trainers on the radiator in the kitchen to dry. He'll wash his stuff tomorrow but for now he decides to go home. Just one more check, still no answer. It doesn't matter, he tells himself. They're still connected. This is still something good. He has faith in her, in them, in what they have achieved so far. He shuts down his laptop and locks the door to the flat on the way out.

In the hallway he can hear that Rose's TV is on upstairs and he presumes she's resting. He hopes she's doing OK, that she hasn't guessed that whenever Eve visits her, Myles now knows she's coming, that he waits for her to arrive and they have a secret look they give one another. It happens like this: when Eve leaves she glances quickly over her shoulder as she steps out of the front door and he raises his hand, she nods and then steps out on to the path and raises her face so she can be seen by Rose who's watching from the upstairs window. Sometimes, they wave as she arrives. Both only take a second but have become a routine without either of them really being aware of them doing so and this matters, it matters very much.

It's dark by the time Myles gets home. He opens the gates and drives in. Celeste's car is there and the house is lit up, warm and welcoming. He knows his sons will be inside and suddenly and very fiercely he wants to be with them.

'Yoo hoo,' he calls as he steps into his house and puts his keys down on the table in the hall. There is the smell of cooking coming from the kitchen but the rest of the house is quiet. It's only seven o'clock but the sky is midnight dark outside.

'Oh hi,' Celeste says, coming out to meet him wiping

her hands on a towel. He is amazed that she's there and not only is she there, but she's dressed in her sweats, she's wearing an apron and her usually perfectly arranged hair is still damp from a shower. She has no make-up on and looks ten years younger. 'You're back earlier than I thought. I decided to come home and cook! It's been ages since I did.'

'Yes,' Myles replies. 'It has.' She doesn't notice any hint of irony in his voice. He goes across to her and gives her a peck on the cheek. 'It smells good,' he says, then adds, 'and the boys? Where are they?'

'Bruno's still up, but he's eaten and I put the other two to bed. Orlando was particularly tired; he had a football match after school apparently. Anka's gone to the cinema. It's just us tonight. Odd, isn't it?'

It is odd. It's how a family are supposed to be and for a moment Myles is wrong-footed, feels that he has been unfair to Celeste, that she can't help the choices she has to make. After all, these choices have given them this house, this lifestyle, allowed him to pursue his writing career, haven't they?

'I'll go and check on Bruno, then. How long till dinner?'

'About twenty minutes I should think. Do you want to open the wine before you go up?'

'Sure.'

The kitchen is, as Celeste dictated when they'd had it

fitted, functional, not fussy; it gleams with shiny appliances, everywhere there are tiny spotlights, there is underfloor heating so the quarry tiles they'd got from a salvage company as a concession to authenticity aren't cold on their bare feet. There's a huge island in the centre of the room surrounded by six leather and metal stools. Celeste has laid it with two mats, cutlery, two glasses and a bottle of red wine. Myles uncorks the wine and pours them each a glass.

'Here you go,' he says, passing her a glass. She's stirring a sauce, pasta is just coming to the boil, there is a salad on the counter and the air is filled with the thick sweetness of cream cooking and the scent of dill. He takes a long drink, puts the glass back down by one of the mats. The wine hits the back of his throat.

Upstairs he looks in on Orlando and Garth. They're both splayed out like starfish; he can see the outline of their limbs under their duvets. Orlando's bedside light is still on and the hideous orange plastic CD player he'd wanted for Christmas last year is playing Book Four of the *Harry Potter* series; Stephen Fry's voice is low and comforting. Myles creeps out and softly closes the door.

He knocks on Bruno's door.

'Hey, you,' he says popping his head round it, 'good day?'

'Yes,' his son nods.

Bruno's sitting on his bed reading and this takes Myles

somewhat by surprise. He'd expected him to be wired up to his Xbox. The dog is curled up on the bed next to him. Bruno's leg is draped across the dog's body; it's like they're holding hands.

'What you reading?'

'*Lord of the Rings*.'

'Good, is it?'

'You know it is, Dad!'

'I'll leave you to it then, shall I?'

'OK.'

And Myles pulls Bruno's door to as well and steps quietly back down the landing as if afraid he might break the spell. Part of him thinks he's walked into someone else's house tonight. Downstairs he has a wife who is cooking him dinner, upstairs he has three amazing children who are happy and healthy and Anka will come back after her trip to the cinema and tomorrow will dawn and everything will be calm and how it should be. Suddenly, all the evenings when Celeste works late or is away on business melt into insignificance. He has this, tonight, and it is wonderful. He lets himself think briefly of Eve too and feels a warm glow at the thought of her. She is someone who adds to this contentment, she makes no demands on him, just gives him her company and the chance to know her. That is all he needs. For tonight, for this moment, that is all he needs.

'It's ready,' Celeste says as he goes back into the kitchen and picks up his wine.

'Anything I can do?' he asks.

'You could dress the salad.'

He remembers when they first got together and how these small acts of togetherness used to thrill him. How he's missed them of late!

He pours dressing on the salad and messes about with the leaves with a pair of salad servers he doesn't recognise. Celeste dishes up. It's salmon pasta and she's added anchovies. She loves anchovies, he hates them. Never mind, he thinks, I'll pick them out. It's so rare she gets a chance to cook for herself, I should allow her this indulgence. They eat; a small mound of anchovies appears on the side of his plate. He drinks more than he should. He is surprised by how little there is to say.

'How was your day?' he asks at last as she motions for him to pass her the salad bowl.

'OK, thanks. Yours?'

'OK.'

Oh dear, he thinks. Is this it? Is this how it's going to be even with her here? He's done the things she'd asked, like paid the gardener more, booked a company to clean the gutters, sorted out the paperwork for Bruno's new school and the many other things she's emailed him about in the intervening weeks and now here they are, sitting in their kitchen with their sons in their rooms upstairs and it seems they have nothing whatsoever to say to one another. This isn't how he wanted this evening to go, not at all. He takes another swig of wine; it feels gritty on his teeth after the smoothness of the cream sauce. He senses it staining his lips.

'Actually,' she says, putting down her fork and resting her arms on the counter, 'there's something I need to talk to you about.'

Oh, here it comes, he thinks. This meal, this being-at-home-in-the-evening bit is part of something else, not just for its own sake.

'I have to go to New York,' she says, 'for a week.'

'Oh.' He's not surprised by this. She practically lives there.

'But it's over half-term and Anka asked if she can go home for her cousin's wedding and I said yes before I knew about this trip and she's booked her flights.'

Celeste is not asking him a question or even seeking his opinion. These are the facts and he knows what's coming next. 'You'll have to,' she pauses, picks up the wine, pours some more into his glass and then some into hers, 'have them for the week. I wondered if you'd like to go camping. Fiona can arrange everything.'

Fiona is his wife's PA; Fiona is the one person who always knows what Celeste is doing. Sometimes Myles thinks it would be better for Fiona to be married to his wife instead of him.

So it's agreed. He is to take the boys camping over half-term; no writing for him that week, no Eve, and he should be pleased that he will have his sons to himself, but deep down in the hidden part of his heart he's thinking that maybe he isn't pleased; he's angry at being manipulated into the position in which he now finds himself. When they begin to clear the dishes away, Myles realises he's drunk too much too quickly. He feels light-headed when he stands and a kind of anger is simmering between his ribs.

Later, after he's said goodnight to Bruno, Celeste has checked her emails and Myles has unsteadily put out the rubbish, taken the dog outside and let him do his business which he's gathered up in a nappy bag and thrown away and then shut the dog in the kitchen, he washes and undresses and gets into bed. He purposely hasn't checked his emails; it would sting too much to read any reply from Eve this evening. He feels he needs some distance from how he feels about her and his head hurts from the wine and disappointment.

However, in bed his wife turns to him and touches him lightly on the shoulder.

'Fancy a quick one? Seeing as I'm here,' she says. She tries to smile but it doesn't fit her face somehow.

He makes love to her but it is perfunctory and he only

does so because he feels he has to. He knows it will be quick and easy and that they will be good at it because they have practised doing it this way for years. She turns her back to him and he holds her open and sinks his cock into her, she straightens her legs to grip hold of him, masturbates while he comes and, as she cries out, it's like he's being emptied out. He hasn't kissed her or touched her breasts and afterwards she passes him a tissue and he wipes his cum off her skin and the sheets.

Afterwards, when he's washing himself in the basin in the ensuite, he glances at his reflection in the mirror and wonders how on earth things could have come to this.

13

Rose is watching the evening news. On the screen is archive footage of people demonstrating in the streets of Athens. Their faces are pressing up against the camera; she can almost feel the heat of the crowd. There is chanting and the reporter's being jostled, his words snatched from his mouth as the microphone is knocked sideways. Back in London, the newsreader is cool and unruffled, her desk gleams and she closes the item with a cool, 'Thank you. That was Athens, as it was.' And that is it. Just a brief glimpse over the heads of the demonstrators to the sky-line, a library shot of the Acropolis, a second's film of the Greek flag, billowing in a hot wind. But in her heart Rose is there, at Hotel Byron off Vyronos Street in the Plaka, looking out of the window to the temple, knowing it was built to please the eyes of the gods, knowing this is the best view of it in the whole city because the sign outside the hotel door tells her this. And Henry is there too. Henry is near.

In October 1963 she, Henry and Mr Georgiadis flew to Athens for the launch of the *Ajax Star*. The preceding months had been hectic as they'd checked and rechecked the plans, negotiated with the port authorities, the shipbuilders, the ambassador and the financiers. Mr Georgiadis's mood had been like the weather; unsettled and stormy with brief interludes of radiant sun when he'd stand in the office, his arms outstretched, and say, 'Ah, Miss Reynolds, life is good. Life is good indeed!' And she and Henry had, of necessity, worked very closely on the guest lists and Mr Georgiadis had asked Henry to oversee the pre-launch reception, so he and Rose had talked about that in great detail too. Mostly they talked about these things in the office, in the boardroom with the door open and Rose would pour them each a cup of tea and she would sit with her notepad and pencil and take notes. But sometimes they'd talk about it when they were alone in hotel bars or restaurants or the time he took her dancing and, after each occasion, she would lie in bed in her room at the top of Verity's house and replay everything he said, each look on his face, every time he touched her hand. Always he was the perfect gentleman and always she felt like she was falling, was suspended in mid-air.

There'd been more dresses too. Since that first one for the races, Henry would send a dress every few months until she had a rainbow of them and there was no room in her wardrobe for them. Yet, the two of them never spoke about the things that really mattered, and after cocktails or dinner she'd hang up her dress, press her face to it to try and track any trace of the lemony zest of his cologne, but find it masked by cigarette smoke and the diesel fumes of the city. And they never walked along a street holding hands, but her fingers would burn at the nearness of him and, when he'd gone home to Penelope, they'd sting at the distance of him.

However, in Athens it was just them. Penelope had stayed in England with her horses and Mr Georgiadis was, of course, staying with family. He'd said expansively, his face beaming, 'You must, you must stay with us. There is much room in our houses for the guests. You will eat our food and drink our drink and be family with us. This is my country. It will be your country.'

When it came to it, though, there were no rooms in the family's houses; these had been taken by relatives from the islands and Sir Reginald and Lady Cuthbert Smythe and their two rather plump, pre-boarding-school-aged children, Agatha and Cedric. So, Rose and Henry were booked into single rooms in the Hotel Byron. His room was on the top floor, hers one floor down. Both of their windows faced the Acropolis and everywhere was the smell of cooking, the sound of horns blaring and the occasional wail of a siren.

The pre-launch reception was to be held at the Ambassador's Residence and, as Rose's taxi drew up outside it in Loukianou Street, a liveried doorman swept down the steps to greet her.

He bowed and said, 'Welcome, lady. Welcome, yes, welcome.'

She was wearing one of Henry's dresses; black taffeta, cinched at the waist, the skirt full and flowing. Verity had lent her a string of pearls and clip-on earrings and Rose had curled and set her hair and carefully applied her make-up. It was an evening when, for once, she felt beautiful, and Henry was close by and his closeness made things that weren't possible seem possible. Or so she thought, anyway.

He and Mr Georgiadis were entertaining a group of investors at a bar near the Royal Garden and would be arriving with them in about half an hour. Rose had got to the Residence early to check everything was ready: that the champagne was on ice, the flowers in the ballroom had been placed where she'd requested them, were elegant, not too ostentatious, and that the waiters were ready in the gardens, that the music was playing.

She walked over the bridge from the drawing room into the garden. The evening was warm and still. The city buzzed in the background but here it was quiet. The sky was a faded cotton blue and there was candlelight and the musicians were tuning up. A small stage had been erected on the far side next to the pergola where, later, Mr Georgiadis would make his speech and the ambassador would reply. The wording of these speeches had been agreed in letters and telephone calls and the cable from the microphone shone black in the flickering light, snaking across the pale slabs of the courtyard.

All was as Rose wanted it to be, so she hurried back to the entrance hall, nodded quickly to the photograph of Sir Winston Churchill taken on his visit there in 1944 and went into the cloakroom, where she washed her hands and checked her hair. In five minutes the guests would start arriving and Henry would be there. It seemed that the whole world was focused on him; that this evening he was at the centre of everything. For this one night only she would allow herself to believe he was at the centre of her.

Later, when the reception was in full swing, the man standing in front of Rose said, 'So, lovely lady, what is it you are here for? You are –' he paused, gathered up the spit which had collected at the corners of his mouth with his tongue. A tongue that was, Rose noticed, fat and glistening – 'you are,' he said again, 'an English rose, are you not?'

Like his tongue, this man was portly and florid. The buttons on his shirt strained across the expanse of his stomach and he'd obviously dropped some morsel of food down his front, for it had left a mark by the side of his tie. He had small eyes and not much hair. His skin shone pinky-brown in the candlelight. Rose had no idea what to say in reply, wanted very much to scan the crowd, to know where Henry was, but she couldn't. This man was demanding her whole attention. He reached out a hand, the one not holding his champagne glass. His fingers were stubby, his nails bitten.

'So,' he said again, touching her arm, 'this is your first time in my country? You must let me take you on a tour of our ancient monuments. We have a beauty here that is to be found nowhere else on this earth.'

Rose took a sip of her drink.

'I work for Mr Georgiadis,' she said. 'I am here to work, for the launch. I doubt I'll have time for sight-seeing, but thank you for the offer. It is very kind of you.'

The man leant in closer. 'There are other things I could show you. Tonight, perhaps? Later, after this party?' The spit was back in the corners of his mouth and he took a further step towards her. She could feel heat emanating from him. He smelled of something stale.

All around was the hum of conversation, the air was heavy with it. It seemed there was no escaping him. His hand was still on her arm and he said, 'After the party? Yes? Mr Georgiadis is my very best, most personal friend.

He would want me to be happy tonight. This will be your job too? Yes?'

Rose took a step back, the man's hand slipped off her sleeve, he wobbled and the glass slipped out of his other hand. It crashed to the floor and splintered. The remaining liquid in it stained the paving stones and the people standing nearest to them looked around and the man whispered angrily, 'You foolish girl. Look, this has happened.' He took another step towards her, his feet crushing the glass, and then there was Henry.

'Miss Reynolds,' Henry said, clearing his throat. 'Is everything all right?'

'There's been an accident,' she managed to say. 'I must get someone to clear up the broken glass. Would you be able to get our guest another drink?'

'Of course, come with me,' Henry said to the man, steering him away by the elbow. 'Mr Georgiadis is just about to make his speech but we have time to get you another drink. There are some people I need to introduce you to as well. Let's allow Miss Reynolds to organise someone to sweep up this,' he pointed to the ground, 'shall we?'

The man's eyes blazed at Rose, who looked quickly up at Henry. Henry wasn't smiling as he propelled their guest away, but he did look back once over his shoulder at her and she mouthed 'Thank you' and he raised one eyebrow at her, his lips set in a tight line. It was then she knew.

He loved her. Despite everything, he loved her and the knowing of this filled the ambassador's garden like a beam of yellow light. It was a certainty and Rose let out a breath which was long and sweet as she motioned to a waiter and told him in slow and quiet English that there was broken glass to clear away. The waiter hurried off to get a dustpan and brush. The incident, it seemed, was over.

After Mr Georgiadis had made his speech and the ambassador had replied, the guests started to drift away. Small parties of people gathered at the entrance to the Residence and discussed where they should go for dinner or more drinks. Henry was swept away in one such group with Mr Georgiadis, the fat man who'd dropped the glass, and Sir Reginald. Lady Cuthbert Smythe had stayed at home with the children because Agatha had been sick after lunch; it had been said it was because the food was so much richer here than at home, but Rose suspected it was because she'd eaten too much of it.

Back at the Residence, however, there was laughter and much back-slapping. Mr Georgiadis was beaming as they left. Henry didn't look back at her this time as she watched him walk away through the drawing room, his hat in his hand. She waited for him to turn round and come to speak to her, but he didn't and she tried very hard not to mind, held on to the love that a little while before had filled the garden with yellow light. It would be all right, she told herself as eventually she turned in the direction of the bar to talk to the staff about clearing up and to thank the musicians. It will be all right. They had enough already. What bound her to Henry and him to her was strong enough. Wasn't it?

The air was still warm. The night sky above the trees was dark and endless and, when everyone had gone and it was just her, the soft-stepping waiters and the chink of glasses being carried away on trays, she sat under the pergola near where Mr Georgiadis had stood to make his speech and put her head in her hands and allowed herself to weep because the moment was perfect, because the pain she was feeling was exquisite, because it meant she was truly alive.

Here, this evening in Athens, she wouldn't have swapped places with anyone. Loving Henry was a gift and, whatever happened in the future, she knew she would always have tonight, that look over his shoulder as he escorted the man away, the fact that although he'd walked through the drawing room and left to have dinner with people she didn't know and never would, he had left most of his heart with her.

The taxi dropped her back at the hotel around ten o'clock.

'Ah, Miss Reynolds,' the receptionist said, her accent thick and soft like honey, 'a good evening, yes?'

'Very nice, thank you,' Rose replied as she was handed

the key to her room and added, 'Would there be any chance of a sandwich and a cup of tea, do you think? I didn't get to eat much at the Residence.'

'Of course, my dear. I will ask Balios to fetch one for you. He will bring it to your room. Yes?'

Rose thanked her and slowly climbed the stairs to her room. Just outside the door, she took off her shoes. Her feet ached. She was very tired. All she wanted was to sit on the balcony, eat her food, drink the tea and then lie in bed and wait for Henry's taxi to arrive. She would hear him ring on the hotel door and the rumble of his voice as he talked to Balios on his way up the stairs. He would stop briefly on the landing where her room was and then go to his, where he would sleep and she would imagine his dreams.

But, when it happened it was of course inevitable, as it had been since that moment their hands had touched when she'd handed him back his jacket after sewing the button on all those years before.

Rose had finished her sandwich and taken off her dress. She'd put on her wrap and had cleaned her teeth. It was nearly midnight but the Plaka was still teeming with people and somewhere nearby music was playing: a bar maybe, filled with cigarette smoke and young couples drinking cocktails. Some of them would be dancing, their bodies pressed up against one another, she thought.

Then a taxi arrived and, from her chair on the balcony, Rose could see Henry step out of it and search his pockets for change. He paid the driver and stood on the pavement as if listening out for something. The taxi drove off and, as Henry walked towards the hotel, he looked up. Rose raised her hand in greeting, found she could not swallow.

It was as she imagined it. She heard him speak to Balios, heard him climb the stairs, heard him stop on her floor and she waited, not breathing, not swallowing. And she knew.

When he knocked on her door, she was waiting on the other side of it and when she opened it, he stepped across the threshold and was holding her, his head bent, his cheek resting on the top of her head. He tasted of spiced food and Greek beer. He seemed tired too, it was like he was inside out and when they kissed his mouth was full of something she could not name, a kind of grief and joy she had never tried to define before, had never needed to, not until now.

Then his hands were inside her wrap. He slipped it from her shoulders and cupped her breasts, fingering the lace of her bra. She undid the belt so the gown fell to the floor. He reached round to unfasten the clasps. She stepped out of her slip and underwear.

'You are beautiful,' he said as he guided her to the bed.

She could feel his hand tremble as it rested in the small

of her back. It reminded her of that time in Simpson's. She smiled quietly to herself.

'Don't ask,' she said as he switched off the bedside light and stretched out on the bed cover. The streetlamp outside glowed orange in the room. The distant beat of music seemed to match the beats of her heart.

'Don't ask what?' He was sitting on the edge of the single bed, unbuttoning his shirt.

Although this was the first time, the sight of him was so familiar to her it was as though they'd done this a hundred times before.

'Whether this is what I want, whether we should.'

'I wasn't going to,' he said, lying down beside her, the inch of air between them both electric and soft. 'It's too late for that. It was too late for that way back when I met you, when we started this.'

And he kissed her on her mouth and her nipples and bent his head until his tongue was in between her legs and she was holding the word 'we' in her fists as they grabbed the bedcover and her orgasm grew in circles until she came and cried out his name.

Then he was in her, all the length of him. He'd had a French letter in his trouser pocket which he'd laid carefully next to the bed and which he'd put on just after she'd cried out and he moved above her and she watched his face in the glow from the streetlamp outside. She could see his lips move as he came in her and then he rested his body on hers and they'd both wept. She'd marvelled briefly that perhaps he'd known this would have happened, that he'd prepared for it, but the thought didn't worry her. She would not allow anything about that night to worry her. And then they slept. There was no real need for words. They'd spoken them all already, to each other, to themselves, out loud and in their heads throughout all the years they'd known one another.

This, she thought, is perfect, and she watched his face beside her, his eyes closed and his breathing steady. She really believed that they would be good at this; that this would be something good.

When she woke the next day, Henry had gone. He had left her a note on a sheet of hotel paper he'd obviously got from the dressing-table drawer. It said, 'Didn't want to wake you. See you at the launch. Love, Henry.'

And later, at the launch, they stood side by side as the ship rolled majestically down the slipway and the crowds cheered and Mr Georgiadis was beaming again as the bottle exploded on to the hull and the band started to play. It was then that Henry looked down and met Rose's eyes and she saw his face. It was suffused. She had kept her promise to him and now she had, she vowed, she would never break it, never let him go.

Rose still believes that no one there that day knew that

mere hours before she had lain with him in a hotel bedroom, that she'd touched him and that he'd been inside her, his body heavy on hers, his mouth on her mouth and that he had slept in her arms. There had been no guilt and no sense of wrong. This was where they were always meant to be.

So, that day when Rose was single, almost thirty, in love, real love at last and Henry was married, forty-three and someone she would always have to share, nothing else mattered because she'd had that night, all of it, from the evening in the gardens of the Ambassador's Residence to waking up with the imprint of his head still on the pillow next to hers. And she'd had the next day, when his arm had brushed against her arm as the *Ajax Star* crashed into the waves in the harbour at Piraeus and the flashbulbs on the cameras of the pressmen and sightseers had flashed and captured the moment for ever and ever and ever.

The news programme has finished. Rose is aware that the girl on the screen is telling her about the weather. 'Rain will ease in the east later in the afternoon,' she says, smiling out of the screen at Rose and sweeping her hand behind her over a portion of Kent, 'but will strengthen towards dawn tomorrow with some risk of flooding in low-lying areas . . .' and Rose thinks of water and of ships and of the note Henry left her which she keeps in the wooden box on the top shelf of her wardrobe and of the black dress which, sometimes, she allows herself to touch and remember, and of the grainy photograph from a yellowing newspaper and the caption underneath it, 'Crowds celebrate the launch of the *Ajax Star*, Piraeus, Athens, Thursday 3 October 1963'.

14

Eve's said goodbye to Debs and is waiting at the lifts at work. It's four thirty on Thursday and she's leaving work early because Max is away and she's managed to clear her emails for once. She's just pressed the down arrow when her phone rings. It's Myles.

'Hi, it's me,' he says. 'Can you talk?'

'Yes,' she says. 'Of course.'

But from habit she looks over her shoulder. The area outside the lifts is empty, there is the distant sound of telephones ringing and people are walking to and from the meeting rooms around the corner but here, for this moment, it is quiet. She moves over to one of the chairs in front of the plate-glass window which looks out over the car park and sits down. She bends forward to shield the phone in her hand. Outside it is not quite dark, the clocks are due to go back a week on Saturday.

'How are you?' Myles asks.

'Oh fine. A bit tired, but otherwise fine.'

'Good day?'

'Yes, thank you. You?'

It's nice to say these things. Normal, everyday things, and she imagines him at his desk in Rose's house and his hair, the curve of his arms, his hand holding the phone.

'Yes, it's been OK. Just trying to clear a few things before next week.'

'Oh yes,' she says. 'Next week.'

He'd told her he's taking the boys camping in the New Forest for half-term before the sites close for the winter. 'Celeste will be in New York, you see,' Myles had said the week before, 'and Anka's going home for a wedding, so I'm in charge!' He'd laughed briefly when he'd said this and she hadn't been able to read his tone, had no idea what he really thought about it all. All she'd known was that they were now able to say these things to one another, that they knew each well enough for this and that this in itself was startling.

'The weather doesn't look like it's going to be too bad.'

'That's good,' she says.

And suddenly she wants to be with him. Not just near him, but to be held by him. She wants to rest her head on his shoulder and be warmed by him. She closes her eyes.

'Will I see you before I go?' he asks.

'I'm not sure. I might come and see Rose tomorrow. Max'll still be out of the office so I could pop over at lunchtime. I haven't seen her this week so far.'

'I know,' he says. 'I've missed you.'

When he says this a chasm seems to open up in front of her, full of danger and light. Part of her yearns to fall into it, part of her knows she should jump it, safely reach the other side where her real life is, where Andrew and Jodie are.

As she searches for something to say in reply, out of nowhere she thinks of The Gables.

The Gables is a house on Church Road which she has driven past almost daily for the last twenty years and for those twenty years it has remained changeless. There've been no children walking up and down its drive on their way to school and back, no Ocado delivery vans arriving and departing, no John Lewis lorries have drawn up with a new dishwasher inside wrapped in cardboard and plastic, no one has paid for a block-paved drive to be laid. Only a carer has come and gone, the standard lamp she could see through the lounge window is turned on and the upstairs curtains are opened and closed. Once she saw someone mowing the front lawn, but mostly the house is as it must have been in the thirties, like something out of an episode of *Poirot*, and then yesterday a For Sale sign had appeared outside it. In the instant she drove by it, she'd known that the man who lived there had died and that she would now not meet him, never know what sort of life he'd led, and she feared that whoever bought the house would change it, put in new windows, build an extension out the back, maybe even convert the loft and brash, shiny cars would churn up the drive and nothing would be the same again.

So as she hunts for something to say to Myles, she thinks of making choices and of change and of that line from *Rumour Has It* when Kevin Costner's character says something like, life has to be wild sometimes otherwise it's just a bunch of Thursdays strung together. And she's caught, firmly in the middle of wanting nothing to change and wanting everything to.

'If I do come over tomorrow,' she says at last, 'will you be there?'

'Oh yes, Fiona, Celeste's PA, is getting everything sorted for the trip. They've even hired me a people carrier for the week, for the boys, all the equipment, the dog! All I have to do is pack it, apparently, and we're not leaving until Saturday afternoon, so tomorrow'll be my last day of writing for a while.'

'I see,' Eve says. 'I'll try, then. If I have time. Shall I text when I leave work?'

But why, she asks herself, should it matter if I'm able to see him if it'll only be for just a moment either on her way into or out of Rose's house? But it does, it's like he's a drug and that moment is a necessary reminder that what she feels for him is real, that him in her life is becoming a fundamental thing and that this matters very much.

'Yes, OK,' he says, but it's not OK and she knows it. It's way too much and not nearly enough. 'How's everything else, by the way?' he asks now.

By everything else she knows he means Andrew and Jodie.

Recently Eve and Myles have taken to speaking in a kind of code. One mention of Celeste's name in a call is enough, she's like a wedge between them, but talking about the boys is allowed and seems to draw them closer together because his love for them is so complicated and something entirely separate from how he feels about his wife or Eve. It's such a delicate balance and Eve knows he'll expect her to say Andrew's and Jodie's names in her reply and that this will be her quota for this call too. Like Celeste, Andrew is a threat. Like his sons, Jodie is accepted but has to be kept safely boxed because she also is too vast a topic to tackle.

'Everything's fine,' she says. 'I got an email from Jodie yesterday with some photos of the children she's teaching. She's loving it over there, really loving it.'

'That's good.'

'Yes, it is.' She pauses, knows she will have to say the next bit because he's mentioned his wife. It's part of the deal.

'Andrew's fine too. Busy now he's back working inside. The band's playing on Saturday at the Jolly Angler.' She can tell Myles this because she knows he'll be in the New Forest, safely at a distance.

'Nice,' is all Myles says, 'that's nice.'

But it's not. Andrew is not fine. Not really. Eve's been aware recently that there is a silence between her and him and it's growing deeper, that she's choosing more and more often not to tell him even the small things she used to; snippets and thoughts that like stones on a beach are separate and tiny, but massed together make a shoreline, a landscape. And he's not whistling, not so much, not any more. Their morning routine is clunky and their timing's out without Jodie's presence to regulate them and she knows that this evening she will cook dinner and they'll eat it on trays in the lounge watching something on TV and tell themselves the quiet is companionable and there's nothing sinister in it at all. And later, they'll kiss each other goodnight and he won't try to touch her and she will try not to mind, is finding that it's becoming easier not to.

The phone line crackles and Eve's aware that there's someone waiting by the lifts. She doesn't look up but knows it's not Debs. However, she's uneasy talking to Myles here like this, senses that whoever it is can see the virtual image of him she's conjured up and that whoever it is standing nearby mustn't know about him, mustn't be allowed to share him.

'Look,' she says, 'I'd better go but I will try and come round tomorrow, I really will.'

'Oh, OK. Yes, of course. You should go. It's getting late. It'll be dark soon. See you tomorrow maybe, then?'

'Yes, tomorrow. Bye, then. Thanks for ringing.'

'Bye,' he says, 'for now.'

They hang up and before she knows what she's doing, Eve is in the lift chatting to Susan from Purchasing about the traffic and the redevelopment of the station and her phone is in her bag and her heart feels cracked with all the things she wanted to say but couldn't.

That evening she watches an episode of *Friends* while she waits for Andrew to come home. She doesn't text Debs, there doesn't seem to be any point in doing so, and when Andrew arrives they eat, chat about the weather and look again at the photos that Jodie's posted online. Eve leans over Andrew's shoulder as he looks at the laptop screen. She is surprised by how strange it feels to be so close to him and finds it hard to touch him. It's like he's a stranger and she doesn't like the person she's becoming, but it's as though she can't help it. Sometimes she feels she's trapped inside a suit of armour, hopeful it will protect her from what she's feeling, stop her hurting others, getting hurt herself.

The next day she texts Myles before she leaves the office. 'Just setting out,' it reads, and he replies, 'OK.'

She'd rung Rose earlier and Rose had said, 'Lunch is on me today. Bring nothing but yourself, my dear.'

'Are you sure?' Eve had asked. 'Is there absolutely nothing I can bring?'

'Just yourself.'

So Eve parks her car in Belle Avenue and locks it and walks towards the house. It had been foggy earlier but the weak October sun's finally managed to burn the fog away and above the town the sky is a type of blue Eve thinks she could reach up and touch. There are vapour trails criss-crossing it and the birds are singing what sounds like one last hurrah. Eve feels odd and dislocated for a moment thinking it could be spring, but tells herself not to be so silly as she opens the gate and walks up the path to Rose's front door. She glances across, hoping to see Myles at the window and for them to nod to one another and for this to be enough for today, but he's not there, he's not waiting for her like she'd expected him to and she's stung by a sense of disappointment that's raw and a little bit ugly. Maybe he'll be there when I leave instead, she thinks.

She lets herself into the house and calls up, 'Hello, I'm here!'

Rose appears at the top of the stairs. 'Oh, come on up.

Lunch is almost ready. I'm just finishing off a few things in the kitchen.' She disappears out of sight.

As she climbs the stairs, Eve listens carefully for the sound of movement in Myles's flat but there is none. His car's parked outside and momentarily she's wrong-footed, like the world has shifted on its axis. How precarious a hold I have on things, she thinks, if something as small as this can threaten to derail me. And then she's in Rose's sitting room and Myles is there and is smiling at her from a chair by the fireplace.

'Hello,' he says. 'Looks like there's going to be three of us for lunch!'

'Oh,' Rose adds, bustling back into the room, 'I see you've been reintroduced!' There is a glint in her violet eyes as she says this and she rests her hand on Eve's arm.

Eve bends down to kiss Rose's cheek, 'Yes,' she says, 'we have. Now, let me help you carry something through?'

'OK,' Rose says, 'follow me.'

Later they are sitting at the table. Its dark wood is solid and uncompromising and the crockery resting upon it looks too delicate for it. The sound of their cutlery on the plates is loud as they eat their soup and then the flan and potato salad and the rhubarb crumble and custard Rose has made and, all through the meal, Myles looks far too large for this place, that he both belongs here and he doesn't. They say small things like 'Mmm, delicious' and 'Looks like the weather's clearing' and Eve feels like she's in a play or a film or something, that this can't be real.

'Ah, that was lovely,' Myles says, scraping his dessert bowl. 'Just what I needed. The danger is, though, I'll need a nap this afternoon rather than cracking on with my writing!'

Rose turns to Eve. 'Myles tells me he's off camping with his sons next week. It's half-term, you know.'

Of course Eve knows, but has to say, 'Oh, that sounds nice,' and looks at Myles and asks, 'Where are you going? Camping, I mean.'

'The New Forest,' Myles replies. He doesn't look at her but starts to fold his serviette.

'Hope the weather's kind to you,' Eve adds. Her head is spinning and her legs don't feel like they belong to her. She never knew she was such a bad actress.

'Thank you.'

Then there's silence until Eve jumps up and says, 'Coffee, anyone? I'll clear. Rose, you sit there, keep Myles company.' It is so wonderful, she thinks, to be able to say his name out loud. She starts stacking the dishes and carries them out to the kitchen saying, 'Coffee? Tea?' over her shoulder and, when she's out of sight she puts down the bowls and spoons and rests her hands on the kitchen counter and tries to steady her breathing.

Then she's back with the tray of coffee cups, the coffee pot, milk and sugar and Myles is leaning across the table and asking Rose, 'So, I'm dying to know. How *do* you two know one another? Where did you meet? When? As a writer, everything I hear is research, you know! I'm not just being nosy, honest!'

'It's a long story,' Rose says, smiling up at Eve.

'Not that long, not really,' Eve replies, putting the tray down and starting to pour. The room fills with the strong scent of coffee; it feels exotic and heady.

'Go on, then, tell me this not-long story. We have time, don't we?'

Eve checks her watch. 'I suppose so. Rose?' she says, 'Over to you?'

Rose is holding her coffee cup and staring down at the surface of the drink. 'It's hard,' she says after a short pause, 'not to believe in fate sometimes. Sense has always told me that we make our own luck and that our decisions and choices are the things that define us, but sometimes, something comes out of the blue and without it, well, life just wouldn't be the same.' She looks across at Eve, her eyes dark now, her expression unreadable.

'I was in the hospital with Mother, it was towards the end. Boy, was she cranky!' Rose stops, takes a sip of her drink, laughs quietly. Eve and Myles don't speak, don't look at one another, but even so Eve can feel him near her, his warmth and the shape of him. Instinctively she wants to move closer to him but knows she can't.

'And one day, I was walking past one of the neighbouring wards and caught a glimpse of a name written in marker pen on a board above one of the beds. You know the sign that says things like "Nil by Mouth" and the name of the surgeon, and anyway the name on this one was "Verity Jones" and I thought, no, it can't be. There must loads of women with that name and anyway, the last I knew, Verity was still living in London. At that stage I didn't know what had happened to Meredith.' Here Rose puts down her cup and reaches across to hold Eve's hand. She squeezes it and Eve smiles at her. It is a sad smile.

If Myles is curious as to who these people are, he doesn't say. He just sits there and listens. Now and then he shifts in his seat, plays with the spoon in the sugar bowl, makes small mounds in the sugar, then smooths them with the back of the spoon.

'There was a girl sitting next to the bed; a tall girl with long brown hair. She was newly pregnant and reading out loud to the person in the bed. I went over, stood and listened for a moment. I knew I should be getting back to Mother, that she would be worrying, but there was something familiar about the patient and then I realised it *was* Verity, thirty years on, but still Verity. She'd shrunk, of course, her hair was almost gone and she was so thin, so painfully thin. But it was her.'

Here Rose looks at Myles. 'I rented a room in her house once, you see, when I was working in London, when . . .' She hesitates, shakes her head slightly and continues, 'But I hadn't seen her since I moved back here, to this house. We kept in touch by letter and Christmas card but then that tailed off and I came to understand that however close you are to someone, eventually life can move on, you can lose them.

'But, there she was and there you were, Eve, and that's how we're here now, isn't it?' She looks at Myles. 'Verity died, about a week later and Meredith, Eve's mother, didn't come back for the funeral. Not sure I can ever forgive her for that. America isn't that far away after all, is it?'

'I don't think Gran would have minded,' Eve says hurriedly. They've talked about this hundreds of times and it hasn't made any difference; Meredith hadn't come back then and hasn't been back since, not even for Jodie's christening. 'Gran and Mum hadn't seen each other for years,' Eve continues, 'and I haven't seen Mum since they moved away and anyway, Gran had you there and me and . . .' Here Eve hesitates too, knows she will have to say his name, knows this will come from her quota. It would be odd if she didn't mention him, '. . . and Andrew,' she says. 'Andrew was around too at the end, wasn't he?'

'Yes, she did. She had us all, at the end,' Rose continues now, busy clearing the cups, 'and since then Eve's been here, has been my link to the past, to the one woman who . . .' Again, she stops mid-sentence. Eve knows better than to ask. She's tried over the years to find out what else linked Rose to her grandmother, what secrets they'd shared, had believed it was something to do with the man in the photograph, the one with the sad eyes, but, like she believes the secret places in her own heart, the corners where she hides what she feels for the man sitting next to her at the table in this flat on this Friday afternoon in October, should stay secret, so she believes that Rose's secrets should stay safe too. So she's never asked to look in the box she lifts down from Rose's wardrobe, never questioned Rose about the dresses or about the man in the picture. She loves Rose enough without knowing all this.

'Not such a long story, then,' Rose says now. 'Just one that covers a lot of years, eh?'

Eve will never forget what Myles does next. He gets up and moves across to where Rose is sitting. Standing behind her, he leans over her and wraps his arms around her shoulders and rests his right cheek on the top of her head. It is such a tender moment, so precious. Eve has to swallow hard to stop the tears from coming and she knows that what she feels for this man, this man who is married to someone else but who is here now, holding Rose like this, is a good thing, is a right thing and that she is wrong to try to deny it. Life is too short not to seize it and take a risk on it. It doesn't have to be just a bunch of Thursdays strung together. Life can be wild and confusing and wonderful.

And now Rose is saying, 'Oh, thank you, my dear. That's a kind thing to do but I guess I'd better let you both get back to work, hadn't I?'

And Myles is letting Rose go, then he's standing behind Eve. He squeezes her shoulder. His touch is like electricity and it's undeniable and she knows Rose has seen him do this and that Rose knows.

Back at work, Eve stares at her computer screen, thinks of all the things she still wants to say to Myles, now more than ever. The lunch with Rose, the story Rose told, the way he held her friend and the way he'd touched her all mean that the stakes have risen. Day by day, minute by minute, they are getting closer. It's a good thing he's going away for the week, she tells herself later as she lets herself back into her house in Byron Road and stands to listen to its quiet humming. Andrew will be back soon and she should start the dinner. She doesn't watch *Friends* but opens the fridge and stares at its shelves.

'Sausages,' she says out loud, 'we'll have sausages,' and inside her head she's telling herself that what she feels for

Myles is indisputable, undeniable, allowed. It is fact and it is not wrong.

A short time later, as the sausages sizzle in the pan, Andrew's car pulls up on the drive.

15

As Myles merges on to the M3 he's struck by a sudden sense of panic. How is he going to cope during the next few days when it's just him, the boys and the dog? He looks in the rear-view mirror at Orlando and Garth in the back, the dog curled up between them. Further back, in the boot, is the equipment Fiona packed for them and there's more in a box on the roof. He feels like Shackleton, fears he won't match up. Next to him Bruno's slouched in the passenger seat, headphones planted resolutely in his ears. He's tapping his right foot to the beat of the music, his head is resting on his hand, his fringe almost covers his eyes.

They'd stopped for a drive-through McDonald's near Basingstoke.

'Aw, Dad, are you sure?' Orlando had asked. 'Mum doesn't . . .'

'Well, Mum's not here, so what would you like?'

He'd barely managed to get the van around the stupidly narrow chicane and had leant out of the window to give the order and money to a smiling youth. This, he felt, was so far away from his detective, so far away from Eve that, for a moment, he felt uprooted, totally unsure as to who he was or what he was doing, but then the boys all started talking at once.

'I want a double cheeseburger with chips,' said Orlando.

'Me too,' said Garth.

'Big Mac meal.' Bruno momentarily unplugged himself from his music. There was a pause and then he added, 'Please.'

The youth passed Myles the drinks, straws and serviettes and Myles distributed them around. Orlando helped Garth put his drink in the holder down by the edge of his seat. Then came the bag of food; it was hot and heavy and Myles rested it on his lap while he manoeuvred the car out of the stupidly narrow chicane and pulled up in the car park. He handed the food out and sat back and closed his eyes. The car filled with the smell of burger and salt and he had to swallow hard to keep down the bile that was rising in his throat.

While the boys were eating he thought about Celeste leaving for the airport the evening before. The taxi had pulled up outside and the driver had pressed the intercom on the gates. Celeste had buzzed him in from the control pad in the hall and then turned to Myles.

'Well,' she said, 'I'll see you at the end of the week. Hope the trip goes OK.'

'Thank you. Safe flight. Keep me posted, eh?'

He took a step towards her but she bent down to pick up the handle of her case so all he could do was touch her on the shoulder.

'Yes, safe flight,' he said again.

'Bye,' she called up the stairs. 'I'm off now.'

There was a chorus of shouting from the boys' rooms. They were so used to her leaving like this it was almost as though she were saying, 'Right, just off to the shops. Back in half an hour or so.'

If Myles was amazed by his children's insensitivity he didn't want to think too deeply about it. After all, maybe it was their safety mechanism, their way of coping with her constantly shifting arrivals and departures, the late nights working at the office or out with clients. He hated to think what the long-term effects of this kind of life might be on them, didn't dare consider the long-term effects this might have on his marriage. And she'd gone and, with Anka already in Poland, he was alone with his sons and the dog.

Back outside McDonald's Bruno had said, 'Hey, Dad, wakey, wakey. We're finished. Shall we set off now?'

Startled, Myles had said, 'Sure thing. Do you all want to give me your rubbish and I'll put it in the bin over there?'

'No, don't worry, Dad. I'll do it,' and Bruno hopped out of the car, opened the back door to receive his brothers' left-over wrappers and cups and jogged over to the bin, checking for traffic as he did so.

Myles watched him go, both stunned by his son's maturity and heartbroken by it. This boy is moving so far away from him so fast he fears he will never catch up with him, never really know him like he thought he did when Bruno had been hip high, holding on to his hand when they crossed roads, when he'd been allowed to kiss him goodnight at bedtime.

Then Bruno came back and they set off and now Myles is pulling on to the M3 and is filled with a sense of panic about this trip. Steady rain is falling and the movement of the windscreen wipers is mesmeric. Orlando and Garth are dozing, as is the dog, and Bruno's plugged himself back into his music.

In this small place filled with the people he loves most of all in the world and in amongst the bustle and hurry of the motorway, he feels very much alone. He knows deep down that this is because whatever love he once had for Celeste has eroded away over the past few years and that this has left him with a gap in his chest which needs to be filled. He thinks Eve may be the answer, but Eve is married to someone else and this is so how it's not supposed to be.

He sighs and indicates, pulling out into the middle lane to overtake a lorry, then tucks back into the slow lane again. He can hear the tinny sound of Bruno's music and the dog is snoring and he thinks of when he met Celeste and how it was supposed to be.

'Oh,' he'd said, 'I'm so sorry.'

'That's OK. These things happen.' The woman is small, she has a look of intense concentration on her face as she studies the pile of papers he's dropped at her feet after Steve from HR had turned abruptly away from the photocopier and bowled into him. 'Here, let me help you,' she says.

She bends down and starts to gather the papers and Myles studies the top of her head, the way the light shines in her hair and the tidy shape of her shoulders, the quick, deft movements of her hands.

'There,' she says, 'all done.' And she smiles at him as she hands him the pile. It's a brief, efficient smile and she turns to go.

'Careful,' Steve from HR adds when she disappears out of sight round the corner, 'she's a pistol, that one.'

'I quite like pistols,' Myles says, surprised by this fact. 'What's her name?'

'Celeste Baker. She's my boss's boss. Sits on the right hand of God on the fourth floor.'

'She married?'

'Don't think so. Doubt anyone will have her. She's scary.'

'I quite like scary,' Myles says, surprising himself again.

He and Louisa had been apart for about six months by this time and never in his wildest dreams had he thought of embarking on a new relationship, or even of looking for one, but this woman, this small prickly, bundle of energy and efficiency, had stirred something in him.

Bet she's a good fuck, he says to himself as he goes back to his desk in IT and scrolls through the company address book until he finds her name.

And she was. She seemed uncomplicated and their first few dates were businesslike and easy and, even when he had to call her to rearrange a dinner they'd booked because he'd been asked to play five-a-side football, all she said was, 'OK. No problem. Let's reschedule.' And they had rescheduled and after dinner they'd gone back to her flat and fucked and he hadn't stayed the night.

So, he wonders now, how has it come to this? Eventually they agreed to get married and 'pool their resources'. It seemed at the time and still does more of a business transaction than anything else. 'After all, neither of us is getting any younger,' she'd said.

Her salary was at least four times his, but he had his writing and she humoured him, calling it a hobby in front of their friends and he tried very much not to mind about this. Her parents lived in Spain at the time and still do, so they rarely see them and this doesn't seem to bother his wife at all. What she thinks about his writing now he's published and can afford a flat of his own to work in, he doesn't know and has never asked. But what's non-negotiable is that they now have a large house in Caversham, three sons, a dog, her BMW, his Mercedes and the car Anka drives the boys to school in and they have furniture and pictures and have taken holidays on Greek islands and Florida, and Spain of course, and not once has he ever felt he really needed his wife with a heart-stopping, can't-live-without-her kind of need he'd once hoped he would and that this is probably the biggest tragedy of all.

A motorbike roars past him, the biker crouched low over the handlebars, his leathers soaked by the rain, and Garth's voice rises sleepily from the back of the car, 'I need a wee, Dad. Can we stop soon?'

'Of course. Winchester Services are about a mile away. Can you hang on until then?' Myles says, glancing briefly over his shoulder and sees his son nod his head.

They get to the campsite as it's getting dark and thankfully it's stopped raining. Fiona had booked them a static caravan with space to pitch a tent for the boys by the side of it.

'Can't imagine you living it too rough,' Celeste had said, laughing a little cruelly, he'd thought when she'd told him of the plan. How does she know he doesn't want just a tent, a fire and a pot to boil beans in?

But now he's here he can see the merits of the idea. Here they have running water, a loo, a table to sit at and the older two can still camp out if they want to.

'Shall we put the tent up in the morning?' he asks them as Benjy Dog snuffles around, relieving himself up against a nearby tree.

'No, now, Daddy, do it now,' Orlando says, tugging at Myles's arm.

And so he does. He struggles in the light from the caravan's windows and the headlamps of the car and Bruno helps to a certain extent by holding things when asked and passing him the mallet when needed, but the other two decide to play night football and Benjy Dog bounds about between them, his tongue lolling out, his mouth stretched wide with excitement so that it looks like he's smiling.

Eventually, they're settled in and Myles is cooking tea. Orlando and Bruno are in their tent making faces at each other by shining torches under their chins and Garth's sitting at the table in the caravan building something complex out of Lego. As the steaks cook, Myles risks checking his phone. There are two messages. One's from Celeste. 'Hope all OK at campsite. Text if any problems.' And one's from Eve, 'Thinking of you,' it reads. 'Hope the weather's good.'

When the boys are asleep, it starts raining again and Myles is in bed listening to it brushing the outside of the caravan and trickling down the canvas of his sons' tent. He looks over at the empty pillow next to his head.

'Daddy? I had a mare.'

It's towards dawn and Garth is pulling at the blanket on Myles's bed. In the light glimmering around the edges of the curtains, Myles can see the silhouette of his son, the tousled hair, the tiny shoulders.

'Do you want to come in for a cuddle?' Myles asks.

The shape nods and then clambers in beside him. His son's body is still warm and crumply with sleep and within seconds he's curled up next to Myles and his breathing has steadied. Myles rests his arm lightly across Garth and soon, he too is asleep again.

After breakfast Orlando and Bruno squabble over whose turn it is to dry the dishes.

'You're oldest so you should go first,' Orlando says.

'You're pathetic, so you should,' Bruno retorts and Myles opens the caravan door to let their words out and fresh air in. He stands on the doorstep for a moment and breathes the bacony, breakfasty air of the campsite.

'Right,' Myles says, 'Bruno, get Benjy's lead, we're off for provisions. The pesky washing-up can wait!'

There is a small part of Myles that feels triumphant

when he says this. They would not get away with this if Celeste were here. But then, he argues, as he picks up the car keys, Celeste isn't here, is she?

They go to Lymington.

'Let's go and see the boats first, eh?' Myles says to the boys and the dog as they park up. It's cold but bright; thick bulbous clouds dot the sky and the sea breeze on their faces is clean and a little sharp. They are all wearing coats and the dog is straining at the leash, keen to explore.

At the end of the high street they follow the cobbled path around to Quay Street and, outside the Ship Inn, they stop to watch. There's an old man sitting on the harbour wall mending nets, elderly people in beige coats are already established on the benches that punctuate the pavements and all around the sound of the halyards knocking against the masts punctures the air and there is salt in the wind here.

Bruno says, 'I'll take Benjy for an explore, OK, Dad?'

'Orlando, you going too?' Myles asks.

Orlando nods and the two of them wander off and, with the sun shining in their hair, Myles follows the bright halos of their heads as they weave in and out of the crowd and down to the end of the quay. Myles has hold of Garth's hand and is saying, 'Fancy going horse riding this afternoon?' when there's a splash and a shout. He doesn't take much notice. After all, this is a harbour.

Moments later, Bruno and Benjy return.

'Where's Orlando?' Myles asks, not concerned, not yet.

'I thought he'd come back to see you,' Bruno says. 'He wandered off.'

'What do you mean he wandered off? Thought you were keeping an eye on him.'

'I had the dog!' Bruno's face clouds over but under the defiance is panic and his lips are trembling.

Myles's heart explodes in his chest. Oh my God, he thinks. My boy, my precious boy. Then he remembers the splash and the shout. No, No. It can't be. Not here, not like this. Not my boy. And, picking Garth up, he runs to the edge of the harbour wall and stares down into the water. Bruno and Benjy follow. Everyone else is going about their business. No one seems to be aware of what's happening, not yet.

Although he's not there, Myles can see his son floating in the water, can see the dark mark on his forehead and the trails of blood in the water. He can see Orlando's coat filling with water and the weight of it dragging him down and he knows he's lost his son, that he's lost his wife's son and that he will remain forever unforgiven.

Holding Garth in one arm, he plucks his phone out of his pocket with the other. He can't control his fingers but starts to press 999. Almost instantaneously he can hear the sirens, see the panic on the faces of passers-by, can't think of his son and the cold of the water, its heaviness and the man Orlando would have become, his grown-up face, the children he might have had. Myles's brain is frozen, there are a million words stuck in his throat and his stomach is heaving. He seems to have grown to be a giant, can't see his feet, can't hear for the buzzing in his ears.

Then through this, through the call handler speaking to him from the other end of the phone, through the seagulls cawing and wheeling above the boats, he hears, 'Dad. Dad!' and he turns and there's Bruno standing behind him with the dog sitting by his side panting, his eyes open wide and shining with excitement and there's Orlando holding up a piece of dried seaweed, saying, 'Dad. Dad! Look. Can we take this home?'

Myles puts Garth down and, not quite understanding but knowing enough to know that there has been and may still be something dreadfully wrong, Garth holds on to Myles's leg while Myles says into this phone, 'It's OK. He's been found. It's OK.'

His breaths begin to slow and he looks down at his son and says, very carefully, 'Yes, of course we can take it home but promise me you won't wander off, not again. Not ever.'

Orlando shrugs and Bruno stares hard at his brother. 'Promise,' he says through gritted teeth. Benjy begins to whine, sensing discord, and a woman pushing a buggy is trying to get past them. She snorts with impatience. Myles feels his temper about to snap.

'Come on,' he says briskly. 'Let's get our shopping and go,' and he starts striding away, Garth clinging on to his hand, the other two following, Orlando trailing the seaweed behind him. It gathers dust from the street and a few of the dried-out air bladders tear off, but Orlando doesn't look back and, if anyone else were to watch them, they'd think, 'Ah, a father, his boys, their dog. What a nice sight.' They're not to know that Myles's heart has been shattered by the thought that he could have lost his son and that he'd thought he had and that the world had stopped turning because of it; that it's shattered by the absolute knowledge that he doesn't love his wife and by the blade-like need he feels now to talk to Eve, to tell her what's just happened, to have her walk beside him, know that in a moment she will reach out and touch his arm and smile her smile at him.

But he doesn't call her.

It's like a test he's set himself, the price he tells himself he has to pay for his son not dying that day like he thought he had, and he feels a better, nobler man for it. It's a bit like what happens in *The End of the Affair*, he thinks as they drive home the following Saturday, and he laughs quietly to himself, thinking how ironic it is that he should be contemplating the end of something before it's really begun.

He'd once read that being honourable is how you behave when no one else is looking, but he did text Eve once or twice during the week, saying things like, 'How are you?' 'How's work?' and she replied saying, 'Am fine. Hope you're having fun.'

And when he gets home with the boys and the dog, Anka's back from Poland and then Celeste returns from New York and asks him for a quick summary of the week: 'Did everything go OK?' she asks, to which he replies, 'Yes, it was fine, thank you,' and he tells himself that Eve is safely boxed like the things Rose keeps on the top shelf in her wardrobe, that she's safely tucked away and not able to hurt him, and he tries to forget what nearly happened in Lymington by sitting at his desk and writing about DCI Derek Pletheroe's hunt for the man who killed the woman and left her body on the beach and how he pores over phone records and CCTV footage and bank statements and can't find any clues that make sense.

But as he writes he knows he's waiting for Eve to come and visit Rose again and because she doesn't he goes running, goes home, wanks in the bathroom when Celeste's late home again and then four days later his resolve falters, there is a tide of pain in his chest and he rings Eve at work, tells her about Lymington and how he thought he'd lost Orlando, and she says, 'Oh my God, that must have been awful. I can't think of anything worse. You should have rung me.'

Yes, he says to himself, I should have rung you, not just

because I wanted to hear your voice but because you have become fundamental to me. And, as Myles admits this to himself one Monday in early November, he begins to see more clearly what he should do, how his life should really be from now on.

16

It's the fifth of November and Rose is in her garden tidying leaves. There's a chill in the air and, as she breathes, the breaths gather and hang cloud-like in front of her for a while. The leaves crackle underfoot. It will be dark soon.

She always begins this job on this day so her bonfire can mingle with the rest; so that the sparks that shoot into the sky can, she tells herself, be her own small firework display. Next door's cat comes to stare at her for a while, just to check that what's she's doing is OK, and then he ambles off. She hopes he'll be safely inside soon, asleep on a chair, not bothered by the rockets and Catherine wheels.

Rose is tired, she seems perpetually tired these days but she carries on, slowly, more slowly than last year, she notices, to rake the leaves from the flower beds into a pile on the lawn and then lift them the pile into a barrow which she trundles to the end of the garden and the incinerator.

She's wearing Father's work coat under her Barbour and has her wellies on. She feels cumbersome and ungainly dressed like this but hey, no one will see her, will they?

Of course she sees the square stone under the hydrangea and she taps it lovingly with the end of the rake, a bit like a caress. She'd had it put there when they did the conversion, as a reminder. There's no inscription on it, but its surface is flat and, in the low light of this autumn afternoon, it gleams up at her.

The flames leap when she sets fire to the leaves a little later. Around her, in neighbouring gardens, she can hear the whizz and whootle of small displays, can imagine the faces of the children as they watch mesmerised, and those of their parents who have come home early from work to fill buckets with sand, bake potatoes, put soup to warm on the stove. She wonders if Myles will be doing these things. She hopes he will.

Then the display at St Peter's School starts and the sky over the church is filled with strobes of colour and sound. It is totally dark now and Sol Joel Park will, she knows, be crowded with families and some of them will be drawing shapes or writing names in the air with sparklers. She prods the contents of her incinerator and adds more leaves. The smoke billows, makes her choke and her eyes water. I'm not crying, she tells herself.

When the pile of leaves has gone she puts the lid on the incinerator and tidies the rake and broom away in Father's shed and then climbs slowly up the steps to the flat, holding tightly on to the handrail and placing each foot down carefully. As she closes the back door the security light switches off and, save for a faint glow around the incinerator, the garden is in darkness.

There aren't many fireworks left now, just the odd one or two, and she closes the curtains, switches the kettle on and turns on the TV. There's a trailer for one of those genealogy shows; some young celebrity is talking about her great-grandfather's service in the First World War. 'I want to find out what really happened to him,' she says, 'why he didn't talk about it when he got home.'

Rose stops stock still halfway across her lounge and has to hold on to the back of the chair. She's taken off Father's work coat and has hung it on its hook in the kitchen and suddenly she's overwhelmed by thoughts of him, how she used to gather the leaves with him, how he'd never told her about his war because it just wasn't something that got talked about in those days.

Later, after drinking her cup of tea and eating a ham and piccalilli sandwich, Rose dozes in the chair. A gardening programme is playing in the background and she thinks she should be concentrating on it, but the front of her mind is full again of Father and of Henry and of what happened in the autumn of 1965.

After Athens, Rose and Henry settled into a routine of sorts. There were dinners and drinks in hotel bars after work but at nine o'clock he'd always drive her back to Verity's and then drive himself home to Penelope. He'd stop the car near Barons Court tube and they would kiss, sometimes hungrily with his hand between her legs, his fingers easing aside the lace of her underwear to find the damp underneath, and sometimes softly, when he would hold her face and look into her eyes and he would sigh and say, 'I want so much for it to be perfect, not like this. A whole night with you, like before. I want nights with you, a countless number of them.' But then he'd open the door for her and she would step out on to the pavement.

She never watched him drive away, never looked back over her shoulder, never told Verity why she was often home so late and Verity never asked. And so it went on.

And then it was the autumn of 1965, a Wednesday. Rose was in the boardroom tidying papers after a meeting and Mr Georgiadis had gone out to meet a distant cousin of his who ran a Greek restaurant in Soho and who was looking for backing to expand his one restaurant into a chain. Henry came in and shut the door behind him.

'Rose?'

Rose turned to face him, a pile of folders in her arms. 'Yes, Henry?'

He cleared his throat, nervous like a school boy. 'Penelope's away for a few days,' he said, 'visiting her mother in the country. I wondered if we could, well, if we could perhaps . . .' He faltered here, came across to where Rose was standing, picked the folders out of her hands and put them on the table. Then he gathered her hands in his, '. . . if we could perhaps book into a hotel for the night. I could take you back to get some overnight things and then we could drive somewhere. It'll mean an early start tomorrow, to get back here, but we could, couldn't we? I could drop you off here, then go home to change my shirt. You can say I've got a dentist's appointment or something. I'll make the hotel booking. No one need ever know. We can even have separate rooms if you like, for appearance's sake.'

Rose smiled, stroked Henry's hand with her thumb and nodded. 'That sounds lovely,' was all she said. Then, 'Yes please, Henry. Yes please.'

Naturally she wished they could book into the same room; call themselves Mr and Mrs Smith like they did in films at the pictures, but Rose and Henry hadn't quite joined the so-called permissive society yet. It wasn't then as it is now, when it's all right to meet at a Travelodge for the afternoon, when the only rules you're breaking are your own and the only real possibility of being discovered is because you've had to enter your car registration number into a computer at reception to get free parking.

To save time, Rose took the bus back to the Talgarth Road during her lunch hour. Verity was out so she left a note. 'Been called away on business. Back tomorrow evening. Love Rose.' She hated lying, but had a feeling deep down in the secret places of herself that this was an opportunity that might not come again soon and that she should grab it while she could. Suddenly the night in Athens which she'd talked herself into believing had been enough to last a lifetime wasn't enough at all and she wanted more, she wanted Henry to herself for another night and then other nights after that. She wanted to cook for him, do his laundry, read snippets from the newspaper out loud to him to make him laugh. She wanted to be Bathsheba to his Gabriel Oak. So tonight would be like sustenance, something to keep them going through the next bit of this, whatever that may be, the bit while she waited for what she wanted to come to pass, what she had to believe would one day be hers.

The afternoon dragged on for what seemed like for ever. Each key on her typewriter seemed to stick and the telephone would not stop ringing. Mr Georgiadis called from his cousin's restaurant to say he would not be coming back and, as the new office girl took the letters for posting, Rose said to her, 'You can go home early today if you like, I'll finish off here.'

Rose tried desperately hard not to look at the door of Henry's office when she said this and, when she thought it about afterwards, wasn't at all sure whether she'd succeeded or not.

It was almost dark by the time she and Henry were getting ready to leave. She put the cover on her typewriter and locked the drawers in her desk, putting the key under the plant pot on top of the filing cabinet as was her habit. Everyone else had gone. They were alone.

'You nearly ready?' Henry asked her, as he carried some papers through to Mr Georgiadis's office to leave on his desk for the morning.

'Yes, almost,' she said, her heart crammed with a type of joy that up to now, she hadn't known existed.

Then he was beside her and holding her.

'I don't think I can wait,' he said. 'Just think, you, me, a night together. Waking up with you, such a simple thing, such a precious thing and,' here he paused and undid a button on her blouse, 'there's the what will happen in between . . .'

She ducked out of his arms laughing and said, 'What, dinner, you mean?'

'Now you're teasing me!'

'Yes, exactly.'

It was heaven to be like this with him. Just them, all the promise of the evening, being free and not having to worry about looking over their shoulders, guarding their words, making do.

He plucked his coat off the coat stand and donned his hat, putting it on at a rakish angle and laughing.

'I feel like Fred Astaire,' he said. 'It's like I could sing and dance and the big band will play in the background and you,' he helped her on with her coat, 'are beautiful.' He kissed her neck. 'You,' he said, 'are my leading lady.'

This Henry was a different Henry from the one she'd known for so long. This was the man who'd lifted her high at the races, who'd rescued her from the fat man in the garden of the Ambassador's Residence and who'd made urgent love to her in a hotel room in Athens two years before. In between had been the careful, considered Henry. The shy man she loved desperately because she knew that underneath his sad smile, underneath the goodness and the doing right by his wife and by what society expected of him, was this man; a passionate, caring man who, for tonight, would let his guard down and be the man she knew was the only one for her, both now and for always, and that this is why she was waiting for him, would wait for ever if need be.

As she buttoned up her coat and clipped her handbag shut and as Henry was whistling 'Cheek to Cheek' and she hummed along stray words like 'heaven' and 'heart' and 'so that I can hardly speak', she knew for sure that this was the kind of love that comes only once in a lifetime.

Then the telephone rang again.

'Leave it,' Henry said. 'Surely whoever it is will ring back in the morning. It's gone five thirty. The office is closed.'

'Oh, I'd better get it,' Rose said, putting her gloves down on the desk and picking up the receiver.

Henry had started to dance now, his hat still askew on his head, his body swaying, his face suffused once more.

Rose was smiling at him as she said, 'Hello. The Georgiadis Shipping Company. How may I help you?'

The call was from Rose's mother. Her father had had a stroke that afternoon and had died. He'd collapsed in the hydrangea bed, had probably been dead by the time he'd reached the ground.

So Henry had driven her home instead of to a hotel in the country. The suitcase she'd packed that lunchtime had leant up against her left leg throughout the journey, a reminder of all the might have beens and, somewhere in Rose's hidden heart, in amongst the breathtaking grief her father's death had brought with it and the dread she felt at the thought of facing her mother, she feared that this missed chance with Henry might turn out to be her last chance, that what they'd planned that night would most likely never happen again.

The woman who opened the front door of the house in Belle Avenue looked like Rose's mother, but there was something so altered about her that, for a second, Rose struggled to recognise her. This woman was small and bent low. It was almost as though as recently as this morning she'd been held up by scaffolding and that suddenly this afternoon, around five o'clock, the scaffolding had been taken away.

'Rose,' Mother said. 'You made good time.'

'Yes, I got a lift. Someone from work.'

'Are they staying? Do they want some tea?'

'No, they've gone. They're driving back to London.'

Rose stepped over the threshold carrying the small overnight case she'd packed that lunchtime. If either woman felt the need to remark on it, they didn't. After all, if Rose had got here so quickly how would she have had time to pack a bag as well? Such things were, it seemed, not important in the face of everything else. She followed her mother down the hallway, her heart shredded by the knowledge that Father would not be sitting in his chair by the fire, a newspaper on his lap, his pipe clamped firmly between his teeth. But also by the fact that she'd just broken her golden rule and had watched Henry drive away.

'Take care of yourself,' he'd said as he'd handed her the case. 'Call me, anytime. If you need me for anything.' And he'd leant down and kissed her gently and swiftly on the lips, a mere brushing of his lips on hers, a dry and warm kiss. She'd stood on the pavement as he'd got back into the driver's seat and wound down the window. He'd reached out a gloved hand and taken hers in it. 'Oh Rose,' he'd said. 'Oh, my darling Rose.'

If she was to be asked to describe the worst moment with Henry it would be this, but bizarrely, it was also the best. It was so fleeting, so full of wonder and love. She watched the car pull out, saw it signal, wait at the junction of the Wokingham Road and then he turned into the flow of traffic and was gone, back on the A4 to London, the light from his headlamps reaching out in front of him, showing him the way. It didn't seem to matter whether anyone had seen them, not at that moment.

'Do you want tea?' her mother said.

'I'll make it. You sit down.'

'People have been telling me to sit down all afternoon.' Her mother's voice was sharp and bitter.

Rose had to hold on to the kitchen worktop to steady herself as the kettle boiled. They'd already come to take Father away but his work coat was on its hook by the back door, his gardening shoes on the mat, mud still speckling the heels. In later years she was to wonder if he'd actually died or whether he'd just decided to leave one day and not come back. She never saw his body and, other than at the funeral when he'd been hidden inside a long pale wooden box, she'd never said goodbye to him.

'Everyone's been so kind,' her mother said now in an attempt, Rose believed, to make up for the sharpness of before. 'Mrs Jenkins from number six came round when she saw the ambulance, said she'd make us a steak-and-kidney pie.'

'That's nice,' Rose replied.

Rose's head was howling with all the things she didn't know. How had it felt when he hit the ground, what had his last thoughts been? How would she ever find out now what had really happened to him in the wars? She knew the facts; he'd fought in the First World War and then had come back and met and married her mother, a girl called Ivy. He'd been a firewatcher and an ARP warden in the Second but what had he seen, whose hands had he held when the bombs fell? These were things she would never now know. It hadn't been talked about when she was a girl and she sometimes wondered if he'd ever told her mother really what had happened either.

They'd met at Suttons Seeds in Market Place. Like Henry, her father, Gilbert, was an accountant. Ivy worked in the Packaging Department. Rose had a feeling that back then, in 1920 when they'd married, her mother had had a sense of humour and mischief, had seen the future as a bright and sparkling thing. Then came reality: a three-bedroom Edwardian semi in Belle Avenue, a quiet, serious husband who read poetry and did the crossword and whose main passion was his garden; and the day-to-day domestic grind of laundry and cooking and war and childbirth and the

Depression, rations, the small social circle she moved in: ladies whose main entertainment seemed to be scoring points off each other about flower arrangements at the church, who manned the cake stall at the Sale of Work and how many times a hat had been re-dressed.

But what Rose hadn't realised until now was that, despite all Mother's everyday disappointments, Father had been the ballast in her life and that without him, she was lost. The next few years were, Rose realised as she carried the tea back into the lounge, going to be very hard.

Mr Georgiadis gave Rose two weeks off work while they arranged the funeral and sorted through Father's things. Rose met with the solicitor. The will was simple. It left everything to Ivy or, in the event of Ivy predeceasing Gilbert, to Rose. There was no hidden love child, no evidence of any secret other life, but there was a good pension and some savings. With Rose's salary to help out, her mother would be comfortably off. Even so and, for a quiet man, Father left a huge hole in the house and, used to having him to orbit around, the two women found it hard to settle with him not there.

The funeral itself was packed. Rose never knew her father had been so popular. Mr Georgiadis sent a wholly inappropriate wreath and Henry did not come because Rose asked him not to. He telephoned and wrote regularly during those first few weeks, but somehow they both knew that whatever chance they'd had had gone and that it was more than her father they were mourning.

Three days after the funeral Rose went back to Verity's to gather up her things. She had to move back home, there was no other choice. She'd also have to find another job as the commute to London and back would not be fair on either her or Mother. This was what unmarried daughters did in those days, what Mother's friends expected of her; Rose did not have a choice. Deep down she told herself she was doing it for Father, that this was what he would have wanted, and so this was how she tried to reconcile herself to not being in London, not being near Henry.

Henry had offered to drive her and the boxes back to Belle Avenue but Rose said, 'No, I couldn't bear it if you did.'

'At least let me come and help you pack.'

'Really, I'd rather you didn't. It's going to be hard enough as it is.'

And, at the house off the Talgarth Road, with the hall full of her boxes, the dresses Henry had bought her in a packing case and the van she'd hired outside, its engine rattling and its driver smoking a Woodbine, Rose sat in Verity's kitchen and wept.

'Oh my dear girl,' Verity said. 'What can I do to help you?'

She sat down next to Rose and put her arms around

her. Rose rested her head on the older woman's shoulder.

As she'd packed the dresses in tissue paper, folding the fabric carefully, trying desperately hard not to linger over each one and remember when she'd worn it, what Henry had said to her when she did, how he'd held her on the few occasions they'd danced, how it had felt to have him make love to her that night in Athens, Rose decided to tell Verity about him. She feared that were she not to do so and go home to Mother without ever committing her secret to someone, she would burst, or go mad, or both.

'What can you do? To help?' she asked Verity. 'Well, firstly you can make Henry unmarried. Let me marry him instead. We'd have Mother to live with us. I might even have children of my own one day.' Rose tried to smile when she said this, but it was a weak, unconvincing smile. The tears were still streaming down her face.

'Has it really come to this?' Verity asked softly into Rose's hair.

Rose nodded.

'Have you . . . you know? Is it too late to go back, be just friends with him?'

'Yes,' Rose said. 'We have. It's too late, much too late to go back to how it was before.'

'When?'

'Athens.'

'And after Athens?'

'No, we didn't have the opportunity. We were going away that night. The night Father died. Penelope was out of town. Henry'd booked us into a hotel near Henley-on-Thames. I'd left you a note when I came to get my things that lunchtime.'

'I remember.'

'What am I going to do?' The words came out slowly, chokingly.

'My best advice, my love, is to move on. Make a life around your mother, the job you'll get in Reading. There are other men, believe me. There's always other men.' She took Rose's face in her hands and gazed long into her eyes. Rose wondered then what heartbreak this woman was hiding. Did all women carry their secret hearts around with them? What is stopping us all from standing on the corner of the street and shouting, 'But I love him! I love *him*, I love only HIM!'?

'I know,' Rose said. 'I know that's what I should do, but inside here,' she tapped savagely on her breastbone, 'it hurts. It started off so simply, just a brush of his hand on mine, but it's been like being in a whirlpool, getting sucked ever more deeper in, becoming so needed and needful until he's become the centre of everything and I have absolutely no idea how I'm going to live without him.'

But she did. She left Verity's house that day and the

man in the van drove her to the house in Belle Avenue. She got a job at the Prudential. The company had moved their Industrial Branch administration from London to Forbury House during that year and sometimes she'd walk to work, through Palmer Park, and sometimes she'd catch the bus and she'd be home by five thirty to help Mother cook the tea and they'd settle in to watch the television; *Coronation Street*, *Z-Cars*, *Peyton Place* and, at weekends they'd take trips into the country, walk along the river in Henley, comment on the boats and have afternoon tea and cake and Rose would try very hard not to mind, not to miss Henry, not to search the windows of the town's hotels for his face.

He wrote, of course, and continued to telephone, but the letters became fewer over time as did the calls. There seemed to be less and less to say because Rose had no idea how to answer him.

In the summer of 1966 he told her he loved her. She still has the letter in the box she keeps on the top shelf of the wardrobe. She did not send a reply. There didn't seem any point.

She packed it away: all the colour and light of her time working for Mr Georgiadis, of living in the bedsit in Verity's house, of loving Henry, and she concentrated on her work at the Pru, on Mother and on tending Father's garden but, at night when she lay alone in her childhood bed, she would rage and boil and imagine herself pulling on her coat and hurrying out of the house, imagine herself catching a train to London and running down the street where he lived. The streetlamps would be glowing orange and she'd hammer on his door and brush past whoever opened it. She'd see Penelope sitting like a toad in the drawing room and would ignore her and she'd find herself standing before Henry and he'd open his arms and she'd step into them. The material of his jacket would itch her skin but she wouldn't mind. He would smell lemony and zesty and he would be warm and always hers and hers and hers.

She's never stopped loving him, not ever, even after what was to come. He'd become lodged firmly inside her, like an extra heart, and it's taken all her energy and concentration to carry on, to learn to live with this love and not to mind.

It's late when Rose clears away her tea cup and the plate the ham and piccalilli sandwich had been on. She has a bit of indigestion so boils herself some water to take to bed. There she settles down with her book. She's reading Hemingway again, *Fiesta: The Sun Also Rises*, has got to the bit at the bull-fight when Romero cuts off the bull's ear and presents it to Brett Ashley. She thinks briefly of the painting in Mr Georgiadis's boardroom and, when she sleeps, she can feel the heat, hear the roar of the crowd, and somewhere in her dreams she picks out Henry's face high up in the bank of seats opposite her and he's smiling. Henry is smiling at her.

17

Eve is curled up on the sofa furious with herself. She's furious because she's drunk too much wine and knows she'll feel awful in the morning; furious because she's angry with Andrew and knows he doesn't really deserve it; furious because she doesn't really know how she feels about her call with Myles earlier and, lastly, she's furious because Jodie hasn't been in touch for a few days and she's worried about her daughter, for her daughter and for herself without the light her daughter brings into her life.

There's one of those property shows on TV where someone takes a ruin and makes it a palace using wattle and daub and reclaimed timber, but Eve's not really watching it. Andrew's in the kitchen clearing up the last of the dinner plates, stacking them noisily in the dishwasher. They haven't spoken much to each other this evening and she hasn't told him how worried she is about the conference tomorrow.

She's due at the hotel in the morning to check the set-up. The delegates will start arriving around ten o'clock and there are meetings and presentations all day, then a drinks reception followed by dinner. What will happen after dinner, she doesn't want to contemplate. Not here, not now with her head fuzzy with wine and this pent-up anger coursing through her. Then her phone rings.

She grabs it from the coffee table in front of her, is convinced it will be Myles, is terrified that it might be. But it isn't. It's Jodie.

'Hi, Mum!' Her voice is breathless and sounds incredibly far away.

'Jodie! How are you?'

'I'm fine. Have just had the best night ever. We danced on the beach, the sand was still hot!'

It's three o'clock in the morning where she is and it's like she's on another planet. Eve's heart constricts with love and fear. She's sure her daughter will have her own heart broken and wants more than anything to be nearby, ready to pick up the pieces.

'Who were you with?' Eve asks.

'Just the guys, you know, everyone. Oh Mum, it's the best night ever! I never want it to end.'

There's laughter in the background and the sound of

the sea. Eve sits up and tucks her legs under her as Andrew walks in and looks at her questioningly.

'It's Jodie,' Eve mouths.

'Can I talk to her?'

Eve is struggling to hear what Jodie's saying; it's something about a bonfire, music, freshly caught fish.

'It all sounds magnificent. But you're all right, aren't you? I mean, you're fine, really, aren't you?'

'Yeah, of course. Chill, Mum. This is the best thing I could have done. The kids are great, it's great. As Al was saying, he has no idea how he's going to . . .'

Her voice trails away as Eve hears someone call her daughter's name in the background and it's then she knows that this guy Al is the one Jodie has been dancing on the beach with, that this is the boy who will break her daughter's heart.

'Do you want to speak to Dad?' Eve asks now, desperate to stop the images playing in her head of this boy, his arms around Jodie, their faces touching.

'Yeah, OK, just quickly. It's dead expensive to call.'

'We could ring you back.'

'No, don't worry. Just a quick word with Dad and then I should go. Got to work in the morning!'

As Andrew takes the phone, Eve panics that he'll see her texts, the ones she hasn't deleted yet, that the words she and Myles have sent each other will burn through the screen and imprint themselves on her husband's skin like a tattoo. Andrew's smiling as he talks and strolls around the lounge. Eve has paused the TV; a woman is standing on a beach, her hair swept back, and she's pointing into the distance. Eve imagines the camera panning round to show the view of this woman's house from the sea and she envies her it and the space around it and the distance it must be from here.

'OK, then, love,' Andrew is saying. 'Yes, speak soon and take care. Bye, love. Bye.'

He hands Eve the phone back, she holds it tightly in her hand. The case is hot.

'She sounds well,' he says.

'I didn't get to say goodbye.' Eve runs her fingers through her hair and stupidly feels like crying, like she's a child denied her favourite sweet.

'I don't think Jodie'll mind,' Andrew answers. He takes one step nearer to Eve and reaches out a hand but then steps back. 'Better go and finish up in the kitchen,' he says.

In bed Andrew is reading a music magazine. He's flicking through the pages and the noise of this is annoying. Eve's head is still thumping and the room's spinning a little. She's replaying the call with Jodie, trying to remember every word to discover how her daughter really is. When Jodie was small, Eve could read her like a barometer, but now it's like she's a stranger and, in trying to capture what she actually said, not what Eve thinks she did, Eve is being reminded of this more and more. All she can see is the surface of Jodie's words: she'd had a wonderful evening, she'd danced on the beach with a boy called Al, it was going to be dawn soon and she hadn't slept, when she did, would probably sleep wrapped up in this boy's arms, his body along the length of hers, and Eve should not mind about this in the least.

After all, she argues with herself as Andrew puts the magazine down and switches off the light, saying, 'Well goodnight then. Glad Jodie called, eh?' and she replies, 'Yes, it was good to hear her voice,' Eve can't claim to be known by her husband or her daughter any more either. There is a huge secret lodged in her chest and it's ticking and the ticking seems to be getting louder and louder each day.

Like today, for instance. Myles had called her at work. They'd gone through the customary polite introductions and then he'd asked, 'So, how's work?'

'It's fine. It's our conference tomorrow.'

'Oh, where are you holding it?'

She told him the name of the hotel.

'Will you be staying, overnight, I mean?'

'Yes, it makes sense to. I have an early start the following morning. There are round-table discussions after breakfast. Debs is coming over to help me corral everyone and man the reception desk!' She laughs a bit when she says this but in reality has no idea how it will go. Max has been twitchy for days. Running this event is a big deal for him and he and Eve have gone through everything with a fine-tooth comb, but still there will be incidents they can't legislate for, won't there?

Myles cleared his throat, then seemed to take a breath and said, 'Celeste should be away tomorrow night, industry thing in Manchester, she's judging an award or something, so I was wondering . . .'

Eve stared hard at the papers on her desk, willing him to continue, willing him to stop. She read the words 'Menu 4 @ £49.50 per head' and 'The second day will start at 9.30 a.m. sharp' and waited.

'. . . whether I could come to the hotel. We could have a nightcap, a chat. It would be nice to see you. It seems ages since I did, properly, I mean. Just you and me. I wouldn't stay long,' he added hurriedly. 'I'd need to get back, but Anka can hold the fort for a couple of hours . . .' Again his voice trailed away.

In Eve's head she could see them in her hotel room. She wouldn't be wearing shoes and for her this would be like heaven. To be in a room with him without her shoes on; it would be almost like they were supposed to be there, that what they were doing wasn't wrong.

Then she found herself saying, 'If you could get away, that would be lovely. Dinner should be over by ten. I could slip away and, as you say, we could have a coffee, or something.' She didn't want to think what the 'or something' might be.

'OK, then.'

He seemed to pull back with those two words, seem less keen suddenly.

'Only if you're sure,' she said.

'Yes,' he replied. 'I'm sure. I'll text you when I leave, OK?'

'OK.'

And with that it was agreed. This time tomorrow evening she could be with Myles in a hotel room and, as Andrew turns to her to kiss her briefly on the lips and says 'Goodnight, Eve,' she has to close her eyes because the sight of what might be is too awful to comprehend. Instead she thinks of the woman on the TV and her house by the sea, and imagines herself sitting at the window overlooking the bay, a bolt of fabric on her lap and the gulls wheeling outside and a boat bobbing in the water, the waves slapping on the hull, a bit like breathing. Eventually she sleeps.

'Why's there a packed case in the spare room?' Andrew asks Eve at six o'clock the following morning as he comes back into the bedroom from the bathroom. He has an early start at the house he's working on.

'It's our conference today. Remember? I told you.'

'Didn't realise you were staying overnight.' Andrew's face is expressionless and somewhat cold. For a second Eve doesn't recognise him. He pulls a clean T-shirt out of the drawer and says, 'Thought you were leaving me there for a moment!' He laughs when he says this but it's a hollow laugh and, turning back to face Eve, he smiles but the smile doesn't quite reach the corners of his mouth.

Eve closes her eyes once more. Her head's still sore from last night's wine and there's no denying it, she's got butterflies like she used to get before school productions or interviews for jobs. She tells herself it's today that's making her nervous, but she fears it might also be because of tonight. A brief image of Myles flashes inside her head. There's a hotel room, soft lighting and Myles is more shape than substance, but he's definitely there.

'Well, I'll be off, then,' Andrew's saying and he bends down to give her a kiss on the cheek.

Briefly she opens her eyes.

'Hope it goes well,' he says.

'Thank you. I'll text you. You'll be OK tonight? There's plenty of food in the fridge.'

'I'll be fine,' and by the time the last strains of his voice have faded, he's gone. She can hear his footsteps down the landing. He goes downstairs, picks his keys up and then the front door closes. He's not whistling. She lets out a sigh and realises her heart is hurting, but she doesn't know who it's hurting for; herself, her husband or Myles. All she knows is that this situation in which she finds herself is painful and it shouldn't be. It's not fair on Andrew or her or Myles. It's not meant to be like this.

At the hotel she sets out the name badges and goes through the catering arrangements with the member of staff allocated to looking after her. She checks the A/V's set up correctly, that the presentations are loaded on the main laptop and that the microphones are working. Then she checks in and takes her bag to her room. She's hanging up the clothes she's brought to change into for the dinner when she has to stop and sit down on the bed. The face she sees staring back at her from the mirror is pale and tired. Myles, it seems, is already in the room. Not like last night when it had just been a brief flash of him. Now she can sense his presence like a physical weight, can hear what he's saying and imagines that should she look out of the window, she will see his car parked in the car park.

Standing, she sweeps up her hair and pins it into a coil at her neck. 'Right,' she says out loud. 'You can do this,' and strides purposefully to the door, checks she's got the key and lets it close behind her with a thwoomp.

Downstairs, Max is waiting for her by the registration desk.

'Oh, there you are,' he says, almost sharply.

'Yes, here I am and everything's set.'

'Good, that's good,' he says. 'Don't suppose you could rustle me up a cup of coffee, could you?'

The conference is for all parts of the Woodward business empire: Marketing, Sales, Finance, Max's team in Design, Customer Service, Human Resources, etc. and the theme is creativity and innovation. The day's speakers will be concentrating on the economic outlook, the recession, new designs, new ways of working, getting rid of the silo mentality. The aim of it is to produce practical checklists, not just engage in round-table discussions for the sake of them, and the CEO, Gavin Woodward, is due to come for the session before lunch and then stay for an hour or so before being swept away again by his team of advisers. Max's nerves in the circumstances are understandable.

So the day wears on. Delegates arrive, are given coffee and then seated in the conference room. When the door sucks shut, Eve sits behind the reception desk and waits.

Gavin arrives at eleven thirty and she feels she should curtsey, but stops herself just in time.

'Here, let me take you through,' she says instead and leads him and his posse to the main room and, opening the door, ushers him in. Max is waiting inside and shakes his hand. They murmur a few words to one another and then Gavin is taken round to the podium. It's seamless, like theatre, and once again, when the door closes, Eve walks back to the desk in the foyer. This time she tidies the badges of those who, for one reason or another, could not attend and checks arrangements for lunch. After lunch she'll go and supervise the setting-up of the room where they're going to have dinner. She tries very hard not to think of Myles.

However, she does look at her phone. The only message is from Debs: 'OK if I arrive 9ish tomorrow? Something to sort in the office 1st.'

Eve replies, 'Yes, no prob. I'm not on mic duty til 9.30 so plenty of time.' She puts a smiley face at the end of the text. Debs sends a smiley face back.

The afternoon session ends at five thirty. Dinner is laid in the Marlborough Suite and the bar for the drinks beforehand is set up in an anteroom. Eve's checked the table plan and the corridors in the hotel are hot as she makes her way back to her room to get changed. She hasn't looked at her phone all afternoon but does now. There's a text from Andrew saying he's home but will probably be going out for a drink later with some of the guys from the band. There's nothing from Myles. Eve is beginning to feel uneasy. She wants to be reassured he's still coming, but then he said he'd let her know when he was setting out and it's not time for that yet, is it?

In her room she showers and gets changed. Then she checks her emails on her laptop, answers a few, highlights others to deal with later and, taking one final look at herself in the mirror, once again she braces her shoulders, tells herself she can do this.

Sipping champagne at the reception she feels disconnected, like she's in a bubble. All around her people are talking, the air is filled with the noise bees make, it's heady and constant and she can't concentrate on anything.

Eventually, it's time for dinner and she stands at the back of the room making sure everyone has a seat before sitting down herself. She stares at the starter, tries to lift her knife and fork but they seem too heavy for her.

'Not hungry?' the man sitting next to her asks.

He works in Marketing and she knows him vaguely. He's a big man with short-cropped hair, is about forty and, under the suit he's wearing, he looks powerful and, in Eve's current frame of mind, slightly dangerous.

'Not really,' she says, 'been too busy to work up an appetite.' She smiles at him.

She's wearing her hair down and a sleeveless black shift dress. Because she's so tall she hardly ever wears heels but tonight she has a pair of silver slingbacks on, which are pinching her toes and make her feel like a giant. She's glad she's sitting down.

The man leans in towards her. His breath smells of wine and the chorizo which has been sliced into the salad starter. 'I was hoping to sit next to you,' he says. There's a tiny piece of fresh spinach from the salad stuck between his two front teeth.

'Were you?' Eve is genuinely surprised. Then she recalls, she'd put herself next to Alexandra from Sales, so why is she sitting next to him?

'Yes, I actually moved the place names so I could!'

'Why would you do that?' She is torn between feeling outraged and afraid.

He reaches out a plump hand and puts it on hers. The knife she's holding slips from her fingers and clatters on to the plate.

'Oh, sorry,' he says but she can tell he doesn't mean it.

'I'd better go and check everything's OK for the charity raffle,' she says hurriedly and, excusing herself to the others around the table, picks up her bag and slips away. She's making her way over to Max's table when her phone buzzes. Veering off to the side of the room, she shelters behind a plant and picks her handset out of her bag. It's a text from Myles. 'Planning on leaving around 9, with you just before 10. Will wait in car until you let me know where to meet.'

'OK,' she replies. 'Drive carefully.'

She asks a passing waitress if she can have a glass of wine and waits while the waitress brings it over. 'Thank you,' she says and takes a long mouthful. It slides down her throat and starts to calm her. It's like running on empty, she thinks, and realises that she's never really felt like this before. Not even in the early days with Andrew; because they slipped so easily from being friends to being a couple, she'd never had this awful rawness inside, this feeling that what she wants most of all is almost within reach but that when it comes it could be dangerous, have sharp edges, that it could hurt her.

Eventually, dinner is over; the raffle called and she's managed to avoid the man from Marketing who, she notices from the other side of the room, is now leaning towards the woman on his right, his large back almost turned away from the others at the table. Eve is glad to have escaped his attentions.

'Is everything OK?' she asks Max.

'Yes, it's fine. You coming to the bar?'

'No, I think I'll turn in. Got stuff to check for the morning. Is that all right?'

'Sure.' Max's face is flushed with a mixture of alcohol and relief. The conference is going well. When Gavin left he was beaming and, having shaken Max's hand again, had said, 'Well done, Max. It's great to see everyone pulling together. You're a star for arranging all of this.' He'd let go of Max's hand then and swept his arm through the air to encompass the room, the hotel, all of it.

'Well, night then,' Eve says now and starts to walk away. Her phone seems molten in her bag. It's five to ten. Myles is probably waiting outside. She needs to call him, tell him her room number, leave an access card for the lift for him at the hotel's reception. Someone had told her once that the heart of a common shrew beats eight hundred times a minute. It feels like hers is too.

But there's no message from Myles. She stares at the blank screen in disbelief. He'd said he was setting out. He should be here by now.

Unsteadily she walks to the lift, presses her floor number, goes to the room and there she waits. She kicks off her shoes; they lie abandoned near the dressing table. When he arrives she'll be wearing them again, but then she'll take them off. This will be how she wants it to be.

And as she waits she's in turn angry, then afraid, then it's like the heart that had beaten so fast earlier has slowed to a stop and she can hear it crank and rattle. It's like it's breaking. Surely he couldn't have had an accident? Surely he couldn't have changed his mind? But where is he? At half past ten she texts him. Then again at eleven. The moments they'd promised one another are slipping away. As each one comes and he doesn't arrive, the time they have on account diminishes until, at eleven thirty, she finally understands he's not coming.

It's then that she cries; huge racking sobs, her face flushed, her hair tangled up in her fingers. She has never in her life felt this kind of pain before and strangely, through the agony of it, she knows she's partly ashamed and partly relieved. She's dreaded his arrival and yearned for it so much that now he's not here, not coming, she has no idea how to feel. When she's calmer, she curls up on the bed and wishes hard that he is next to her and it's like he's there and not there; he's everywhere and nowhere and if she were ever to think it, this would be the time to give him up, right here, right now, but she doesn't, can't. Instead she gets undressed and climbs into bed and is just about to switch off the light when her phone buzzes once more. It's Andrew, she tells herself. It should be Andrew and I should be pleased that it is.

The message is from Myles. 'I'm so sorry,' it reads, 'something came up. I couldn't get away. I'm really sorry. More sorry than you will ever know.'

He doesn't say what the something was that came up and he doesn't suggest another time for them to meet and Eve tries very hard not to be hurt by either of these two omissions. She sends Andrew a text saying she hopes he's had a nice time and that she'll see him tomorrow and allows another half an hour to pass before she summons up the strength to reply to Myles. 'I'm sorry too,' she says. 'It would have been lovely to see you.'

He replies within seconds. 'Good night. Sleep well. Speak soon xxx.'

He's never put kisses at the end of a message before.

She hugs this knowledge to herself as she tries to sleep. Towards dawn she wakes and checks her phone again. Andrew has not replied, nor are there any further messages from Myles.

And, as she lies there and the red light on the smoke alarm blinks down at her, she remembers the dream she's just had. In this dream Myles is walking beside her, the sun threading gold in his beard. His eyes are shining. He is smiling.

'You look crap,' Debs says when she arrives at the hotel the next morning.

'Thank you!' Eve replies, not a little stung by her friend's forthrightness. 'Actually, I didn't get a very good night's sleep, nor did I eat much last night!'

'It shows! Seriously, though,' Debs puts her hand on Eve's arm, 'are you OK? Is anything wrong?'

'No, just a bit stressed about all of this.' Eve points to the conference room and to the knots of people standing around drinking coffee before the restart of the conference. 'I'd better go and check the set-up again,' she says and hurries off, leaving Debs to charm a delegate who has lost his name badge.

At the mid-morning break, Eve checks her phone. Myles has texted: 'I'm still so sorry,' it says, 'I really really wanted to see you.' Eve decides to wait before replying; she doesn't yet know what she wants to say to him.

There are no messages from Andrew.

The conference ends after lunch and the delegates begin to fade away. Some are dashing for the door to get back to the office to meet deadlines or make calls; others are ambling, taking the chance to network, finishing flirting a little maybe.

Max is still beaming and, coming over to where Eve and Debs are stationed, says, 'Presume you two will take the rest of the day off? Once everything's packed away? Don't you dare come back to the office! OK?'

'Oh, OK. Thanks, Max,' Eve says, suddenly longing for the quiet of her house, a hot bath and the chance to gather her thoughts. She hopes Andrew will need to finish something off tonight and therefore work late. She's too confused to face him. She's not yet ready to face herself. All she knows as she starts to tidy the reception desk and instruct the courier about taking the display stands and brochures back to the office, is that she's overwhelmed, not by guilt or relief, but by disappointment. She'd wanted so much to spend time with Myles, just them, just her without her shoes on. It didn't have to be anything more than that, but even that she hadn't been allowed to have and still she doesn't know why he hadn't come.

'You sure you're OK?' Debs asks. As usual she's immaculate, she reminds Eve of a gazelle; totally poised, elegant, contained.

It's now that it happens. There's no one else around; Max and the team have gone to the bar for a debrief, the A/V guys are busy with their cables and screens, the courier has left, all the delegates have gone. Eve sits down heavily on one of the chairs behind the desk. She's exhausted, not just because of the conference, but because she's realised how much energy it takes to want something she can't have and pretend she doesn't mind.

'No,' she says to Debs. 'I'm not OK. Not at all.'

'What is it? Is it Jodie? Andrew? Rose? Is there something wrong with you? Don't tell me you're ill. God, not that.' For the first time ever Debs appears unsettled.

Eve's inner turmoil magnifies. Yes, these are the things that should preoccupy her, not this yearning, this inexplicable need to be with another woman's husband.

She looks at Debs.

Debs eyes widen. She says, 'It's a man, isn't it?'

'How do you know?'

'How do you think I know?'

'You too?'

'A long time ago now. But I remember. He's still here somewhere.' She taps her chest where her heart is. 'Maybe I should have fought for him at the time but it just seemed insurmountable. I was so young. He was so . . .' she pauses, takes Eve's hands in hers, 'married. That's it, isn't it? With you, I mean? Who is he? Not someone at work, surely? Not Max!'

'No, it's not Max and I can't really say who it is, but it's just so hard pretending all the time.'

The need to tell someone, anyone, what's sitting at the top of her own heart floods out of Eve at that moment. She repeats, 'It's just so hard pretending,' and then adds, 'pretending to him that what we're doing is really OK, that it doesn't break any rules when it does; pretending to Andrew that nothing has changed, when it has; pretending to Jodie that I'm still the person she always thought I was; but most of all pretending to myself that it doesn't hurt. I know it sounds corny, but it's just impossible: I can't live with him or without him. I'm stuck, and whereas I want this connection we have to be a good and perfect thing, I'm afraid it's not good and will never be perfect, not entirely. Maybe there will be moments, but if I ever step back from the perfection of the now, the times he calls, the sound of his voice, how he looks at me, the rest is chaos. And,' she continues, 'what's more is that I have no idea how it's all happened. It seems like it's been a matter of moments since I first met him and then, it seems like I've known him all my life and the rest of it, all of my marriage, has concertinaed into the tiny space that's left when I'm not thinking of him.'

Eve realises she is crying. Not small, tidy tears but large, ungainly ones. They are coursing down her face and most of all what she feels is relief. It's like a dam has burst.

'I'm so sorry,' Debs is saying. 'Oh, my love. My poor sweet love. Here,' she lets go of Eve's hands and fishes a tissue out of her handbag. 'Wipe your eyes. It will seem better in a minute. It always does. It has to.'

'He was supposed to come here last night,' Eve finds herself saying now after she's blown her nose and wiped her eyes. She hates to think what she looks like, is grateful there's no one else around. 'But, he cancelled, didn't explain why. I mean, I know family must always come first, but it's just a reminder of how hard it is to feel like this for someone; all the compromises we have to make. Do you know what I mean?'

'Yes, I do. Of course I do,' Debs replies. 'But,' she continues, 'things do have a way of working out. I mean I was able, in the end, to walk away from my . . .' she hesitates, 'my situation . . . It wasn't easy, it still isn't, but there are always other options. I got married, as you know. That was also a mistake, as you also know, but hey ho, that's life for you. Curved balls being thrown at us from all directions!'

They laugh quietly, sadly, and Debs hugs Eve and, as Eve holds her friend, beneath her expensive jacket she feels how fragile Debs's bones are, how thin she is, how much she too is holding in.

'What a pair we are!' Eve says disentangling herself, and then her phone rings. She looks at the screen. 'It's him,' she says to Debs.

'Answer it, then; I'll get on here.'

Eve looks at the name 'Myles Stephens'.

'Hello?' she says into the phone.

Andrew is late home that evening. Eve has had her bath and is sitting on the sofa with a glass of wine watching an episode of *Friends*. The house is warm and cosy around her; she is incredibly tired. Her mind is numb. She texts Debs, 'Season 6, Episodes 15–16. The One That Could Have Been'.

18

'You have got to be kidding me!'

Pletheroe is standing at the front of the incident room staring belligerently at his team.

'All this time and all we have is this?'

He sweeps an arm to indicate the photographs, the arrows drawn in red marker, copies of the victim's bank statements and itemised phone bills pinned to the display board to his right.

'This tells us nothing,' *he says.* 'Nothing!'

He is exhausted and hasn't been home for two days. He's snatched some sleep in the armchair in his office and has lived off coffee and thin sandwiches. He didn't quite trust the egg and cress one he'd had yesterday, has felt somewhat bilious since.

He's also afraid. He's afraid that tomorrow, in an hour, in two minutes' time, the door will open and in will march a young athletic detective, freshly promoted, with ideas about databases and new techniques in forensics and that he, DCI Derek Pletheroe, will be consigned to the wings with his lifetime's worth of experience and pockets full of paper scraps. There's something in Pletheroe's bones that tells him this may be his last case.

As Myles types the words 'his last case', he realises his heart is thumping. Could he really do this? Is he brave enough? And yet, just the thought of it lifts a weight from his shoulders. He stands and stretches, looks down at the time on his laptop. It's ten thirty. He'd rather hoped Eve would have got in touch this morning, but so far she hasn't and, when he thinks about it, he can hardly blame her. The call yesterday afternoon hadn't gone well.

'Hello?' she'd said into the phone.

'Hi, how are you?'

'OK. It's been a busy couple of days.'

'I guess it must have been.'

'How are you?'

'Oh OK.' But he wasn't. He didn't know what to say to her. 'I am sorry about last night.' It sounded lame even to his ears.

'Yes, it was a shame.'

'I'm even sorrier I can't tell you why I couldn't come.' There, it was out in the open: the reason he didn't go and the fact that he couldn't tell her, didn't want to because it would spoil everything even more.

'That's OK.'

Her voice sounded weary. There were noises in the background, but he couldn't make out what they were.

'Where are you?'

'Still at the hotel. Debs and I are just tidying up.'

'I'd better let you get on with it, then.'

'I guess so.'

'I am sorry, Eve, really I am.'

'I know. Look, I should go.'

'OK, bye then. Hope you have a restful evening.'

'Thank you.'

'Speak soon maybe?'

'Yes, of course.'

But when she'd said 'Yes, of course' she'd sounded sad, resigned almost. How far they'd come in so short a time, he thought. How much could depend on so little.

He saves what he's written and makes a coffee. Should he go upstairs and see Rose? Would that help? He decides not to, it probably wouldn't.

Instead he stands by the back door and looks out into the garden. Everything is so incredibly still, like a photograph. Most of the leaves have fallen now. Rose has been burning them diligently over the last few weeks and the branches of the trees are bare and pointing to the flat white sky. It seems the garden is waiting, like he is waiting – for spring, for something to change.

He hesitates. He doesn't want to think about it again, not now, but, wrapping his hands around the coffee cup, he takes a sip. The drink scalds his tongue. He has to think about it. There's a lot to consider. He reflects on the evening in question.

He'd asked Anka, 'Are you sure you'll be OK for an hour or so?'

'Of course, Myles,' she'd said. The sibilants in 'of course' and his name seemed to take an age to travel through the air to reach him. It was as though she knew.

'I just need to drive about a bit, clear my head. Sort out a plot line.' It was a lame excuse and he knew it. He had never done this before.

She'd nodded and picked up the TV remote, had started flicking through the channels.

The boys were in bed and he wondered briefly if she had a boyfriend yet, was hoping that he, Myles, would leave soon so she could call him. He rather thought she didn't, but also wondered if she'd guessed what was going on with him. After all, he felt that Eve's name was emblazoned on his forehead, that it should be obvious to anyone he met that half his heart was elsewhere these days. How could anyone not realise this when it seemed so obvious and so right to him? He thought about Eve then; Eve waiting for him at the hotel and the chance they had of spending time together there. He didn't want to think where it might lead. For now all he could think about was driving there, arriving, finding her, her resting her head on his shoulder, of being able to breathe again properly. Just recently it was like he'd been holding his breath and the effort of doing this was making his ribs ache.

Anka glanced away from the TV screen and at him. 'You have your phone with you?' she asked.

'Yes.'

'And Celeste? She will be staying away tonight?'

'Yes, I believe so.'

'Very good. I shall watch the television for an hour and then go to bed. I will leave the lights on outside and you can let the dog out and lock the doors when you come back. Yes?'

At the sound of the word 'dog', Benjy lifted his head briefly and looked at them from his place in front of the fire and then slumped it to the floor again. He closed his eyes. His tail twitched a little and then he was still. Behind the noise of the TV Myles thought he heard the dog snore.

'Yes, OK.' Myles likes Anka. He likes how definite she always is. More often than not, he wishes such certainty for himself. 'Right, I'll be off then,' he said.

'Yes, goodnight, Myles.' Again the long sss; it followed Myles out of the den and into the hall.

He picked up his keys from the table and checked his phone. No messages telling him not to go. Nothing from Celeste either. He was aware of a noise outside and that the security light was on but thought nothing of it. Maybe it was the wind.

Then the front door opened. His wife walked in. They looked at one another.

'Celeste?'

'Who were you expecting?'

'Oh, no one. I didn't know you were coming back, that's all.'

Then she must have seen the keys in Myles's hand. 'You going out?'

'No, just getting something from the car.' The lie came quickly and effortlessly like he'd already prepared it.

'But you've got your jacket on.'

'I thought it would be cold outside. What are you doing here?' There was a pause. He played back the words in his head and thought they sounded harsh, an obvious change of subject. But he was disappointed to see her, disappointed that it meant he could not now leave. If only he'd gone five minutes before . . . But still, what he'd said had sounded unkind and he wasn't an unkind man. 'It's lovely to see you. I'm just surprised, that's all.' He was aware that he was trying to smile, hoped it sat more comfortably on his face than it felt.

'We finished early so I decided to come home,' she said. She was still holding on to the handle of her overnight case as if at any minute she could change her mind and leave again.

Then Anka came out of the den.

'Ah, I thought I heard your voice,' she said.

The TV was still playing in the background. Benjy obviously was still asleep.

Anka looked questioningly at Myles and then at the keys in his hands.

'I was just getting something from the car,' he said again, feeling like he was in a scene from a movie and that Columbo was watching from the wings and would, just as Myles put his keys back thinking he'd got away with it, say, 'Ah, just one quick question if I may . . .'

The look on Anka's face was unreadable and Myles felt stung with guilt. He should not be involving her in this. It wasn't fair. He decided to take action.

'How was your journey?' he asked his wife, going across to her, putting his keys back down on the table in the process and taking the case from her. He wheeled it to the bottom of the stairs.

'Not bad,' she said, at last taking off her coat.

Myles took his jacket off too. The air around them seemed to settle slightly.

'Thought you had to get something from the car.'

'It can wait.'

Anka was still watching them.

'I shall,' she said at last, looking directly at Celeste, 'finish the programme upstairs. You will be tired and need quiet here.'

'Thank you.' His wife's voice seemed softer than usual, kinder. This unsettled Myles yet further.

'Do you fancy a drink?' he asked her as Anka slipped past them and went upstairs. The light bounced off her long fair hair. For a second he envied the apparent lack of complications in her life.

'Sounds nice. I'll unpack later,' Celeste said, slipping off her shoes.

'You hungry?'

'Not really. You?'

'No.'

In the kitchen Myles looked at the clock. He should have been halfway there by now. He should have texted Eve to say he'd set off.

Celeste came in as he was cracking ice cubes into two tumblers. The whisky poured over it in a golden blanket. The room smelled spicy with it.

'Here,' he said, holding out a glass.

'Thanks.'

She sat on one of the bar stools at the counter, her drink

in front of her. She ran her fingertip around the rim of the glass; it made a faint whistling sound.

'Myles?' she said quietly.

Myles was leaning up against a cupboard on the other side of the breakfast bar, could feel his phone in his pocket. It seemed to be burning him. He wanted to find a reason to leave the room so he could text Eve, but his wife had said his name, he had to stay.

'Yes?' He shifted his feet, took a sip of his drink. It tasted sour on his tongue.

'I have some news.'

'Good news?'

'I hope so.'

And then she told him.

'I've been offered a job in New York. A promotion, obviously. It's been on the cards for a while. My last trip there was . . .' She stopped.

'New York?' With his free hand he gripped on to the counter, felt he might fall otherwise.

'Yes.'

'You won't take it, though, will you? I mean there's the boys, your parents, the house, Benjy, and . . .' he didn't want to say it but felt he owed it to himself to do so, 'there's my writing.' Eve's name was branded inside his head and it was loud and there and he couldn't say it, he mustn't say it.

Celeste took another mouthful of whisky. She looked

tired and very small and he felt tall and vast and angry. He thought he knew what she would say next. And she did.

'I already have.'

'You've already accepted the job?'

'Yes. I had to. These offers aren't made twice, you know. If I hadn't have done, it would have been curtains for me. You really don't get it, do you?'

'Obviously not!'

'No, I'm sorry. I didn't mean for it to come out that way. Look,' she slipped off the stool then and came over to where he was standing. He could smell her perfume and somewhere deep down inside him there was a dull pain, like a tired muscle being made to work. 'Look, I'm sorry I didn't get a chance to talk to you about it, but in the end it happened so fast. There was a conference call while I was in Manchester today, we agreed terms and so I came home, came here to tell you as soon as I could.'

'But, what about the boys? You can't leave the boys, surely?'

'Oh Myles, you are a dolt.' She'd laughed, a little unkindly he thinks now as he holds his cold coffee cup and still nothing seems to have moved in Rose's garden. 'We're all going. They're paying for us to relocate. The boys will go to school there. We'll get the dog over, rent out this place. Hopefully, Anka will come as well.' She looked at him, her eyes wide. 'Do you think she will?'

Was this, then, her main worry; that their nanny might not go with them?

But, he thought, what about him? What about his flat? Pletheroe? He feels a sudden surge of affection for his beleaguered detective, doubts he could actually transfer him to the streets of New York. DCI Derek Pletheroe is a British cop in a British town; he puts brown sauce on his chips and likes mushy peas. DCI Derek Pletheroe is, it seems, on his last case after all. And then, as Celeste turned away from him and moved back to her seat to pick up her drink, he thought of Eve again, the real Eve, not the name stamped in his head. Eve would be waiting for him in a hotel room less than an hour's drive away and here he was certain in the knowledge that in a month or so he would not only be separated from her by his house, his sons and wife and dog but by a time difference of five hours and the vastness of an ocean.

'I'll take my stuff up, then?' Celeste said, her voice quivering slightly.

'OK, I'll let the dog out and follow you up.'

At the door, Celeste turned back and looked at him and, in a rare moment of uncertainty, said, 'We will be OK, won't we?'

And of course he said, 'Yes, we will.'

'We'll talk more about it in the morning, yes?'

'OK.'

Oh, how he wanted to be an honourable man and do the right thing. And, for a second as she stood there with the hallway light behind her, he remembered what sort of marriage he'd hoped he'd have and how much it hurt that it hadn't worked out the way he'd expected and then, suffusing everything right then, right there, was Eve and the way her hair caught the light, the flares in her eyes, how when she walks into a room the air seems to stop to listen.

He went into the den and started switching off the lights.

'Come on, boy,' he said to the dog. The animal staggered lazily to his feet. 'I know, the thought of peeing out there in the cold and wet isn't nice, is it?'

While he waited for Benjy, Myles checked his phone. He was amazed by how much time had passed since Celeste had got in, since he'd been in the hall with the keys to his car in his hand. There were two texts from Eve. Oh my God, he thought. Nothing about this is fair.

Benjy came back in panting and looking pleased with himself.

'Well done, boy,' Myles said and gave him some fresh water and biscuits. 'Night, then.'

The dog snuffled as he gobbled the biscuits and then settled back down in his basket by the door to the utility room. Myles checked everything was locked up and turned off the hall light. Standing by the table, the screen of his phone glowed and lit up his car keys as he sent Eve a text. 'I'm so sorry,' it read, 'something came up. I couldn't get away. I'm really sorry. More sorry than you will ever know.'

Celeste had been asleep when Eve's reply came through. The screen on his phone lit up when it did and he took it into the ensuite where, in the ambient light from the bedroom, he texted her back: 'Good night. Sleep well. Speak soon xxx.' He'd never sent her kisses before. The floor beneath his feet seemed to shudder when he pressed Send.

Now, two days later, Myles still doesn't really know how he feels about the move. They haven't told the boys yet because they want to have something more definite to tell them than, 'Oh, by the way, we're moving three thousand miles.' He's insisted they wait until they have a house and schools sorted and have made plans to take Benjy and that Anka has agreed to go too. For the moment Celeste is busy arranging things at work. 'It's like I've been given a whole new set of plates to keep spinning,' she'd said to him that morning. And he knows that, although she's pretending otherwise, she's in her element. What he's going to say to his agent and editor is another matter and then there's Rose and Eve. How on earth is he going to be able to tell Eve?

It's started to rain when he goes running a little later. The rain trickles down his face but he quite likes it. It feels like a sort of punishment. Meatloaf's 'Bat Out of Hell' is blaring from his headphones and ricocheting around his skull. He runs round the block, smiles a little to himself and when he gets back to the flat he realises that once again he's been running round in circles. Story of my life, he says to himself as he bends to take off his trainers.

He knows he won't write any more today. There are too many other things to think about, but he checks his emails before he closes down his laptop. There's one from Eve. His hands are trembling when he clicks on it to read it.

'Hi there,' it says. 'Hope you're OK. It's Rose's birthday coming up soon and I'd like to take her out for the day, to the races. She went once before, I think, and talks about it so fondly. Would you like to come too? I'm sure she'd be pleased if you did. No worries if you can't, it's just a thought. Let me know, though. Love, Eve.'

He feels blessed, like he's been given a new start with her. The abortive evening at the hotel is behind them. They are moving on.

He replies immediately. 'I'd love to come! Let's talk details soon, OK? Love, Myles.'

As he presses Send he gasps, surprised yet again by how much what he feels for Eve hurts and yet, how much he relishes the pain of it. He will have to tell her about New York soon. He really will.

The dialogue box says, 'Your message has been sent.' There is a large green tick next to it.

19

Rose can't sleep and knows full well why this is so. The clock by her bed says it's three in the morning. Outside there's the sharp bark of a fox and in her mind she can see it slinking amongst the bins, cold, low to the ground, crafty, ultimately tragic. She gets up and puts on her dressing gown and slippers.

Pulling back her bedroom curtains, she looks out at the quiet road. It's foggy and slabs of yellow light hang under the streetlamps, there's a fine mist hovering above the pavement and it seems to sparkle like millions of metal filings. The cars sit hunched by the kerb, the train tracks on the other side of the river are silent; not even goods trains are running at this hour. The town is mothballed, waiting for dawn, and when it comes it will be 1 December and this is why she can't sleep.

In the kitchen she makes herself a cup of tea and carries

it through to the lounge, where she switches on the electric fire in the hearth. Its convector whirrs into life; there's the smell of hot dust in the air. She sits and cradles her cup, tries very hard not to look at the mantelpiece but fails. She always fails at this time of year.

When she was at school Rose had read Faulkner and had been struck by his theory of the present past. There is, he'd said, no such thing as was; the past is. And whereas, over recent months whenever Rose had remembered Henry, it had been like she'd been telling herself a story, a once-upon-a-time thing with a beginning and a middle, but when it comes to the next bit, this bit, she can't bear for it to be in anything other than the present tense.

Sitting in the lamplight Rose thinks she can hear the fox again. For some reason she imagines it to be a vixen, thin, maybe limping. She can see her slanted amber eyes glinting; her breath appears as small puffs of smoke from her open mouth, her nostrils, as she runs.

There's no need to get the photograph down, not yet. What's lodged behind it is, like the contents of the wooden box in the wardrobe, imprinted on to her, like a pattern of tiny indentations on her skin.

It's 1 December 1966. On the bus, the man next to Rose is reading a newspaper; there's an article about Harold Wilson's meeting with Ian Smith on board HMS *Tiger* in the Mediterranean, and above it a headline about the independence of Barbados which had finally happened the day before. Rose glances at the words; the man rustles the paper meaningfully, stretches out his arms so one is nudging up against her as if to warn her not to pry. Perhaps he thinks the news belongs just to him, she thinks. She smiles wryly to herself, says, 'Good morning.' He doesn't reply.

She's on the eight fifteen. The conductor's been round and she's bought her ticket. He leant against the back of her seat and swayed as he punched the details into his machine. It chuntered out a ticket; she's holding it in her hand inside her glove, and its cardboard corners are pressing into her skin.

The roads are icy and boys outside Alfred Sutton School are skidding across the frozen puddles, their mouths are open with laughter but Rose can't hear the sound of it through the bus window.

Henry's letter is in her handbag. 'Dearest Rose,' it says, 'Thank you so much for agreeing to meet me. I shall be arriving on the five thirty train from Paddington on Thursday 1 December and shall see you at the station. I do hope you will allow me to buy you a cup of tea and a cake! It will be truly wonderful to see you.'

In the six months since Henry had told her he loved her, Rose had promised herself she would not answer his letters or his telephone calls. It hurt her too much to do so; there was too much distance between them. She had Mother to care for and her job; he had Penelope and his work. However, despite her resolve, not a day had passed when Rose hadn't regretted this promise, had wished it otherwise. And then, the week before, he'd written asking to see her. He'd said he had something of import to tell her. It was the word 'import' that did it. It was just so Henry and, with that one word, her resolve had disintegrated. She'd written back agreeing to meet and so, this was the day.

This is the day, she says to herself as she steps off the bus outside Forbury House and enters the building, although how she's going to survive the hours until five thirty she has no idea.

The morning drags. There are interminable letters to type, a twenty-page report to transcribe and a sheaf of papers to file. She stops at one o'clock for lunch and, wrapped in her hat, coat and gloves, sits on a bench in Forbury Gardens gazing at statue of the Maiwand Lion, his eyes cast halfway between defiance and sorrow. The sandwich she'd made that morning sticks in her throat and she finds it hard to swallow. It's almost impossible not to think of Henry, of what he might be doing at that very moment, how his day is moving inexorably towards the time he'll leave the office, cross the road, catch the Tube and arrive at Paddington. She sees him buy his ticket and show it to the inspector, then climb on the train and sit by the window. The fields will flash by covered by darkness and he'll look at other people's houses as they pass through Slough and Maidenhead and notice how they're lit up inside. Maybe he'll imagine what kind of lives are being lived in them, maybe he'll think of her and the thing of import he says he needs to tell her.

The afternoon drags. She telephones Mother at four o'clock.

'Hello, Mother,' she says. 'It's me. Rose.'

'Hello, dear. How is your day?' Mother's voice is flat and monotone. She isn't really interested in Rose's day, hasn't been for as long as Rose can remember.

'Very good, thank you, Mother. I just wanted to remind you I shall be late home. I'm meeting a friend for a cup of tea after work but hope to be home by seven. We'll have the rest of that gammon for supper, if that's all right.'

'Yes, that's fine, I suppose, if you have to. Meet your friend, that is, although why you can't invite her here I don't know. Then I could have my supper on time rather than having to wait. You know if I eat too late I get terrible indigestion and then I don't sleep.' The voice is whiny now, a little snide.

Rose takes a breath and says, 'It's the first time I've been late home for months, Mother. Be reasonable, please.'

'Well, who is this "friend", anyway?'

'Just someone I used to work with in London, an ex-colleague, you could say.'

'They're not going to make you go back are they? You know I couldn't do without you. Not now, not since Father . . .'

Father's death is always wheeled out in such circumstances, like a kind of blackmail. It keeps Rose in Reading; it's stopped her from returning to Henry over the last two years. But now, with that one word, 'import', the defences her mother has built around Rose have been breached and nothing is going to stop Rose from meeting Henry this evening; nothing, absolutely nothing.

At last five o'clock comes and Rose covers her typewriter and puts her In and Out trays in the cupboard and locks the door. Like when she worked for Mr Georgiadis, she puts the key under the plant in the plant pot on top of the filing cabinet. She slips on her coat.

'Good night,' she says to the receptionist, Gloria.

'Good night,' Gloria replies. 'Hope you have a nice evening.'

'Thank you. You too.'

The cold hits her like a hand as she leaves the office. The pavements glisten and exhaust fumes hang everywhere. The shop fronts in Friar Street and Broad Street are bright, a little gaudy, she thinks as she makes her way down Blagrave Street towards the station. She thought the walk would take longer than this, but here she is already. It's only a quarter past five.

The Paddington train is on the arrivals board. She waits. The minutes tick by.

At five twenty-five a train from Wales pulls in. She sees people get off and on it.

On the platform opposite another train arrives. It's Henry's train. Rose can feel this in her bones. She looks at the board; the letters have flipped over like the numbers do on cricket scoreboards and it says 'Arrived' next to the time. She waits. The station clock clicks from five thirty to five thirty-one.

Crowds pulse through the station. She cranes her neck to see him in the throng. She knows he will stand taller than most. She hopes she will remember what he looks like, remembers him that last time in the office with his hat on at an angle as he danced with her on the day Father died.

Henry doesn't come, but Rose still believes he will. He's not on this train, but he'll be on the next one, she tells herself. Maybe he missed the first one, was late leaving the office, got held up on the Tube. She sees him anxiously looking at his watch as he arrives at Paddington, the sag of his shoulders as he realises he's missed the five o'clock and will have to wait for the five fifteen. Then she can see him on this next train, like a replay of the first journey and when the board in Reading says 'Arrived' once more, she searches the crowds for him, confident that this time he will be here.

But still Henry doesn't come.

Rose waits for two more trains and then she leaves. She's shaken and disappointed, of course she is, but she still has faith. She knows he will contact her to explain and that the explanation will be truthful and plausible, will be something to do with Mr Georgiadis most probably, a late-running meeting or something, and that Henry will arrange to come on another day. He will tell her this thing of import then.

She stamps her feet to warm them as she waits in the queue for the bus home, knows she will lie to Mother when asked how her evening went. 'Yes, it was lovely,' she'll say. 'We had such a good catch-up; it was great to see each other again.'

Then she'll make supper for herself and Mother and she'll wait for Henry to telephone or to write and that one day soon, maybe tomorrow, maybe next week, she'll be back at the station waiting for him and that this time he'll come. Henry will come.

'Hello, Mother,' she calls as she opens the front door of the house in Belle Avenue.

She puts her keys on the table and hangs her hat and coat on the stand next to it. She's tucked her gloves into the pockets of the coat and bends down to pick up her handbag. The cold hangs on to the material of her coat.

'Hello,' she calls again.

Mother is in the doorway to the lounge. She's holding a telegram.

'This came for you,' she says, 'about an hour ago.'

It will be from Henry, Rose tells herself as she says, 'Thank you, Mother. I'll read it in the kitchen while I put the kettle on.'

It isn't from Henry.

It's from Mr Georgiadis.

It reads: 'Henry killed today in road accident ~STOP~ Will telephone later with more information ~STOP~ I am sorry for this news, G ~STOP~'

When her mother finds her, Rose is slumped on the kitchen floor, her mouth a huge O of pain, the telegram still in her hand.

'Rose?' she says, 'Rose, whatever's the matter? Talk to me. Talk to me, Rose. You're scaring me.'

Rose doesn't tell Mother; she can't. All she says is, 'I've had some bad news. About someone from work. The telegram's from Mr Georgiadis.'

'Anyone I know? Anyone important? Did the girl you met tonight know them?' Mother asks.

'No,' is all Rose can say in reply. How could she start to explain, where could she begin? This man, this Henry, had been the only one, would always ever be the only one, and Rose had wasted so much of the time they could have had together and now, now she'd never know what this thing of 'import' was; Rose would have to live the rest of her life not knowing the only thing that might have made sense of it.

Mr Georgiadis telephones at nine o'clock and tells Rose that Henry had left the office early that afternoon, had told the people in the office he had a meeting out of town, had stepped on to Welbeck Street to cross to the other side to walk to the Tube at Oxford Circus and had been hit by a taxi cab. He'd died instantly. He hadn't suffered. No one would be pressing charges. It was an accident, pure and simple, and for this we should all be grateful, Mr Georgiadis says, adding that he is sorry she had to learn this awful news by telegram. There were so many people to tell, and it had seemed the quickest way.

Rose says she quite understands, thanks him for calling, says of course she'll be at the funeral to pay her respects and that she'll wait for Mr Georgiadis to give her the details when Henry's widow has decided where and when it would be.

'I expect it will be family flowers only,' Mr Georgiadis says before hanging up.

'I imagine so,' Rose replies. 'Family flowers only.'

She makes Mother her supper and, pleading a headache,

goes to bed early. Mother tuts and fusses and complains that she'll have to do the dishes herself this evening.

Rose answers, 'Yes, Mother, if you wouldn't mind. That would be kind of you.'

That night Rose's head is filled with pictures of Henry and she can smell the lemony zest of his cologne, she can see the way he walks, walked, into a room. She wraps her arms around herself and keens quietly, letting herself remember his weight on her, his weight in her, how he'd stepped into Welbeck Street the day he took her to Simpson's, the bitter irony of how he died, how he had loved her that night in Athens when the sky had gone on for ever and the stars had been diamond bright.

The funeral takes place a week later. Rose takes a day's annual leave from work and sits next to Mr Georgiadis and the rest of the staff from the office in Welbeck Street. She holds on to the order of service as if it is a lifeline. She stands and sings when instructed, can hardly bear to look when they carry his coffin in. It is so long that there is space for eight pall-bearers; the flowers on top of it quiver as it is carried down the aisle of the church. Wherever she looks it seems she sees the back of Penelope's head, the rigid line of her shoulders, how the black feathers in her hat ripple when she moves.

The church is almost full and, like at Father's funeral,

Rose has no idea who half the mourners are. Some she recognises as contacts of Mr Georgiadis, people they've worked with throughout the years, but the rest are complete strangers and she finds herself filled with rage and a kind of jealousy that they should know Henry in ways she didn't and now can't. And yet, when the minister says, 'Let us pray,' she closes her eyes and knows that only she knew the Henry who danced, the Henry who bought her dresses, who kissed her at the races, took her to drink cocktails after work, who had held her that night in Greece, who had booked a hotel room for them the day Father died, who had told her he loved her. And it was only she who had made his face suffuse with joy. Only she.

When Mr Georgiadis speaks, his eulogy is impassioned and full of movement. He calls Henry 'limitless', and Rose believes that only she knows the full extent of the truth behind this word. To her Henry was, is and always will be limitless. He was her beginning, is her middle and will be her end. This she promises herself as they carry his coffin out and she swallows hard. Tears are coursing down her face but she will not sob, she tells herself she must not sob. Henry would not want her to do this. She doesn't go to the private burial or the wake and the journey back to Reading is made in a haze. It feels as though she will never sleep again, although it is the only thing she can think of doing or wants to do.

The days afterwards are monochrome. December limps its way towards Christmas, but Rose can't join in the festivities at work and says she has a do on at the church when the staff in the office at the Pru invite her out for a Christmas meal at Sweeney & Todd's pie shop in Castle Street. It's like her life has slowed to a crawl. Whatever had kept her going through the months after Father's death as she struggled to make Mother's life less sad has been punctured, like a balloon is punctured by a pin. She gathers together the things that remind her of him; his letters, the bus ticket, the tissue paper from the packaging around the very first dress he gave her, and she puts them in a box Father had made. It is about eighteen inches by eighteen inches, has the initials GR on its lid. It is made of pine.

She hadn't realised how much strength it had taken not to mind that she'd had to give Henry up, but even though she had done so, there'd always been, she now knew, the chance that she would have another opportunity to be with him, and this had been her solace. Now that too is gone and she is left with nothing. The days are dark and it rains and the shop fronts blaze their wares at her and mostly she feels sick; it's like there's a toad lodging in her chest and it's bilious and septic and she oozes grief. Sometimes she's angry, but mostly she's paralysed, has no idea how she will go on, what there is to hope for.

At noon on Saturday 17 December, when Mother is out

arranging flowers at the church for a christening the next day, Rose is sitting in the lounge reading a book. She's supposed to be writing Christmas cards, but finds she can't concentrate for long enough and that she doesn't really care which of Mother's so-called friends gets cards this year.

It snowed lightly in the night, the kind of snow which is crisp and sparkly, the kind that crunches underfoot. Mother has worn her overshoes and taken her stick, but still Rose is worried in case she falls and believes even now she should have insisted more vehemently that she accompany Mother on the walk there. When the doorbell rings she assumes it's someone from the church bringing Mother home, but it's not. It's Penelope.

'Good day, Miss Reynolds.' Her voice is businesslike, brisk. 'May I come in? In case you hadn't noticed, it's perishing out here.'

It is not really a question and Rose replies, 'Yes, yes, of course. Come in. Please come in. Let me take your coat.'

'Thank you. I shall also have a cup of coffee. Hot, strong, barely any milk. No sugar.'

Rose takes the coat and hangs it up.

'Certainly,' she says. 'Please go through, I'll put the kettle on.'

The white light from the snow outside is such that the lines around Penelope's eyes seem deeper than usual. This fact makes Rose feel much, much younger than she has a right to. When Penelope takes off her hat, her hair is sprinkled with grey. This too shocks Rose. It reminds her how much older than her Henry was.

'This is a nice house,' Penelope says at last when Rose has brought in the coffee and they are sitting on either side of the fireplace. Penelope is perched on the front of the seat, the bulky material of her tweed suit has formed itself into bunches around her breasts and hips. Her legs are crossed at the ankle. Her hands lie impassive in her lap.

'Thank you. It's my parents' house. Mother's out at the moment. She should be back soon.'

'I see.'

Rose is struggling to know what to say to this woman who had been Henry's wife. What is she doing here? What does she want?

'You're puzzled as to why I'm here, I suppose?'

'Well yes, I must confess I am.'

'It hasn't been easy, getting here. Not just the weather conditions but whether to come at all.'

Rose remains silent because she has no idea what she should or could say.

'It's about Henry,' Penelope says.

Now suddenly Rose knows that Penelope knows and that perhaps she always has.

'I thought it might be,' she admits.

'I imagine you're relieved your mother's not here,' Penelope continues. 'I suppose you wouldn't want her to know that you were my husband's . . .' She pauses as if searching for the word adequate to describe what Rose might have been. 'My husband's bit on the side?' she says at last.

'Was I?' Rose is angry now. How dare this woman come here, say this? Never had she considered herself his 'bit on the side'. Surely, she'd been more central than that? Surely she deserved to be treated with more respect after sacrificing her happiness the way she had?

She tries to keep calm, believes it won't help to challenge Penelope yet. She will have to pick her moment.

'Well, weren't you?' Penelope's eyes are flinty.

'I never claimed to be anything more than someone who loved him,' Rose says finally into the silence which rests like a weight between them. 'I was prepared to wait.'

'Wait for what?'

'I don't know. I don't actually know. I just knew that while he was still married . . .'

'Ha!' The word explodes out of Penelope's mouth. 'Ha! Well, he *was* married. He was *still* married when he died so you didn't win, you didn't win! Did you?'

'Win what?' Rose is puzzled, has no idea what this woman is talking about.

'Him, you little fool. Him! However hard he tried to get away; he left it too late, didn't he?'

'What do you mean, "he tried to get away"?'

Penelope takes a deep breath, picks up her coffee but her hands, Rose notices, are trembling. She's not as fearless as she appears, Rose thinks.

'I've come to tell you because I don't want you hearing it from anyone else and because legally I have to, but you have to realise that it's hard, so very hard.' Penelope's voice is softer now; she puts the cup down and leans forward. 'You see I haven't quite made sense of it myself yet.'

'What? What is it?'

Rose looks at the clock on the mantelpiece and at a photograph of her parents standing outside the house. It's a quarter to one. Mother will be back soon, wanting her lunch. Rose doesn't want her to find Penelope here.

She wishes her gone, but then Penelope says, 'Two weeks before he died Henry asked me for a divorce.'

The words drop on to the carpet at Rose's feet. 'He did what?'

'He also said he'd changed his will, that he'd named you as a beneficiary. You!' She spits out the word as if it's poisonous. 'He said he assumed I wouldn't give him a divorce but that he had to ask anyway and that he was leaving you thirty thousand pounds in his will, money he'd inherited from an aunt, his mother's brother's wife apparently, so I'm here to tell you what the fool wanted, what he did. And,' she curls her lip and almost snarls at

Rose as she says, 'if you ask me it's a good job he died when he did.'

'How can you say that? Surely, you don't mean that?'

The strength then seems to leave Penelope; she seems diminished by its going. 'No, I don't mean it. I don't know what I mean,' she says. 'All I know is that until about a month ago I had no idea and now he's gone everything's changed and he's not here for me to blame. I thought I would have time to make him change his mind.'

Rose rises and goes across to Penelope. She kneels down in front of her and takes the older woman's hands in hers.

'Oh, I'm sorry. I'm so sorry, about everything,' she says.

'I expect you are but,' Penelope looks down at her hands and at Rose's fingers intertwined with hers, 'we just have to go on, don't we? We just have to do right by him, I suppose.'

'But the money? I can't accept the money,' Rose says.

'But you must. I have plenty of my own. It's not the amount, it's the principle and the fact I didn't know and now it's too late. You can see that, can't you?'

Rose nods and, disentangling her grasp from Penelope's, stands and moves to the other side of the room. It feels easier to cope with their separate griefs when they are at a distance from one another.

'Will you stay? Have some lunch before you leave?' Rose asks. She is finding it hard to look at Penelope.

'No, no thank you. I have a driver waiting outside and no, I won't stay. I've said what I came to say. I've always been a firm believer in honesty, but it appears to have back-fired on me this time! I wish very hard I hadn't needed to come.' She attempts a laugh but it doesn't quite work. It comes out more like a cough, or a sob. 'Just tell me one thing,' she asks after a pause. 'Did you love him? I mean really love him?'

'Yes, yes I did. I do.' Rose closes her eyes and for a second she can see him; the pale blue of his eyes, the wideness of his smile, and she knows him for the good man he was, the man who tried to do right by both her and Penelope, and now she knows what the 'thing of import' was that he was on his way to tell her when he died. She would have tried to argue him out of it, of course, but in the end just knowing not only that he loved her, but also the nature and goodness of that love, would have been enough to be some kind of vindication for the long nights alone, her decision to stay in Reading, the pain of not seeing him every day, the pain of it when she had seen him every day. She would, she knows now, have felt cherished and safe in the knowledge that if she couldn't have him as a fixture in her life, he loved her enough to have asked Penelope for a divorce, to have made provision for her in his will and that maybe, maybe one day Penelope might have agreed to end their marriage, that there'd been hope.

So Rose hadn't been wrong to believe in Henry and she knows now as she tells his widow that yes, she loved him, really loved him, still loves him, that the thought of this would be the one thing that would sustain her through the years to come.

Rose watches as Penelope is driven away, promises herself she will honour Henry's wishes but that she'll never spend the money, that she'll leave it to a good cause when she dies. That way it will be handed down intact and his legacy will live on after her. She also promises herself that she will be kind to Penelope in her thoughts. After all, they both have a right to grieve the fact that Henry has gone. The one thing they share is the certainty that Henry will now never come home to either of them.

It is soon after this that Rose decides that she will put a small square stone under the hydrangea in the garden. She will not get it inscribed; it is enough to know that it is there. It will signify that Henry's love for her was a solid, impermeable thing. It takes her years to do it, but finally she does. It is there now in Father's garden, near the spot where he too died.

It's almost dawn when Rose finally stands after her long, sleepless night. She moves stiffly over to the mantelpiece and picks up the photograph of Henry that had been in the boardroom at the office and which Mr Georgiadis had sent her when he retired twenty years ago as if he too had known, and slowly she turns it over and unclips the fixings. Behind the board at the back is the telegram dated 1 December 1966. Rose stands and holds it to her cheek. The paper is yellow and fragile; Henry's voice whispers to her. It says, 'Sleep now. All is well. Sleep now. I did not die.'

20

'Are you sure you don't mind me going?'

Eve's making the bed and Andrew's paused in the doorway of their bedroom on his way downstairs. It's 27 December, the day she and Myles are taking Rose to the races.

'No, of course not,' Andrew replies. 'I've got to pop into Mum and Dad's and then the band's getting together. We've got that gig tonight at the Jolly Angler. You can come along if you like when you get back, if you're not too tired.'

Now he asks me! Eve thinks. All those evenings during the summer and autumn, especially after Jodie left, when she'd have loved to have been invited and he didn't say a thing and now she's made plans of her own and he's asked her if she'd like to join him!

'I'll have to see how I feel, if that's OK. It could be quite a long day. I'll let you know when I get home, OK?'

'You're going with that guy who lives in the downstairs flat, right?' Andrew's tone is conversational; there seem to be no hidden corners in what he's just said. Eve is sure he doesn't know, that he can't know.

'Yes, Rose thought it best we were accompanied and apparently this guy says he owes her a favour so he's agreed to drive us.'

'Don't lose too much money betting!' Andrew says in a half-joking, half-serious kind of way, looking back at her over his shoulder as he starts walking down the landing. He's whistling but it's a half-hearted whistle. Eve finishes plumping up the pillows and straightens out the duvet. It looks like no one has slept in the bed for weeks.

Christmas had been hard without Jodie but they'd talked to her via Skype and Rose had come for lunch on Christmas Day and afterwards all three of them, Rose, Andrew and Eve, had fallen asleep watching the afternoon movie. Then Eve had cleared up while Andrew walked Rose home. 'I like walking at this time of year,' she'd said as they were leaving, a glint of mischief in her eye. 'It's great looking into people's windows and seeing what's going on inside.'

'Really, Rose, you rascal,' Eve had said and she'd laughed and hugged Rose to her.

That night Eve and Andrew made love. It was slow and uncomplicated and very familiar and when Andrew had fallen asleep, Eve had cried, had tried hard to muffle the sound of it, and Andrew hadn't woken or, if he had, he didn't say anything or ask her why she'd been weeping. Lying there, the darkness pressing down on her, Eve had felt strangely alone. Here she was with her husband to her right, her skin newly brushed with the warmth and familiarity of his touch and with the memory of him inside her, and yet if she turned to her left and reached out a hand, Myles would be there and she believed that should he take her hand, his touch would be warm and familiar too.

Myles is playing Connect 4 with Garth in the playroom, or a version of the game anyway; the one which Garth always wins. Celeste is checking emails on her laptop sitting at the breakfast bar in the kitchen, the other two boys are upstairs and Anka isn't there, she's been at home in Poland over Christmas. Benjy Dog is asleep in his basket.

For a split second Myles feels a sense of communion, that everything is as it should be. Garth sits back on his heels and raises his arms in triumph. 'I've won again, Daddy. Look!'

'So you have. You're a professional at this, aren't you?' Myles says.

Then Celeste appears in the doorway.

'Look,' she says, 'do you really have to go out today?

Something's come up and I could do with a couple of hours of uninterrupted time to get it sorted.'

Myles's heart sinks. The sense of well-being, of everything being as it should, vanishes.

He walks over to where she's standing and says quietly, 'Yes, I do think I should go. I'm sorry, but I've got to break it to my landlady that we're moving and that she'll have to find another tenant. I also want to negotiate being released from the lease and taking her out for the day is the least I can do. This friend of hers told me that going to the races means a lot to Rose, I owe it to her. I really do.'

Celeste sighs. She's wearing dark blue jeans and a check shirt. She looks almost boyish standing there, only the hard set of her mouth and the bitter look in her eyes remind Myles that she's in her mid-forties, she's the mother of three sons, is the woman he's spent the last fifteen years of his life with and that he hasn't really loved her for a long time, not in the way he should.

'But taking two old biddies out for the day,' she continues, 'and over Christmas too, when you should be here with us, I just don't think it's right.'

Myles turns to his son and says, 'Why don't you set up one more game? I'll be back in a jiffy.'

He doesn't tell Celeste that Rose's friend isn't an old biddy, but that she too is in her forties and that for the past six months his dreams have mostly been about holding her in his arms and being able to say her name out loud. Instead he puts his hands on Celeste's shoulders.

He can feel her bones through the material of the shirt and says, 'Why do you think I'm doing this? I'm giving up everything I've got here to bring the boys out to New York so you can take this job. Just give me this one day to do something I think I ought to do, something I owe Rose. OK?'

Celeste shimmies her body and Myles's hands drop to his sides.

'Oh, OK,' she says offhandedly. 'Just don't be back too late. OK? I'll take them swimming or something, or to the cinema, and then perhaps I can get the chance to finish what *I* need to do this evening.'

In his heart Myles knows that the overriding feeling he should be experiencing is disappointment that his wife could be so monumentally selfish but instead all he can feel is relief, like he's been given a get-out-of-jail-free card. He goes back to where Garth is crouching on the floor next to the game and squats down next to him, saying, 'Right then, boy, let's bring it on. One last chance for me to beat you.'

Garth wins the game and Myles kisses the top of his son's head.

'Next time, eh? Maybe I'll win next time,' he says.

Ten minutes later Myles is pulling out of his driveway

and turning left into Darell Road. It's nine thirty and the morning sun is sharp. There was a hoar frost in the night. The trees look like they've been sprinkled with icing sugar. Diamonds of light reflect themselves out at him as he drives down St Peter's Hill.

Rose is waiting for Eve and Myles to arrive. She's in her coat and stout walking shoes. She's holding her gloves in her hand and is picking at the stitching around the hem of the right-hand one. Today is going to be wonderful, she tells herself; hard but wonderful. Already she can feel Henry's presence next to her and the years are rolling back and she's standing next to him and he's lifting her in his arms at the moment St Paddy won the Derby at Epsom in 1960.

Eve is squashed into the back of the Mercedes for the journey but she doesn't mind. She loves the throaty sound of its engine and watches the muscles in Myles's arms flex as he drives. They pull off the M3 and make for Kempton Park. The course is heaving with Winter Festival punters and the cold clear air is alive with the babble of the crowd and the round scent of horse. A man is gabbling over the tannoy and the race track and the horses' coats are gleaming in the winter sun.

They bet on a few races. Rose has two winners, Eve and Myles have one each. They eat fish and chips in the Best of British restaurant, Myles has a pint of bitter, the ladies each have a half of lager.

Rose looks for Henry in the crowd, thinks she sees him but then the man turns round. It's not him. Of course, it's not him.

And all day Eve and Myles speak in short sentences about practical things. They try very hard not to touch one another. They concentrate on making sure Rose is comfortable, that she doesn't get too tired.

The weather stays cold and bright. Rose dozes in the car on the way home. The sun is low in the sky when they reach Reading.

So, when it happens it is, of course, inevitable, as it had been since that moment their hands touched the summer before.

'Well,' Rose says when the three of them get back from the races, 'I think I'll go upstairs. It's been a long day.'

'Are you sure?' Eve asks, bending down to kiss Rose's cheek. 'Won't you have a hot drink, warm yourself up a bit?'

Eve straightens and looks across at Myles. He's standing by his desk. The late afternoon sun is falling in layers through the louvred shutters, making a pattern on the floor.

'No thank you, dear. It's been lovely, so lovely, such a

wonderful reminder of long ago, but I think I'll go up, settle in for the evening, rest these weary bones.' Rose laughs a little as she says this and turns to go.

The door closes softly behind her and Eve and Myles can hear her slow footsteps as she climbs up to her flat. The quiet she leaves behind her is astonishing.

'Would you like a coffee, or . . .' there is a pause, 'tea perhaps?' Myles asks, his voice travelling across the room in gulps, 'if you can stay a while, that is. Or, do you need to get back?'

Eve looks at her watch. She can stay. Andrew won't be back until much later so she nods; it's a tiny nod, barely perceptible, but Myles must have seen it because he begins to move towards the kitchen. As he passes by her she can smell horses. Even though they'd only visited the paddock a few times, the sweet scent of the animals seems to cling to his clothes and when he's gone she sees the strength of them, the sun glinting on their coats, and it reminds her of summer, the summer before and the light threaded through Myles's hair, the light lodged in his eyes, and she's aware she's not breathing. She gasps.

'You OK?' he asks, switching on the kettle.

She hadn't realised he'd heard her.

'Yes, fine.'

As she waits she touches a few things on his desk; she doesn't move anything, just lets her fingers brush the lid of his laptop, the back of the chair he sits in when he writes. The sun is lower now, the central heating has come on; she cannot hear Rose move around upstairs, and outside, the sound of the traffic in Belle Avenue is sketchy and muffled.

Then she senses him behind her. He leans in and puts the mugs on the desk next to the laptop and a blue folder with the number nine written on it in emphatic black ink. His movements knock a pen which rolls very slightly and she reaches out to stop it, then turns to face him, the edge of the desk pressing into the back of her thighs, and his arms are around her and it feels like this is what perfect is.

His lips, when they kiss her, are warm and dry and the kiss travels through her sternum and into her belly; the space between her legs starts to howl.

'You OK?' he asks again.

She nods. She cannot speak.

This is the inevitable moment, not what will follow, or the fact they're here in his flat on this December afternoon and Rose is upstairs and that she knows. This is the culmination of the emails, texts, calls, the snatched lunches they've had together in anonymous bars and tucked-away pubs, that November evening in the hotel, all the times they'd told themselves they were nothing more than good friends but when her skin had hummed at the nearness of him.

It's getting dark in the room now as he cups her face in

his hands. She loves the shape of him, everything about him; hadn't thought she would ever feel anything like this again. But it's here, it's like instinct and, in this particular place at this particular time, it is totally and irretrievably right.

And there's no guilt. Not yet.

The mugs stay on the desk, the streetlamp flickers on and the light in the room becomes like old gold. He leads her to the bed and afterwards she will remember his mouth on her breasts, the smooth length of him inside her, the rise and fall of him and the rhythm and release of him, the warmth of his skin on hers. She will remember the fist unfurling inside her when she comes and that she heard the sound of the sea.

This is perfect, she thinks later as she watches his face on the pillow next to hers. His eyes are closed and his breathing is steady. For now she really believes they will be good at this; that this will be something good.

The light has gone completely when Myles wakes. For a moment he has no idea where he is, then Eve moves slightly next to him.

'Hi there, you,' he says, turning to face her.

'Hi,' she answers.

'What's the time?'

'Around six thirty, I think.'

'Not too late then.'

They can hear the soft murmur of Rose's TV upstairs and outside there's the sound of a car door closing and someone laughing.

'Are you OK?' he asks.

'Yes, you?'

'Yes,' he says. 'I am very OK.'

He leans down to kiss her. She still tastes of salt and vinegar from earlier. Her skin is silky and smooth in the gold light from the streetlamp outside the window.

'I'm not going to ask,' she says. Her hair is tumbling around her face. It too is glowing.

'Good.' He chuckles and kisses her again, running his fingers over the curve of her shoulder. He tracks down until he finds her breast. He circles her nipple. She lets out a moan. 'Ask what?' he says after a brief silence, his hand is resting on her belly now. She shifts in the bed next to him, their feet touch. He can't seem to stop smiling.

'What happens next,' she says. 'You see I don't think I want to know.'

There's part of Myles, the part that's a writer, which thinks it should know the script from here on in. After all, he's written enough scenes like this in his novels. But there's another part of him, the bigger non-writer part of him, which feels he's on the cusp of something amazing and dangerous and perfect and flawed all at the same time. He doesn't want to know what will happen next either.

'I understand,' he says. 'But we're here and it can't be undone. I don't want it undone. In fact, I want it again and again and again, a thousand times again.' He lifts himself until he's lying on her once more and he's inside her again and her head is thrown back to reveal the soft skin of her neck, her eyes are open and her back is arched. They come; their orgasms are smaller and shorter this time but still wonderful and he kisses her afterwards, runs his tongue lightly over her teeth. The world is just them. At this precise moment there is no one else.

But he has to tell her what he's avoided telling her for over a month. Each time he's got close to doing so he's changed his mind and now it's too late; what they've done can't be undone and now he has to tell her.

The duvet's slipped off her, exposing both of her breasts and the points of her hips. Her pubic hair is still dark and damp. She stretches languorously. She reminds him of a wild cat: the colour of her hair, her eyes, her sinuousness. It's all come to this, he thinks: the months of calls and 'How are yous' and 'Talk soons' and 'Take cares'. The coded conversations about Celeste and Andrew and the lives they've led in the spaces between their emails and lunches and kisses hello and goodbye and the occasional touch of her hand on his or his on hers, have brought them to this and what he feels about her is raw and necessary and impossible.

'Eve,' he says.

'Oh no. Don't,' she says.

'Don't what?'

'Don't say it's a mistake.'

'I wasn't going to.'

'Oh, that's OK then. What is it, what's wrong?'

She's sitting up in bed beside him. All he can see is shapes and shadows and he can feel the warmth emanating from her. The sheets are sticky. The rooms smells of sex and something wanton, something beautiful.

'There's something I have to tell you.'

He'd never explained why he hadn't come to the hotel in November and she'd never asked, but now he knows without looking that her eyes are wide and fearful. The last thing he wants to do is to hurt her. Maybe he should have stopped it earlier, he thinks, before it came to this. But he knows he wouldn't have been able to, just as he wasn't able to stop from happening what had just happened and what this may mean to her marriage and to his.

'Yes?' she says so quietly it's almost a whisper.

'Celeste's been offered a job in New York,' he says. 'We're moving out there at the beginning of February.' He doesn't pause so there can be no space in which she can speak. He daren't hear what she is going to say. His sentences roll out in an unstoppable flow. 'I don't know how long for, a year or two, three at the most maybe. I'll have to come back now and then to see my publisher so we could see each other then perhaps? And there's email and the phone but it's not going to be easy. It hasn't been enough, the waiting in between, even when we're only a few miles apart, but we can make a go of it, can't we? We have to now, don't we? Now, I mean, after this. After . . .'

She reaches out and puts her finger on his lips to stop him from saying anything more. Then she asks, 'Why? Why didn't you tell me before?'

'I didn't know how to. I couldn't. I'm so sorry, Eve. So sorry. Lousy timing, I know, but . . .'

She's silent for a while and it's like he can hear the thoughts in her head.

Finally, she lies back down beside him and rests her head on his chest. 'I guess we're in for the long haul anyway,' she says. 'What's three years and three thousand miles between friends?'

'Don't cry,' he says. 'Please.'

'I'm not crying.'

'Yes you are.'

'Yes, I am but it's OK. I'll be OK. I heard someone say once that grief is the price you pay for love. I think it was the Queen after Diana died. If I didn't love, it wouldn't hurt.'

'You love me?' he asks her now, tipping her face up so their eyes meet.

'Why else would I be here, now, like this?' she says. 'If I didn't love you, I mean. I wouldn't be here, would I?'

Eve is in the bath when Andrew comes home.

'Good day?' he asks.

'Yes, thank you. Rose had fun, I think. Sorry I wasn't able to join you at the gig in the end.'

'The journeys went well?'

'Yes, no hold-ups.'

'That's good, then. Did you win much?'

'No, not much. How was your gig?'

'Fine, yes, it was fine.'

'And your parents?'

'They're good too.'

It's either the temperature of the water, the fact she hasn't eaten anything for a while or the fact that her heart is about to burst that makes Eve's head spin. She feels she is falling. It's like she's thrown a stone into a lake and the ripples are reaching ever outward. One day, she knows, they will find the shore. It is inevitable that they will.

'Sorry. I'm a bit later back than I thought, but did you get your work done in the end?' Myles asks Celeste as he gets into bed beside her later that night.

'Yes, thank you.'

'And the boys were OK? What did you do in the end?'

'Went to the cinema.'

'That's good.'

Myles lies down next to his wife.

'Oh, by the way, the quote for the shipping costs came through,' she says sleepily. 'I've accepted it. And the rental agreement's arrived for the house in Connecticut. Looks like we can book our flights now.'

'Oh, OK,' Myles replies, turning off the light beside the bed, relieved she didn't ask if he'd spoken to Rose about the lease, assumes in the welter of her own thoughts, she has forgotten about it, but still he doesn't sleep. Instead he thinks of Eve and of how she tasted, how she moved under him, how she moaned softly when he touched her breasts, and he has no idea how he will ever reconcile where he is right now to where he really wants to be.

After they get back from the races Rose makes herself a cup of tea and turns on the TV. They're showing a re-run of an episode of *Dad's Army*, the one where Corporal Jones marries Mrs Fox.

As she watches it, Rose tries very hard not to think of Eve and Myles, of Andrew and of Myles's wife, but the thoughts of them are insistent and she finds herself praying to whatever god might be listening that they will all find a way to be happy. After all, she knows how painful it can be not to follow your heart and she knows about the obstacles and about loyalty and duty and about the countless kinds of love. If only Eve and Myles were freer to make the right choices, she thinks. Losing Henry like she did taught her that life's too short to make the wrong ones.

When she hears Eve leave around eight thirty, she watches from the window as she gets into her car and drives away. Myles leaves a few moments later.

It's going to be another cold night, Rose says to herself as she watches them both scrape ice off their windscreens. Their exhaust fumes stay hanging in the air long after they each stop at the junction and then pull away in different directions and disappear from view.

21

The next day Rose hears Myles arrive just before ten o'clock. It's comforting to hear him moving about downstairs, the noises familiar to her now, like the background hum that had been there when she'd lived with her parents as a child and then later, when it was just her and Mother.

She hears the door to Myles's flat close and then his footsteps up the stairs. There's a knock on her door.

'Hello!' she says brightly as she opens it. 'I'm surprised to see you here today. Inspiration struck, has it?'

'No, not really.'

He looks subdued, different from yesterday when he'd seemed so confident and capable, an ideal companion at the races. She tries not to think about the silences afterwards when he and Eve were downstairs, but these silences are fact and she wonders now if this is why he seems so chastened. Perhaps today's the day everything is going to change. She has been expecting it for a long time.

'Do you want to come in? I can put the kettle on,' she says.

'Yes, that would be great. I'd love a coffee.'

Again he seems vast amongst her furniture. She's so used to it just being her here, or sometimes her and Eve and sometimes her and the ghosts of those who have gone, but not often this certainty of muscle and bone, this maleness. He sits down in an armchair.

'How are the family?' she asks as she hands him his coffee.

'They're fine, thank you. Getting a bit stir crazy from being inside over Christmas, so I'll probably take the boys for a run about in the park this afternoon. Take a football or something. It'll do us all some good, most likely.'

He's awkward, ill at ease. She wants to put a hand on his arm to steady him.

'Will your wife go with you?' She's fishing, she knows this, but senses something's wrong. Myles is studying his nails; as he bends his head she can see a few grey hairs flecked amid the brown. His whole body seems tired, she thinks.

'No, I doubt it,' he answers. 'I think she's going into work later. She's got some stuff to sort out.'

'Over the holidays?' Although Rose has mostly stopped

being surprised by what Myles tells her about the choices Celeste makes, this one does surprise her.

'Well, it's a busy time for her and actually that's what I've come here to talk to you about.' The words come out quickly, clipped, like they've been practised. He picks up his coffee she's made him, blows on the surface of it, takes a sip, puts the cup down on the table in front of him, turning the handle so it faces away from him. 'There's something I've got to tell you.'

So this is it, Rose thinks. He's going to tell me about him and Eve and it'll be out in the open and everything will find a way of working out, as things normally do, as Verity told her once that they did and that what she'd helped to make happen had been the right thing, that Myles is more right for Eve than Andrew is.

She thinks briefly of Penelope then and how, in the years after Henry's death, the two women had found a way of working things out too, how they'd come to a sort of understanding. Not that they were in regular contact, not after Henry's will and the money had been sorted, but when Rose thought of Penelope, both before and after her death, it was with a kind of affection and acceptance. And when Mr Georgiadis's son had written to tell her that Henry's widow had died, she'd thought, and still does, that, despite everything, it was better to forgive Penelope for what she did to stop Henry from being with Rose as he'd obviously wanted to be, as she too hoped to be forgiven for loving him when he was not free to be loved.

And it was the same with Mother. Long before Mother's illness and her brief stay in the hospital where Rose had met Verity again and had got to know Eve, Rose had decided to forgive Mother too for expecting her to come home after Father's death and for moulding her life into that of spinster daughter and carer. There was no point in being resentful; it would take up too much energy, energy Rose found she needed when Mother finally died. Her grief then had been unyielding and demanding; it had taken her longer than she'd expected to recover from the loss. Thank goodness for Eve, she'd thought at the time and still does, and so, sitting there waiting for Myles to tell her what he'd come to say, she silently prays a small prayer that it will be something good.

'Yes?' she says. 'What is it? Nothing's wrong, I hope?'

'Well, I have to give notice, I'm afraid. On the flat, the tenancy. You see Celeste's been offered a job in New York and we're all going over there, at the start of February actually. But obviously I'll pay you for the months left on the lease if need be.' Myles's voice trails away. The room seems to spin.

'New York?' Rose is struggling to understand and what she says next bursts out of her before she has time to think or to stop herself. 'But what about Eve?' she says.

'Eve?' Myles stands up and walks over to the window. He has his back to Rose. Then he turns to face her and his eyes are filled with such deep sadness, the kind of sadness she'd seen in Henry's eyes. 'How long have you known?' he asks.

'Since the start. Since that day in the summer when you met on the doorstep. I knew then.'

'How? How did you know?' He jingles the change in his pocket, takes out a coin, looks at it and puts it back.

'I just did.' Rose rises and walks over to where he's standing. She feels tiny and, even more than usual, he reminds her of Henry.

'How?' he asks again.

'Because something similar happened to me once,' she says and it feels so good to do so.

'Oh Rose,' he says and wraps his arms around her and they stand there for a while totally silent, totally still.

Eventually Rose moves. She realises she's crying and needs a tissue. When she's wiped her eyes, she asks him again, her voice steadier this time. 'So, what *are* you going to do about Eve?' she says.

'We're going to try and carry on, as best we can. I can't . . .' he pauses, begins pacing up and down in front of the window.

Rose is now standing in front of the fire, the tissue crumpled and hot in her hand. She watches him closely.

'I can't,' he says again, 'leave Celeste and the boys. Not now, not with the move and everything.'

'But is it what *you* want? This move?'

'To tell you the truth, Rose, I don't know what I want. Or I do, but what I want I can't have, so I have to try and stop wanting it. I need to put Eve's marriage first too. It's not the right time for us. It's just not the right time. I thought at the start it would be manageable, would be perfect, but then I started to, started to . . .'

'Started to what?'

'To love her.' He says this so quietly Rose fears she has misheard him. 'And she loves me, or so she said yesterday.'

'Oh Henry.' Again the words are out before Rose can stop them.

'I beg your pardon?'

'I mean, Myles,' Rose says. Then she adds, 'Just be careful. That's all I ask, just be careful with her happiness, with yours. Life's too short to make the wrong choices.'

'I will,' he says. 'I will be careful. After all, we both have so much to lose.'

They are quiet for a moment. The room that was spinning a moment ago settles around them once more. The outside sounds which had seemed suspended start up again.

'About the rent,' he says.

'Don't worry about that. Go, get your family settled. Come back. Just come back often to see me, to see Eve.'

'I will,' he says again. 'I promise.'

But he doesn't or, at least, he doesn't come back in time. He leaves like he said he would and, by the middle of February, all he's sent is a card with his new contact details on. He's written 'With love, Myles. Will let you know as soon as I know when I'm coming over,' on the back. Rose puts the card on the mantelpiece next to the photograph of Henry and even though she can't quite get used to the quietness in the flat below, she hasn't yet spoken to the letting agency about getting a new tenant. Some days she thinks she can still hear the sounds Myles used to make but then she stops and listens carefully and realises he's not there.

Eve's seen the card on her weekly visits since but hasn't commented on it. In fact they've never spoken about him, or of that afternoon in December when they came back from the races. To this day Rose assumes Eve thinks she doesn't know and this knowledge weighs on her heavily.

And now it's nearly the end of February and Rose looks out of her kitchen window at her garden. It's a brisk day; there is a flurry of activity in the air, a hint of spring. Yesterday it had rained sharply and in bursts and the ground is still damp, but she decides that today she will cut back the sedums, so she puts on her coat and pulls on Father's work coat over the top of it and steps into her boots. Carefully she goes down the steps, holding on to the railing. The metalwork is cold and wet. By the time she gets to the bottom her fingers are numb.

After getting the secateurs and trug from the shed, she starts trimming the stalks. The flat flower heads are brown and crisp. She can already see the new growth at soil level, tiny furls of green that look like they're made of plastic. She hopes there won't be any surprise frosts as they go into March.

The phone rings inside the flat. Slowly she climbs back up the steps and slips off her boots just inside the back door. It will be Eve, Rose is sure of this. Eve always lets the phone ring for a long time in case Rose is in the garden. Rose answers. 'Yes?' she says into the handset.

'Hi, it's Eve.'

'Hello, how are you?'

'Fine, thanks. At work. Were you gardening?'

'Yes, dead-heading the sedums.'

'Don't stay out there too long. You might catch a chill.'

'Oh, I'll be fine. Was it something in particular you wanted, my dear, or just a chat?'

'Well . . .' Eve hesitates on the other end of the line, 'I was wondering if I could pop over later? There's something I'd like to talk to you about.'

'Of course, come anytime. I'll have the kettle on and I made some flapjack yesterday. It rained, didn't it, so I couldn't garden. We could have some of that too. Does that sound nice?' Rose knows she's filling space with words because she thinks she knows what Eve wants to tell her. Jodie will be coming back in the summer and then will be gone again in September, to university this time, and Rose can sense that soon Eve will have to tell her about Myles.

Whatever Eve feels about Myles has changed her, and Rose wants to be able to help Eve find a way through whatever it is she's feeling now for this man who writes detective fiction is living with his wife and sons on the other side of the Atlantic. She wants somehow to help Eve reconcile these emotions with what she believes she owes her husband and daughter.

Maybe it was better my way, Rose thinks as she waits for Eve to answer. There weren't so many people to hurt; it was just me and Henry, and then Penelope, and now it's just me. At least there were no children. She daren't think about this, though; it still pains her to think that she and Henry might have had a family, that they could have done.

'Lovely,' Eve says. 'That sounds lovely. I'll see you later, around five, I should think. Now don't stay outside too long, will you?'

Rose looks at her watch. It's half past one. 'No,' she says.

'I'll just tidy up outside and then come in and have some lunch. I'll see you later. OK?'

'OK.'

'Drive carefully, my dear.'

'I will.'

'Bye, Eve.'

'Goodbye, Rose. See you later and thank you. Thank you for everything.'

I haven't done anything, not really, not yet, Rose thinks and she hangs up the phone and goes back into the kitchen. She steps into her gardening boots and out of the back door. She thinks of Eve and of Myles and then she thinks of Henry. She's smiling, albeit a little sadly, as she reaches out for the handrail, but this time she is not so prepared. The step underfoot is more slippery than she's expecting. This time she stumbles and falls, comes to land at an angle on the platform between the seventh and eighth step where she keeps her fuchsia pots in the summer. Her head crashes against the metalwork, one leg is tucked underneath her body, her left arm is flung out to the side, the cuff of Father's work coat half covering her hand.

It is around the fifth step down that she dies.

22

When Eve pulls up outside, she's surprised to find the house in Belle Avenue in darkness. Usually, at this time of day, the stained glass in the door would be lit by the lamp in the hallway and the small light on Rose's dressing table in her bedroom would glow behind the closed curtains. But today, there's no sign of life, not there, nor in the houses on either side. They must all still be out at work, Eve thinks, and perhaps Rose has dropped off to sleep in her armchair as she sometimes does after working in the garden.

She parks her car and tries, but fails, not to look for Myles's Mercedes. Of course she knows it won't be there, but there is a tiny part of her heart that wishes it was. 'I've rented a lock-up in Caversham Park Village,' he'd told her about a week before he left, 'for the car. I can't face selling it.'

'Nor should you,' she'd replied, somewhat astonished by the strength of her anger. She'd vacillated in the days after he'd broken the news to her between a kind of acceptance, tinged with a slither of relief that he'd be gone and she wouldn't need to be so torn by her love for him, and bitter surges of fury at the prospect of the distance and the fact that she would know so little about his life over there, even less than she did about his life here; the secret bits of it that were, of necessity, closed off to her. Moreover, she was often cross with Celeste for making this choice and for dragging the family over there with her. Surely, Eve thought on occasions, some things are more important than work?

The last time they met before he left had been hideous. Neither had known what to say, the time had flown. Just enough to drink a coffee in Starbucks in town, to say meaningless things over the noise of a child wailing in a pushchair nearby and then, like in *Brief Encounter*, he'd touched her hand and was gone. At the time she thought she'd never be able to forgive him for going.

However now, as she unlocks the front door of Rose's house, Eve hesitates and closes her eyes, trying to summon up the image of Myles standing at the window, his arm half raised and that smile on his lips, the one that had floored her so completely that first day last summer. She steps inside. The house is unusually cold. She can hear the hum of the central heating but behind it there's a deep and undeniable chill in the air. Without knowing why precisely, her heart skips a beat and she finds herself swallowing hard, so hard it hurts the back of her throat. She climbs the stairs.

'Yoo hoo,' she calls as she knocks on the door of Rose's flat. 'It's me, Eve.'

There's no answer.

She unlocks the door and, as she goes inside, the cold and dark hit her hard.

'Rose?' she calls, her voice shrill now. 'Rose, where are you?'

She remembers back to before when she'd arrived and Rose wasn't there and that she'd gone downstairs and waited in Myles's flat and Rose had come back and all had been all right again. But this time she feels something's different, not that she knows what yet. But it's the cold and the absolute silence that makes it different this time.

Hurrying through the flat, she turns on the sitting-room light. All is as it should be: Rose's newspaper is on the table next to her chair, the crossword half done and the card Myles sent from New York is still on the mantelpiece looking out at her as if to say 'Don't forget me'

The back door's open. Ah, so that's why it's cold, Eve thinks. Rose must still be in the garden. But even from here she can see the garden is in darkness. The security light isn't lit as it should be if Rose were still working on the sedums like she said she was earlier. Eve spots the flapjack tin on the counter but all she can taste in her mouth is bile.

By now she knows something must be very wrong, and it is.

In the light from the kitchen Eve can see what looks like a pile of clothes on the small platform halfway down the steps. She can see the brown material of Rose's father's work coat and a pale slice of flesh that resembles a hand.

'No!' she cries out. 'No, my God. No.'

At the sound of her voice, something next to the work coat moves. The security light snaps on. It's next door's cat. He stares up at Eve with his auburn eyes and opens his mouth but no sound comes out.

'Have you waited with her until I came?' Eve asks him, trying to keep her voice calm.

He looks at her again and then disappears down the steps and away, out of the arc of the security light's beam and into the black of the undergrowth. Eve is alone now and Rose is so completely still.

'Rose?' she whispers. 'Rose?' She crouches down beside her.

There's no answer. Eve reaches out to touch Rose's hand. It is cold like winter stone is cold and the skin is tight on it. Rose's eyes are still open. The violet of them is almost black in this light.

Eve sits down on the last step before the platform. All the strength has left her legs and her hands, she realises, are shaking. She too is cold. Of course she knows Rose is dead and she knows she mustn't move her, but wants to. She wants to gather her up and hold her in her arms and warm her but she can't because she's too cold herself and she mustn't because, because . . . She can't think why not, but instinct tells her that she mustn't.

'I must phone someone,' she says out loud and she knows that the one person she wants to speak to now is Myles. Her heart is telling her this, but what would be the point? What could he do? He's three thousand miles away, for fuck's sake. No, she tells herself. Ring Andrew. You should ring Andrew. With trembling hands she plucks her phone from her bag and tries to find his number in her address book. It's hard. She can't concentrate. She keeps thinking Rose will sit up at any moment and say, 'Oh dear. That was unfortunate. I'm all right now, though. Shall we put the kettle on, my dear?'

At last she connects to Andrew's number. It rings. It goes to voicemail. Shit, she says to herself. Shit you for not being there when I need you. She leaves a garbled message and scrolls through her contacts until she finds Myles's number. He answers on the third ring.

'Hello, you,' he says. His voice is bright and a long way away. 'How are you?'

'Myles.'

He must have guessed from that one word that something is terribly wrong because he says, 'What is it? What's the matter?'

'It's Rose. She's fallen. I found her. She's cold, on the steps, down to the garden. I don't know what to do.'

'Oh my God. Don't move her.'

'I haven't.'

'Have you rung for an ambulance?'

'No. Not yet. She's dead, Myles. Dead.' And then Eve starts to weep, her tears are hot on her face.

'Do you want me to fly over? I can get the next flight.'

'No, not yet. Don't come yet. Let me let her be pretty again. I need to make her comfortable.'

'Ring me as soon as you can. But now, you must call 999.'

'I know. I will.'

She hangs up and immediately Andrew rings. He says he's on his way. After this she dials 999 but as soon as she's said the words, she forgets what words she's said. Everything is a blur now. Myles's voice is still in her head and she can imagine Andrew's van as he drives through Reading, the scuffed nearside wheel arch, the specks of rust above the back bumper. He will be here soon, and so will the ambulance, and soon she will be able to hold Rose. Soon she will be able to close Rose's eyes for her.

Later, at the hospital, there are questions to answer, details to give. Eve hates to think that she's under suspicion, but guesses the staff are just following procedure.

She tells them, 'I left work just before five. I drove there. I found her. I'd spoken to her at one thirty. She was gardening.'

Of course it all gets sorted. There's CCTV footage of Eve leaving work. There are phone records to cross-check. There's the fact that Eve has no idea what's in Rose's will, or even if she has made one. Her only motive when it comes to Rose, she tells the WPC who's standing in front of her in sturdy shoes, her trousers a little tight over her hips, is love. After all, Rose has been like a grandmother to Eve.

And Andrew's there and he holds Eve's hand in the small room off a long corridor with its squeaky floor and smell of disinfectant and he says, 'We can find someone for you to talk to about this. You know, if you need help dealing with it. A professional. Someone who knows what they're doing.'

And she wants to scream and say, 'No. All I need is for you to hold me. For you to talk to me, for you to understand.'

They decide not to tell Jodie until the next day, until they know more about how Rose actually died and when the funeral might be, not that Eve expects Jodie to come back for it, and, as Andrew is researching undertakers on the internet, Eve emails Myles to say that the ambulance came and that Rose is now in a chapel of rest and she'll call him when she can. He replies straight away, saying that wild horses won't keep him away from the funeral, and Eve weeps quietly over the keyboard at the thought of him being here. Andrew is busy and doesn't notice and right now, Eve doesn't want to think about Andrew, or about the fact that both Myles and he will be in the same place at the same time and that they each have their own reasons to mourn the loss of this wonderful woman who has been the foundation of Eve's world for as long as she can really remember.

And that night when she thinks back to the hours they spent in the hospital and then seeing Rose laid out in the morgue, her amazing eyes shut, her skin luminous, soft now like silk, Eve is shocked to realise that amid all the trauma of arriving at the house, of finding Rose, of realising that Rose was dead, the main thing she remembers is how, with his speech about getting professional help, Andrew had seemed to fail her. Where is the man I married? she asks herself. How can I have travelled so far away from him, not like the man he has become?

And, as Andrew sleeps and she lies awake next to him, it's like the start of an ending. As yet, she doesn't quite know what sort of start or what sort of ending. All she knows is that, even more so than the day in December when she slept with Myles, her life is fundamentally altered. The person she was when she woke that morning is someone who, if she looked at her reflection in the mirror, she would definitely not now recognise.

And, as dawn breaks the following morning, under the weight of her grief there is a small fluttering thing, a bit like a butterfly, which seems to be telling her that from now on, maybe, she doesn't have to pretend any more.

She phones Max at eight thirty and he says that of course she must take the time off work, they will cope.

'I'll check emails later,' she says.

'You'll do no such thing,' he says. 'Just do what you need to do and let me know how you are. Come back in when you're ready. There must be a lot to sort out.'

When she hangs up the phone, Eve is touched by Max's kindness, terrified by the thought of having to go back to Rose's house. She is weeping again; the muscles in her face are tired with crying.

'I'll stay home this morning,' Andrew says. He's standing in the doorway to the lounge. Eve is sitting on the sofa with her laptop on the coffee table in front of her. 'I called the people I'm working for and explained.'

'Thank you.'

'I will have to go over there later, though, or else I'll get behind.'

'That's OK.' She scans her inbox. There is an email from Myles sent during the night. He will be sleeping now, she thinks. 'When shall we call Jodie?' she asks.

As with Myles in New York, Eve finds it difficult to reconcile herself to the time differences which frame her life. Myles is always and relentlessly five hours behind her and Jodie is five hours ahead. She is always adrift somewhere in the middle of these two points.

'I've already texted her and arranged a Skype call in about ten minutes.'

'You've done what?' Eve is outraged. How could he do this without having agreed it with her first? Just one more example of it being him and Jodie and not him, her and Jodie.

'I was trying to help.' Andrew's tone is unnecessarily belligerent and he goes and clatters about in the kitchen for a bit, ostensibly putting the kettle on. Eve is too exhausted to care very much, but a residual layer of anger remains. She will, she decides, save Myles's email for later. Meanwhile, she starts researching how to register Rose's death. It has been a long time since she had to register Verity's and the process might have changed.

The minutes tick by.

'Hi, love,' she hears Andrew's voice from the kitchen. Wearily she closes her laptop down and stands. It seems that every bone aches as if she's run a marathon.

Andrew's sitting at the kitchen table. Jodie's face is on the screen, her movements are jerky and distorted because the signal isn't good. She looks tired.

Rain is pattering unconvincingly against the window and for a second Eve shudders, thinking that Rose is still on the steps down to her garden, that she's been there all night and that she'll be colder now and her clothes will be getting damp.

'Hey, Dad,' Jodie smiles. 'What's news?'

'How are you?' Andrew asks.

'Fine, just finished work for the day, going to find something to eat later, then prep for tomorrow's class.'

'That's good. Oh, look, Mum's here.' Andrew turns his head briefly to look at Eve.

He still seems put out, like he's sulking. Eve tells herself it's because he's grieving too.

'Hello,' Eve says bending down to look at the screen, but she can't. She can't do this. It's too hard. Telling Myles, telling Max was different, it was necessary. She can't tell her daughter that Rose is dead. Rose has been Jodie's touchstone, has been there through everything: all birthdays, her first days at school, her first broken heart, exams and the 'I'm so fat' complaints when she'd been fourteen. She touches Andrew on the shoulder. 'You tell her,' she says. 'I can't.'

She waits by the sink looking out at the rain while Andrew explains to Jodie what's happened.

'You mustn't come back. Rose wouldn't want you to. It's too far and you'll be back soon enough anyway,' he says.

'But I want to come to the funeral.' Jodie's voice is low and soft and she speaks slowly. Eve imagines her wiping her eyes with the back of her hand.

'It's too far to come,' Andrew is saying. 'It will be too sad for you.'

'I don't want to be protected from it. I want to pay my respects.'

'No, please don't come. Mum wouldn't want you to.'

The anger bubbles up again in Eve's chest. How dare he assume he knows what she does or doesn't want? How dare he not know that what she wants most of all is for Myles to walk through the door and how ashamed she is that she should be thinking this?

Andrew and Jodie talk for a few more minutes but Eve's head is full of a kind of white noise, like a tap running at full pressure. Nothing seems to be making sense and she knows she's letting her daughter down, but she's empty; her body's here, her hands are resting on the draining board, but the inside of her is somewhere else. It's holding a pen and signing something to say Rose is dead, it's bending down to empty Rose's fridge of perishable items, like milk and cheese, and it's in Myles's arms with his breath on her neck, the rough of his stubble against her skin and the zesty scent of him and he's here and not three thousand miles away and he, the inside parts of her know, is the only one who will understand.

When Andrew's said goodbye to Jodie and she's disappeared from the screen, he turns to Eve and asks, 'Do you want me to come with you to the house later? We could go this evening, when I get back from work.'

Eve is silent, can't decide. Her mind is full of Jodie, of her daughter's pain, not her own. Shit, she says to herself. I am not doing this well, but says, 'No, it's OK. I'll go on my own. I think I need to be alone there. I need to do the official stuff . . .' She stops mid-sentence. 'Do you think,' she says, 'there'll need to be a post mortem? Did they tell us that last night?'

'Yes, they did.' Andrew is unplugging his laptop, is curling up the cable.

'This is like a nightmare,' she says.

'Yes, it is.' Andrew is walking out of the kitchen now, carrying his laptop – his back is broad and unflinching. Eve is confused, is uncertain suddenly who this man in her house is and what happened to the boy she married.

At the house in Belle Avenue, Eve is yet more confused. She keeps expecting Rose to say something from another room, for there to be the bustle of her movements around the flat. But it's quiet, everything is so utterly quiet.

After Andrew left for work, Eve read Myles's email.

It said, 'How are you? I hope you're getting some sleep.

Do let me know how you are in the morning and what, if anything, I can do from here. It feels awful being so far away. I see things when I close my eyes. I see you and want to be there. I want to be there more than anything right now. As soon as you know the date and time of the funeral, let me know and I'll book my flight. All love for now, Myles.'

It's odd, Eve thought, how far we've travelled from the first messages, the ones about books and the weather. Now it's him and me and we are an us and we shouldn't be, not even now, not when we're connected by this awful thing, this loss. We shouldn't be because there are so many other people to consider. This is what Eve was going to tell Rose when she planned to see her yesterday. She was finally going to tell her about Myles and ask for Rose's help in deciding what she should do. Was it only yesterday? Eve says to herself as she opens Rose's wardrobe, runs her hands over the fabric of the dresses hanging there.

Before she left home, she replied to Myles's email and said of course she'll tell him about the funeral as soon as she knows. How he will explain the need to be there to his wife, though, is hard to imagine. After all, Rose was only his landlady, had only been so for a short while. How would he justify flying halfway across the world for her funeral?

Now, however, she does what she can at the flat. She

empties the fridge, tidies, takes stock of the bigger tasks that will need doing, like sorting out Rose's paperwork, her finances, her belongings, but mostly she sits in Rose's armchair by the fire and it gets dark outside and the central heating hums in the background and she thinks about the difference between yesterday and today and how losing Rose has made her realise what she'd been too afraid to admit to before. She doesn't love Andrew, not now, maybe never has. Not in the way she should, not the breath-catching, needful way she feels about Myles. Has she ever? she asks herself. Even in the early days? She doesn't know, all she does know is that whoever she was before, she has changed. Does it, she wonders, take more courage to leave or to stay?

Around six o'clock, she manages to get up from the chair and turn on a lamp. She takes down the photograph of the man with the pale eyes from its place on the mantelpiece and she scrutinises his face.

'Who are you?' she asks him, her voice inordinately loud in the silence of the flat. She turns the photograph over; the corner of a piece of paper is sticking out next to one of the clasps that hold the back of the frame in place. Carefully, she prises the clasps away so the backing slips out. The piece of paper is yellow and crisp with age. She lifts it out, puts the picture down on to the seat of the chair and there in the small pool of light and the silence, she reads a telegram dated 1 December 1966. It says, 'Henry killed today in road accident ~STOP~ Will telephone later with more information ~STOP~ I am sorry for this news, G ~STOP~'

23

'So,' the solicitor says, 'I think that's everything. Do you have any questions?'

Across the table Eve is looking at her hands. They are resting on its pale smooth surface and next to them is a cup of coffee. She has not drunk any of it. The room is decorated in pastels, there's an abstract print on the wall and a plant in a pot on the floor in the corner. The chairs are the colour of charcoal. Outside the window the late-February sun brushes the glass and reveals the smears where someone sometime has tried, unsuccessfully, to clean it.

Eve is wearing black trousers, tan low-heeled boots and a light grey woollen tunic and has wound her hair into a knot at the base of her neck, although a few tendrils have escaped and are curling around her ears. It is Tuesday, two weeks after Rose's death.

'I don't think so,' Eve replies. She looks up at the man.

He's not what she'd expected when she'd got the letter. Instead of a serious middle-aged man in a dark suit, a crisp white shirt with his hair greying slightly at the temples and the bedside manner of a kindly doctor, this man is young, a little brash. His suit doesn't quite fit him properly and he's tried to tame his unruly hair with gel but has only succeeded in making it look greasy and uncared-for. Despite this, he has a nice smile and his voice is oddly comforting, with a trace of a Welsh accent. Eve wonders where he was born.

'As I said, we sent a similar letter to Mr Stephens,' he says, 'and Mr Stephens has rung in and said he will meet with us when he comes over for the funeral. It's on Friday, I believe?'

Eve nods.

'Again, I am so sorry for your loss,' the young man says.

'Thank you,' Eve says.

'And,' he continues, 'if you'd like any investment advice, please ask. We have a specialist department here in the office.'

'Actually,' Eve says, 'I do have a question.'

'Yes?' He looks somewhat nervous, had thought maybe that the meeting was drawing to a close and he could move on to the next item on his long list of things to do today.

'When did she . . . ? I mean, when was this new will drawn up?'

He flicks through the paperwork. 'August last year,' he says.

'What date?'

He tells her. So, she thinks, that was the day she visited and Rose wasn't there and she went downstairs to Myles's flat and he made her a coffee and they waited and Rose had come and all had been OK. Had Rose known then what was going to happen between her and Myles and, if so, how had she known? And now there was this.

'Ah, I see,' Eve says, twisting her wedding ring around her finger, lifting it up towards the joint and scrutinising the slight indentation the gold has made in her skin.

'So,' the solicitor says again. He's growing impatient with me, Eve thinks. 'We'll process the necessary paperwork and when probate's sorted, we'll get the monies to you both.'

Eve nods again. It's like when she'd gone back to Rose's flat the day after she died and had realised that what had been before was now changed; today has changed things yet again.

In Rose's will, this sheaf of papers on the table in front of her and which the young man in the solicitor's office had just gone through with her, Eve is named as benefactor. Maybe a copy of it is in the flat somewhere amongst the pile of papers she hasn't yet had the courage to look through, but she is to inherit the house in Belle Avenue and all of Rose's belongings and most of her money. There is an amount, the solicitor has told her, however, which is ring-fenced, and which is to be divided equally between Eve and a Mr Myles Stephens. This amount, he says, is a sum of £30,000 which Rose herself had inherited in 1966 and which, after careful investment, has now reached what this young man in front of her calls 'a substantial legacy'. He shows absolutely no curiosity as to who Mr Myles Stephens might be or why Rose has left him some of her estate and Eve tries very hard not to mind this when inside her head a voice is shouting 'Help me! Please help me!'

On the pavement outside the offices, Eve hesitates, has, it seems, forgotten how to walk, what she has to do to cross a road. Her bag is a dead weight on her shoulder and she knows that deep within its folds is a phone and that she should take out this phone and call someone. She should phone her husband and tell him about Rose's will and she should call Myles but is fearful of doing so, doesn't know how she will cope with hearing his voice. Once again she seems stuck between where she wants to be and where she should be, between who she wants to be and who she is, and she has no idea what will happen next.

It's getting late and there's no point going back to work and if she did, she wouldn't be able to concentrate, so Eve goes home and busies herself with tasks around the house.

She believes that putting on some washing, hoovering the hall carpet and putting out the rubbish will help her make sense of what's happening.

And when Andrew gets in from work, she has to say it at once before she loses her nerve so, as soon as he's through the door, she says, 'I went to see the solicitor today. You know I got that letter. I told you about it?'

'Oh yes?'

He's put his keys on the table in the hall as usual and his shoes in the cupboard. His movements are familiar and yet he's like a stranger to her. Rose's death, the will and Myles have established themselves between them like a filter and Eve doesn't know how to behave in this new order, is at sea and adrift.

'Rose has left me the house and her money,' she says.

It's like she's speaking into a void; there had been a thing which had been her marriage and now this thing has gone.

'Really? That's staggering. Did you have no idea? Had she not told you?'

'No.' The energy seems to seep from Eve and it's as though she can't be bothered to explain anything further to Andrew.

'How much? What does it mean? She'd really never told you?'

He's hungry for information and Eve has to concede

that it does seem odd that during all the years Eve and Rose have been friends, they'd never mentioned what would happen when and if Rose died, Eve never asked about the man in the photograph and Rose never said things like, 'Well, when I was young, it was like this, you see. Let me tell you the story of my past.' Instead theirs had been a relationship of equals and of now. Their concerns had been of the everyday and the immediate. Rose had come into Eve's life whole, unselfish and uncomplicated and Eve had basked in her love and companionship and now – well, now Rose has given Eve yet another gift, one she and her husband had never thought to discuss before now, and one Eve hasn't a clue how to deal with.

'I don't know the exact figures,' she says, a little impatiently. She needs time to herself to think, doesn't want to have to tell Andrew about the other money that Rose had divided between her and Myles. Instead, she wants to email Myles and find out what he's been told. She wasn't brave enough to call him earlier, but now the need to know is gnawing at her. However, she says instead, 'I guess it'll all get sorted. I just want to concentrate on Friday, really; that's what's important, surely.'

Andrew takes a step towards her and she looks at him, is shocked to realise how impatient she is with him, how cruel she's being to him. But she can't help it. It's as though the evenings she's watched *Friends*, the gap between his life and hers, his seemingly exclusive relationship with their daughter, the months and years of her driving to work and driving home again have emptied her and she's been filled with something else, something new, and what's arrived is bright and permanent, is what she feels for Myles, the grief of losing Rose and the possibilities of what Rose's legacy may bring. These are not nebulous things, they are concrete, and, beneath Eve's expectations of what she should do, who she should be, is this other world, peopled by Myles and a life other than the one she's been living up to now.

This is, she realises, the new order. What was before has ended, what will be is to come. Rose's funeral will be the pivot. After the funeral she will have to decide.

'Yes,' Andrew says, as he starts to climb the stairs. 'Let's get Friday over with and then we can concentrate on what comes next.' He glances back over his shoulder halfway up and then takes the rest of the steps two at a time. He is whistling and Eve has to close her eyes and steady her breathing to shield herself from this. How dare he whistle now? she thinks. How *dare* he?

At work on Thursday morning, Debs is predictably forthright.

'You look crap,' she says to Eve as they walk from the lifts to their desks.

'Thanks!' Eve tries to smile but it doesn't quite work.

'I guess it's about tomorrow, right?'

'Yes.'

'When does Myles arrive?'

'Around ten thirty. He flew overnight.'

'And where's he going to stay?'

'At Rose's. It seemed the right thing to do. I left a key in the hanging basket this morning on my way in.'

'Have you spoken to him recently?'

'No, we haven't been able to but we've emailed, you know, about the will and arrangements for tomorrow.'

'What's it going to be like having both of them there?' Debs asks as she slips out of her coat and hangs it on the stand by her desk.

'I have no idea,' Eve replies. She picks a tissue from her pocket and crushes it in her hand. 'But at least you'll be there, right? You'll be there to help?'

Debs bends down to switch on her computer. Since the conference, Myles had been something acknowledged but unspoken between them. Eve had told Debs the basic facts but none of the details; after all, neither of them could do anything to change the situation, could they?

'Of course I'll be there,' Debs says and she reaches out to touch Eve's arm. 'Of course.'

At her desk Eve waits for ten thirty to arrive. She answers emails, takes calls, talks to Max and is aware that outside it's raining again, steely rods of rain, and finds it odd, not for the first time, that she can't hear it through the thickness of the glass.

Myles's appointment at the solicitor's office is tomorrow morning. The funeral is at noon. It's all going like clockwork. Eve knows about every piece in the jigsaw and has spoken to Jodie who is finally reconciled to not coming back for the funeral and they've both cried again and she's wanted more than anything to hold her daughter and tell her that everything will be all right. Eve is everywhere and nowhere. Rose is everywhere and nowhere and so is Myles and it's ten forty-five and Eve is checking the arrivals page on Heathrow's website and sees that the flight from New York has landed.

Now Myles has arrived, Eve allows herself to think of her mother. It's a subject she's avoided of late, having told herself that this is the one thing she's unable to fit into everything else that's happening, but now, now Myles is in the same time zone, is waiting for a taxi, will be on the M4 travelling towards her, she remembers the phone conversation with her mother.

'I won't come to the funeral,' she'd said.

'Why not? You knew Rose when she lived with Gran, right?'

'Yes, but not very well. She came, she went. Mum seemed to like her but I was doing my own thing by then. It's too far to come for someone I barely knew, and if I did it was years ago anyway.'

'But Rose has been so good to me.' Eve recognises the voice she used to use when she was a girl and wanted something she couldn't have.

'That's your business, not mine. Look, Eve, I have to go. Thanks for letting me know about Rose and I do hope it goes OK but really, I have other things, other priorities . . .'

Isn't it odd, Eve thinks, how some people can be so impervious and others so pervious? Since the call, she's struggled to understand her mother's reaction, but as she waits by the coffee point at work and a text buzzes in on her phone, she thinks she might know the reason why. Maybe her mother's always been jealous of Verity's relationship with Rose. Maybe that's it, she says to herself, as she takes her phone out of the pocket of her trousers and opens the text.

It's from Myles. 'Have landed,' it says. 'Speak later. Love.'

Eve tries very hard not to, but on her way home from work she drives past the house in Belle Avenue. A light is shining in the downstairs flat, the coloured glass in the door is glowing and, for a second, Eve struggles to remember that Rose has gone and that behind the window and door is Myles and that, like her, he is waiting for tomorrow, for the funeral.

She tries very hard not to stop her car outside the house, not to park it, get out and lock the driver's door and she resists walking up the path and letting herself into the house with her key, but she fails and does all these things and she's standing at the door to the downstairs flat and she's knocking on it.

Myles opens it.

'You,' he says. 'You came. I didn't think you would.'

24

They hadn't spoken of this but, of course, Myles had hoped she would come. She steps into his arms and he holds her. He doesn't try to kiss her but touches her hair lightly with his lips while she cries. They are huge wracking sobs and he knows without her having to tell him that she's crying both for Rose and because he's here, because she wants him to be but not for this reason, certainly not for this.

'Come, sit down.' He steers her to the sofa.

So much is the same, yet it's not. He'd left the flat furnished for the next tenant. After all, what need had he of the furniture and fittings? So on the face of it, it's just like it was before and yet the place feels different; it is filled with the hours and days they've spent apart and with the absence of Rose, the sounds she used to make upstairs.

And the house in Caversham is let to a family from Sweden and he won't visit it, he doesn't need to. Despite the fact that his family once lived there, he is surprised by how little it means to him, that he doesn't care about its windows and bricks and the trees in the garden or the lawn he used to mow.

The streetlamp is shining through the shutters as he pulls Eve to him and she nestles into him, her head on his chest.

'How are you feeling?' she asks. 'You know, from the flight. Are you terribly jet-lagged?'

'Not really, not yet. Not quite sure how I feel. Just got to get through tomorrow morning and then the funeral.'

'You still going back on Saturday?'

'Yes, I have to, I'm afraid. Bruno's got a soccer match on Sunday. I promised I'd be back for it.'

'Soccer?' He hears her chuckle quietly. Even though her eyes are still damp from crying, it's a nice sound.

'OK, football! I'm sorry!'

'You've only been gone a little while.'

'I know, but it's hard. The culture's invidious out there, it seeps into everything.'

'And into the book too?'

'No, Pletheroe's remaining resolutely British, all Marmite and PG tips. Although I'm still finding it tricky to close down this case. This killer just doesn't seem to want to be found . . .'

He's stroking the back of her hand with his. It feels so right for her to be here and yet so wrong. The bed is in the other room and he wants her and doesn't want to want her. It's not right, not tonight.

They don't speak for a while and then she says, 'I'd better go. Andrew will be expecting me.'

'OK.' He's relieved and sorry at the same time. It's been wonderful, this visit, but like it was before, with every minute that's passed, he's known she'll have to go. They've always been on borrowed time and always will be. There is nothing perfect about this situation at all. He will fly back the day after tomorrow and she will stay here and nothing will change, even though everything has.

It had been hard enough explaining to Celeste why he felt he should come in the first place; he can't risk staying any longer than absolutely necessary. In fact, he'd let her believe he was also meeting Tom, his agent, while he was over so that the timing had been nothing more than a fortunate coincidence. Even now, he feels no shame about this.

Friday is clear and bright and the cold is sharp. Myles arrives at the crematorium at eleven thirty. His meeting with the solicitor didn't take long and although he's still amazed that Rose should have left him half the original

£30,000 legacy, with each passing day he's growing more accustomed to the idea. The final amount is, he knows, way out of proportion to the length of his friendship with her, but something tells him why she's done this, it's as though she wants him to have a choice, one that has nothing to do with Celeste and her job or even with Pletheroe and the books. It's like Rose has led Myles to the outside edge of the life he's known and said, 'Here, take this gift. Use it to venture somewhere else, somewhere new.'

As he waits for the cortège to arrive, a shiny black Bentley pulls up. The driver gets out and opens the passenger door. A short, squat and dark-skinned middle-aged man emerges. Everything about him exudes wealth and ease. He walks over to Myles.

'Christos Georgiadis,' he says, extending his hand.

Myles takes it. It's warm and firm.

'Miss Reynolds worked for my father, many years ago, in London. I am here to pay my respects.'

'That's kind,' Myles says. It takes a moment for him to realise who Miss Reynolds is, then he adds, 'Rose would be pleased to know you're here, I'm sure.'

'How did you know her?' Christos's eyes are dark brown and intelligent. His teeth are exceptionally white.

'I rented the downstairs flat in her house for a while. I used it for work. I'm a writer, you see.'

Christos shows no interest in this last comment but instead says, 'And we expect many people today?'

'I don't think so,' Myles answers. 'Just a few friends. She had no family, not really.'

It is then that the hearse arrives; silent, creeping, its engine purring gently. The funeral car is behind it and he can see Eve in the back of it with the man he saw working on the house opposite his in Darell Road last summer. He is broad and strong, and he takes Eve's arm as he helps her from the car. The sun is glinting off his hair.

There are twelve of them in total. It is sad to see so few people, Myles thinks as he picks up the Order of Service sheet. For all of Rose's generosity, she was, he realises, a very private person. He tries very hard not to look at Eve but it's difficult. Her head is bowed and her husband stands stiffly by her side. He does not touch her. She looks incredibly beautiful and very vulnerable.

Rose's coffin is on the dais and the dark pink curtains are poised, ready to obscure it from sight. The congregation sing three hymns very badly; even Christos Georgiadis's voice is muffled and scratchy – Myles had expected better from him. The minister says some prayers and some nice things about Rose and it's when he talks about Rose's smile and the violet of her eyes that Myles realises whose eyes he's always been reminded of when he looked at Rose: they were Elizabeth Taylor eyes, he says to himself as the curtains close and they can hear the rollers roll the coffin away. He shouldn't be able to hear them, it is wrong of the people who run this place to allow this to happen and, in his mind's eye, he can see the flowers on top of the coffin vibrate, their petals shaking as though buffeted by the wind.

Afterwards they gather around this small wreath. It bears a card with the words, 'With love always, Eve, Andrew and Jodie' and there is murmuring amongst Rose's neighbours and the few friends from her church who have come and who exchange words he can't quite hear.

Myles sees Christos Georgiadis speak to Eve, hold her hands and then kiss her on both cheeks and then he is gone. His driver opens the door of the Bentley once more, Christos climbs in and the car slides away. So much history, so little to show for it, Myles thinks as he watches the car disappear down the driveway.

'So you're Myles.' It's not a question.

'Yes,' he says to the woman standing in front of him. She's tall and slim with straight, bobbed hair. She looks brave and fearless. 'And you are?'

'Debs,' she replies. 'Eve's friend from work.'

'Ah,' Myles says.

They shake hands.

'By the way, Eve's told me,' she says quietly. She still has hold of his hand.

'I see.'

'Don't hurt her, please.'

'I won't.'

'Promise?'

'Yes.'

She lets go and there is no time for more because suddenly Andrew is there, is saying, 'Thank you so much for coming,' to Myles as if he were a stranger who'd been passing and thought he'd pop in. 'Eve tells me you rented the downstairs flat for a while. It was odd we never met, eh?'

'Yes, I did. It is,' is all Myles can manage to say.

It's bizarre being here with Eve's husband; this man who's been a shadow and a threat in his life since last July. But here he is, with bones and blood vessels and muscles and hopes and fears and it's unsettling to know he's real, like Celeste is real. The knowledge that whatever it is that Eve and he have had together over the past few months is not a thing in isolation like he thought it was, hits Myles with a force. They have, he realises, been part of this collection of people with their myriad connections and expectations. This is what makes what he and Eve have done more wrong than he'd thought. And yet, and yet, now Eve is next to him and she's touching him on the arm and saying, 'It's sad not more people came.'

'Yes, it is. But you're here, that's what matters.'

And she's beautiful and her eyes are the colour of topaz and she is everything to him and he can't see past her or around her, she fills his vision and his mind and he knows it's as impossible not to love her as it's impossible to love her.

Andrew is clearing his throat and saying, 'We'd better go. We're expected at the hotel. Although it'll be a bit of a paltry affair with just the few of us. Even that guy in the car's gone.'

'That's Mr Georgiadis's son,' Eve says a little sharply. 'It was good of him to come at all.'

Being at the wake is hideous. Myles makes small talk with two of Rose's neighbours over sandwiches and weak tea, who say, 'I didn't realise you'd moved out. We used to like seeing your green car. Had wondered why we hadn't seen it of late. So, you're living in America? That must be exciting.'

And Myles is polite and charming and inside he's seething and just wants to be alone with Eve, but Andrew and Debs are always near her and all he can do is look across the room at her and when their eyes meet, he imagines she knows what he's feeling and that she understands.

Eventually, when everyone else has gone and it's just the four of them left, he finds Eve at reception. Andrew and Debs are finishing their drinks and Eve is paying the bill. She turns to him as the receptionist hands her back her credit card and smiles. 'Well,' she says to him, 'at least it's over.'

'Will I see you later?' he asks in a whisper. He feels he should hurry, say everything he needs to say in the next few seconds.

'I don't think I can get away. Andrew will expect me to stay at home tonight. It would seem odd if I went to the house and anyway, he might offer to come with me. I'm sorry.'

Her eyes are huge and full of pain as she says this and he's filled with the need to kiss her mouth, to touch her breasts, to feel the hard bones of her hips beneath his and this wanting hurts so much, it is as if someone is cutting his skin with a knife.

'That's OK,' he manages to say. 'I'll call you tomorrow sometime, before my flight, maybe.'

And then Andrew and Debs arrive through the doors from the function room and he leaves the hotel without touching her or holding her and he drives off in his hire car back to the house in Belle Avenue and Andrew drives Eve and Debs away and Myles has never felt so surrounded and so alone. He orders a Chinese takeaway from the New Happy Garden on the Wokingham Road and is asleep by nine o'clock. He has no idea how he's going to face going back to the States in the morning with so much left undone, left unsaid; with so much done, so much said.

Spring, a year later

25

Myles looks out of the window of the cabin on to the garden of the house in Norwalk, Connecticut. Above the trees the sky is a cerulean blue and the blossoms hang heavy on their branches. Up the sweep of lawn he can see the deck outside the back of the house, a baseball bat is leaning up against the railing and someone, Anka most probably, has taken the cushions off the steamer chair where he'd sat the night before, drank a beer and looked at the stars. He can see Anka now, moving about inside the kitchen, is comforted by the sight of her, is glad she has come with them and that she seems happy here.

He looks at his laptop screen. He's nearing the end of the copyedits for Book Nine. The whole process has taken longer than planned because of the move here last year and the time it took to settle the boys into their new schools. Myles had told himself that he would buckle down after

Christmas and finish the book, which he did, and now it's spring and the ending is in sight but it's been a slog, each word wrung from him, and he has no idea what he should do next. His head is full of words that make no sense. He really believes he will never write another novel again.

The back door opens and Benjy bounds out, skitters about the garden for a while until Anka calls him in. He lifts his head and his ears twitch and then he's gone. In his head Myles can hear the patter of the dog's claws on the woodblock floor.

The house is satisfactory. Colonial, it has five bedrooms, three bathrooms and a finished basement. They've rented it furnished but he feels no connection with anything there, not the tables, chairs, beds, pictures. Sometimes he thinks the only things keeping him here are the boys and the dog.

They have three cars: Celeste's sleek Mercedes, his Jeep and the Honda Pilot Anka drives. Garth is in first grade, Orlando in fifth and Bruno's in seventh grade in middle school. The two older boys are due to sit their CMT later in March but other than the names they call some things being different, life is much the same. Garth may call the rubbish trash, and pavements sidewalks, but Orlando is still bewitched by trains and when Bruno gets in from soccer practice, he plugs himself into his Xbox like he did in the UK and talks even less frequently to his father.

While the boys are at school, Myles spends most of his time in his cabin. He still runs daily and sometimes when Anka's out getting groceries at Stew Leonard's, he wanks in his and Celeste's ensuite and thinks of Eve.

Yes, life is satisfactory and yet it's not.

The main thing that's remained the same, though, is Celeste and her job. She commutes to Lower Manhattan, taking the I-95 south, tracking Long Island Sound and parks her car in an underground car park and Myles has no idea what she does all day. About once a month she flies to the UK and when she's gone he wonders why they moved here at all. He wishes very hard that they hadn't.

Before the move, he'd hoped that things would change once they got here; but what he's coming to realise is that wherever he and Celeste are, his marriage is a sham. He'd believed it was OK to be one of the ninety-five per cent of people who can live knowing their life is a compromise, but since being here, since having had the distance between himself and Eve, he knows that he wants to be one of the other five per cent and he wants this fiercely.

But there's been no need for him to go back to the UK before now and, although he thinks he knows what he wants, he doesn't know how to go about getting it. All his dealings with Tom and his publisher have been done by email and phone and anyway, progress on the book's been so slow, he's not yet had promotional stuff to do. The adaptation of the series is, it seems, on the back burner because the actor the film company wanted has been snatched up by the BBC for a show about a wind farmer with terminal cancer; a show badged as a conflict between ecological goodness and pharmaceutical compromise. So, Myles stays here in Norwalk and he runs, speaks to his neighbours, goes to parents' meetings at the boys' schools and sometimes he catches the Metro-North to Grand Central and does the sights. He calls it research and says that one day he'll take the boys to the Guggenheim and they'll not spend the whole trip asking when they can have a McDonald's or where the gift shop is.

And, in the midst of all this, he allows himself to contact Eve about once a week. They talk about the weather and the news and she tells him how Jodie's getting on at university and he'll tell her about the book, or what there is to say about it anyway, and they avoid the massive subjects like Rose's death, her legacy, whether they are making the biggest mistakes of their lives by doing what they're doing.

He's banked Rose's money in a separate account and avoids talking to Celeste about it too. Sometimes he convinces himself he's saving it for the boys' college educations, other times it scorches a hole in his pocket so huge that all he can imagine is himself scooping up the bank notes from the sidewalk, folding them into the hands of a clerk at JFK and buying a ticket to Heathrow, then driving in his green Mercedes to where Eve works and taking her to live by the coast, to somewhere where the sea meets the sky.

It's odd, he thinks now, as he scrutinises the page proofs, how he's managed to shut his heart off from Eve. It's as though he's been living in a perpetual state of denial, mostly because it had hurt too much to love her and not be able to be with her, but also because he's not been able to make up his mind as to which bit of him is fraudulent; the man who's the husband and father he'd signed up to be, or the man who made love to the woman with the topaz eyes and huge heart. Whoever he is right now, he's stuck between these two. It's impossible to stay and impossible to go. He wants to want to do what he thinks is the right thing for his sons but knows that even as it is now, they have only a portion of his attention; the rest is three thousand miles away. Whichever way he looks at it, he is torn. He thought it would get easier in time, but it hasn't.

Take last night, for example. He'd sat on the deck and drunk his beer. The sky had seemed vast and inexplicable and he'd gone over in his head the conversation he'd had with Eve earlier.

'So,' he'd said, 'how are you?'

'I'm fine, thank you. You?'

'Yes, fine.'

'Any news?'

'Not really. Just more of the same. What about you?'

'Ditto.'

'What you got planned today?'

'Work this morning, then I might go out for a walk later if it doesn't rain. It'll be good to blow some of the cobwebs away. How's the book, by the way? You still pleased with the ending?'

Recently, she hadn't been saying much about her daily routine, it was all general stuff and, like just then, she'd turned the conversation to questions about him as quickly as possible.

He'd heard a seagull cawing in the background, imagined the tin-plated surface of the Thames near her office and her sitting in her car in the car park looking up at the windows and the sun bouncing off them and her walking along the towpath later, watching the boats cut their way through the water.

'Not pleased as such,' he said. 'Relieved, maybe. It's kind of the only way it could end.'

'And has Tom said anything about what may happen next?'

'No, we haven't really discussed it in any great detail. I think I've got an idea but it needs to ferment a bit longer. If I can face starting another book, that is!'

'Ferment? Like a fine wine, you mean?'

'Yep.' He'd laughed then and so had she and it was wonderful and awful and he'd closed his eyes and wished very hard that he could conjure her here, that she would be standing behind him with her hand on his shoulder and looking at the screen and pointing and saying, 'I think that should be a semi-colon there.'

As he'd finished his beer, Celeste had come out of the house. She'd just got in from work.

'Boy, I'm whacked,' she said. 'That was some day.'

'Uh huh.' He twisted the empty bottle around in his hands; the glass was warm now and he didn't want to put it down, didn't want to have to move from there.

'I think I'll go up. Got an early start. You coming?'

'In a minute.'

Celeste shivered. 'You sure you're not too cold out here?'

'No, I'm fine. Will be in, in a little while.'

And as she'd stepped back into the kitchen, she'd said casually, 'Boys OK today?'

'Yes, they're fine.'

It was probably the most inane conversation they'd ever had and it left him thinking, What the fuck am I doing here?

Later, she'd turned to him in bed and he'd felt the heat from her skin and she'd taken him in her hands and stroked his cock and he'd closed his eyes and made love to her for the first time in months but afterwards had felt empty, hollowed out, and she'd said, 'Well, night then,' and he'd said, 'Yes, goodnight. Sleep well,' and he'd lain there listening to her breathing and to the house clicking and settling around him.

So today, before the boys get home from school, Myles goes for a run. He runs down Frances Avenue, along McAllister, up Hollow Tree Road, down Taylor Avenue until he gets to Flax Hill Road and back to Frances Avenue. He listens to 'Eye Of The Tiger' by Survivor and 'You Get What You Give' by the New Radicals and once he's home and has showered, he sits in his cabin in the garden of the house in Norwalk, Connecticut and skips through the document on the screen until he gets to the end. Occasionally, as he goes through the document, he does this to remind himself, to reassure himself that the story ends the way he wants it to.

And it does.

The case of the murdered woman on the sand dunes remains unsolved. It is the only case DCI Derek Pletheroe has not closed down and he's replaced in the Homicide Department by a younger man who walks around the office like a panther, confident, elegant and powerful in his designer suit and his whiter-than-white shirt. Myles hopes that in the TV adaptation, if it ever happens, this character will be played by someone like Rupert Penry-Jones or Idris Elba. The team have farewell drinks for Pletheroe. He stays half an hour and then leaves with the carriage clock they've given him and tells them he's got a holiday cottage booked and will be taking up bird-watching. He travels north to where the moors are and tramps through the bracken and tries to get the air down into the bottom of his lungs and it's there on a Wednesday afternoon in the middle of October that DCI Derek Pletheroe slips, falls into a river and knocks his head against a rock and, as he gasps for air, the waters swirl around him. His body's carried by the rapids until it comes to rest in a tangle of tree roots. The very last scene of the book shows Myles's DCI with his eyes closed and a bruise darkening on his temple, the shallows lapping around him . . .

26

The next day Tom calls. It's ten in the morning in New York, three in the afternoon in London.

'Um,' he says, clearing his throat, 'how are you?'

'Fine, thanks,' Myles says. 'How are you?'

'Very good. Um, well the thing is . . .'

Myles has an uneasy feeling that it's not going to be good news.

'The publishers are wondering,' Tom continues and Myles can imagine his agent, his eyes dark, his face with its high cheekbones and his swept-back silver hair, drumming his slender fingers on his wooden desk, 'if you'd come over for a meeting. They're keen to know what you've got planned next, you know, after Pletheroe. They'd like to know if there's anything for them . . .' Tom's voice tails off.

Myles looks out of the cabin window. The scene is the same as yesterday. Anka is in the kitchen with the dog, the boys are at school, Celeste is at work but now suddenly and tantalisingly, a mere flight away is England: good, sturdy, familiar England, so different from this glossy American dream he'd promised himself he'd be living with a wife who actually loved him. How wrong he'd been to believe it could be any different over here.

'I'll come,' he says, not stopping to wonder whether the idea he thinks he has as to what he could write next is an idea at all, and whether any publisher anywhere would want anything to do with it even if it was.

It is surprisingly easy to leave. Anka is in charge of the boys and, like when he'd gone back for Rose's funeral, Celeste shows only a cursory interest at the prospect of him going. All she'd said, and as she'd done the last time, was, 'As long as you're back in time for Bruno's next match. It's our turn to do the car pool and Anka will be taking Orlando to swim club and I won't be able to . . .' He didn't listen to the rest and three days later he is in mid-air with the drone of the aircraft's engines thrumming like music through him and Eve doesn't yet know he's on his way because he hasn't known how to tell her that he is.

Being in transit is liberating. Up here, where the air hostesses glide through the cabin and people stretch their cramped limbs and wander up and down the aisles, watch movies, peel the plastic lids off trays of in-flight food, doze, chat to one another the way that strangers do, he feels free. He's no longer a homeowner, husband and father but he's Myles, the boy in the headmaster's office, the man who writes novels, the man who made love to Eve that late December afternoon when the light fell through the shutters and striped the floor like a tiger's coat.

The meeting with Tom is scheduled for the following morning so, when he lands, Myles shuffles with the rest of the passengers through passport control and then, with his carry-on bag, he's out in the terminal, standing stock-still in the crowd. The air is cold on his face, everywhere is shiny and vast. He longs for trees and narrow lanes, for the sound of birdsong.

He picks up his hire car from the Hertz desk. Outside the terminal the afternoon is sparkling, full of spring promise. The sky's the colour of cornflowers and it gladdens his heart. He should be driving into London; to the hotel he's booked which is a short walk from Tom's office. But instead, he finds himself heading west on the M4 and the signs for the M25 are a blur to his left and then there is junction 8/9, the stretch to junction 10. He takes the exit, sweeps round the corner to merge on to the A329M. The fields are plump with green, the light's soft. Outside it will be hot, a foretaste of summer, but here, cocooned by the car's air-conditioning system, he is cool and wondrously happy. Even so, he lets himself acknowledge that he's finding it odd driving on the left, odd driving a manual car again. Underneath the thrill of this unexpected journey, he is hoping he's not too late.

The flood plains next to the river are dry and firm and filled with people walking their dogs, playing football, just sitting and looking at the water, and the car park outside Eve's building is half-empty by the time he gets there. It is as though a public holiday has just been announced and he laughs a little to himself as he parks in a visitor's space and walks briskly up to the door. If he stops to think about what he's doing, though, he'll lose his nerve. All he can think of now is Eve and the sure knowledge that he was wrong to go the States; he knows now that he should have stayed and fought for her, that this is why he is here now. He had told Debs he wouldn't hurt Eve so, at last, has come to find her. He has come to say the things he left unsaid, do the things he left undone after Rose's funeral.

The rotating doors make a shushing noise; the metal of the handle is surprisingly cold to his touch. He puts his hands on the counter in front of the receptionist and asks for Eve. His voice is extraordinarily loud in his head.

'May I ask who's enquiring?'

The receptionist is flawless; her lips are painted carmine, her eyes shine out at him with a kind of glittery brightness.

'Just a friend,' he manages to say. He's lost five hours

of his life crossing the Atlantic and has no real idea what time it is.

The receptionist taps some keys on her keyboard with her perfectly manicured nails. She looks at the screen in front of her. This is taking for ever, Myles thinks.

Then she looks up at him. Perhaps, he wonders, she wishes she were not here but outside in the glory of the afternoon. For a second he feels some kind of compassion for her but then she says, 'I'm sorry. We have no one of that name working here.'

'You must have!' He knows he's shouting.

'I can assure you we don't. She left us last October.'

'Where did she go? Why did she leave? Do you have her forwarding details?'

'Again, I'm sorry, sir – ' she says this with a hint of disdain – 'I'm not at liberty to divulge any details. I'm sure you can understand.'

Myles searches his mind for hints in Eve's recent emails or their brief and unsatisfactory calls as to where she's actually been all these months. He'd always thought of her here, following her daily routine, going home to her house in Byron Road, talking to Debs . . . Ah! Myles says to himself, Debs!

'What about Debs?' he asks. 'Is she here?'

'Do you have a surname for this . . .' again there's an uncomfortable pause, 'Debs?'

Myles is convinced this woman is enjoying his discomfort.

He doesn't. He has no idea what her surname is. 'She looks like Mary Portas,' is all he can think of saying. 'But her hair's not as red.'

'Oh, I know who you mean.'

She waits, he shifts his position. His legs are aching; his head is starting to hurt.

'Well?' he asks. 'Is she here?'

'Again, I'm sorry, I really am . . .'

He doubts this somehow.

'. . . she's away on holiday at present. Back next week.'

Myles has had enough. He swings round, doesn't even say goodbye, but is out the rotating door and back in the car park before he knows where he is. The heat hits him this time and doesn't seem so benevolent now and, as if he's compensating himself for Eve not being there, he tells himself that before he goes back, he'll go to the lock-up, swap this hire car for his Mercedes. He will drive his own car again.

But for now, he drives to Byron Road and sits in the car outside the house where he believes Eve still lives. She'd obviously told him where she lived, but he'd never been here before; had never had the nerve to drive by it because he'd been afraid of what he might have seen. However, her car is not on the drive. Nor is her husband's van, the one he'd parked outside the house he'd worked on in Darell Road a couple of summers ago. Instead there is a young woman emerging from the front door, she is pushing a double buggy, has a small dog on a lead. It is obviously time for its afternoon walk. They get to the end of the drive.

He presses a button, the car window slides down. 'Excuse me,' Myles says.

The woman looks suspiciously at him. 'Yes?' she says. She is thin, looks tired, the children in the pushchair are flushed and sleepy.

'Does Eve still live here?'

'Oh, no, sorry. We moved in just after Christmas. The previous owners have moved away, I think.' She looks down at her children; the dog is pulling on the lead. She says, 'Billy! Sit! We won't be long.'

'Oh, well, thank you.' Myles can't think of what else to say. He closes the car window. The woman turns the buggy, the dog leaps up. They walk away.

'Where are you?' he asks Eve when she answers her phone a moment later. 'Where have you been all this time?'

27

She tells him, as she always knew she would have to eventually, if and when he'd ever said he was coming over, which he hadn't, not yet. When he rang to ask her where she was, he'd sounded like he always did, like he was an ocean away. Over the past year it had been as though the promise they made one another that winter afternoon had been preserved in a piece of amber which both of them had been too afraid to break open and discover what actually was inside.

And, two days later, she flexes her fingers, then attaches the buttonhole foot to her Janome Memory Craft sewing machine. She smooths out the fabric and bends her head towards the light from the anglepoise lamp on her work table. Every time she picks out a bolt of fabric from the chest on the other side of the room, she pauses and remembers Rose because each piece of material is redolent of her.

It took ages for Eve to reconcile herself to using Rose's dresses for her sewing business, but once the decision was made, it seemed so right that she often wonders why it took her so long, and now she's settled in her cottage overlooking Newgale Sands in Pembrokeshire and all of everything that happened before is miles and months away.

The house is at the end of the seafront, is an end terrace, has bay windows at the front, two bedrooms, and inside she's painted the walls a soft white. The floorboards have all been stripped back and there is a small front garden between her and the road, a cobbled yard at the back. She traded in her car and bought a new one which she parks in a lay-by three doors down. It is a simple house and it's wonderful to sew here like this with the sea outside her door and the sky stretching above and along it and, despite the constant conversation of the waves and the cries of the gulls, it's peaceful here.

And her business is going well. She's called it Scribble & Stitch and what started out as a few commissions for families nearby has grown and she now has jobs coming in from her website and a constant stream of orders. The kids' drawings are great and she replicates them faithfully, so if Daddy is drawn with an orange face, he gets an orange face; if Stanley the Stick Insect has ten legs, she gives him ten legs. Dave Jones from the pub makes the stands for the toys for her and she orders the brass plates from a company in Crewe. She stuffs the toys with Minicraft Supersoft stuffing and next to her work table the drawers of her sewing stand are crammed with buttons and pipe cleaners, scraps of leather, bits of lace.

Eve is happy here. She sews in the mornings and in the afternoons she walks along the sands or visits Dale and sits outside the Griffin Inn and scans the horizon across to Milford Haven. Sometimes she drives to Wooltack Point and, when the boats run, she crosses over to Skomer. Last autumn, just after she'd moved here, she saw the seal cubs basking in the shallows at the foot of the cliffs, their cries reminding her of something ancient. She's not lonely, has made friends in the village, has money enough, thanks to Rose's legacy and the proceeds from the house in Belle Avenue, and when it's wet or cold outside, she curls up in front of the fire and reads the detective stories Myles has written. She is on Book Four, is one of the few people who knows how Book Nine is going to end. She hasn't watched an episode of *Friends* in months.

There are, however, a few things which, when she lets them, cause her pain. She grieves for Rose and will often dream of her and wake confused as to why she can't call her up and hear her voice. She misses Jodie but consoles herself with the fact that even if she were still living with Andrew, Jodie would not be there most of the time but would be studying Law in Durham and working part-time as a waitress at the Marriott Hotel across the road from the Elvet Bridge, and all she'd have of her daughter would be snapshots of conversations and Skype calls and three days of her company over Christmas.

But mostly it's the thoughts of Andrew that are the most difficult to bear. She knows he doesn't really deserve to have been left the way he was but, in the months following Rose's funeral, Eve was filled by a kind of fury that took her completely by surprise; each day her heart seemed to grow heavier in her chest and her teeth felt too large for her mouth, just as they had done that moment before she first met Myles. And all the doubts and worries and uncertainties of the weeks between that day and when she'd slept with him and all the hours she'd spent missing him after he'd gone to America and before and after Rose died seemed to concertina and leave her raging. She wanted space and time and to be alone. To put it simply, she didn't want to be married to Andrew any more, she didn't want to work at Woodward Electronics. After years of being wife, mother, PA, friend, she wanted to discover if the person she thought she was when she was with Myles was the real Eve.

Telling Andrew had been awful.

It was a Saturday night in late September. They'd eaten spaghetti and he'd said, 'Don't forget I have a gig tomorrow night,' and she'd said, 'Oh, OK, we can eat at lunchtime if you like.'

'I'll probably be at band practice from about eleven and then we'll go straight from there to the gig.'

'Via the pub, I presume?' She'd sounded as bad-tempered as she'd felt.

'Mmm,' Andrew said. 'Most likely.' And he'd changed channels on the TV without asking her what she wanted to watch.

'Andrew?' Eve had had no idea she was going to say what she said next. It just came out from somewhere deep down, somewhere unexplained and uncharted.

'Mmm,' he said again, this time studying his phone and pressing a few of the keys. It made a whooshing noise as the text he'd typed was sent. She did not know who he was messaging.

'Andrew. I've made a decision.'

'Oh.'

'Could you turn the TV off and put your phone down, do you think? This is important.'

Grudgingly, he did both. And it was the look on his face which convinced Eve. If she'd been in any doubt before, now she was certain that what she had to say couldn't not be said. It's strange, she thought, how this can have happened, how we can be so different from the children we were when we met, when he first kissed me behind the science block after double Chemistry and how we bought a house together and furnished it and had Jodie and lost Verity and Rose and how his parents had never really liked me but had tolerated me through Christmases and birthdays and the occasional holiday in Kent. There was then and there is now and Eve doesn't really know what had happened to them in between. All she knew was that the passion and conviction had gone and all that was left was old affection and the expectation of loyalty and that neither of these was love.

She remembered back to when her husband had come home from work the day she'd first spoken to Myles and how familiar and good Andrew had seemed but how, over the months that followed, she'd come to realise that this familiarity and goodness were more likely constructs of her own making; they were not fundamental or necessarily real. The distance had grown and spread until even their love for Jodie couldn't bridge it and here she was on the brink of telling him she was leaving.

'Well?' he said impatiently. He tapped his foot on the carpet.

'I want to go.'

'Go where?'

'Just go.'

'What do you mean?'

'I want to leave here, move somewhere else, do something else.'

'I don't.'

'I know. I want to go on my own.'

'On your own?' His voice was scornful, disbelieving. 'What do you mean, on your own? What could you possibly do that's different from this? Where could you go?'

'I'm thinking of using Rose's money, buying myself a house by the sea, setting up a sewing business like I've always wanted to.'

'Have you? I mean, have you always wanted to do that? If so, why didn't I know?'

Andrew looked at her then, his eyes filled with something she could not describe; it was a mixture of sadness and defiance.

'Yes, I have,' she said.

There was a pause. She didn't dare say anything further, didn't know what she could say.

He stood and walked over to the fireplace and then turned to her. He seemed very tall and he said, 'Is there someone else? Is that it? There's someone else!'

And she could reply honestly that there wasn't. 'No,' she said, 'there's no one else,' and there wasn't. If he'd said, 'Was there someone?' she would have had to say, 'Yes.' If he'd said, 'Do you want there to be someone else?' she would have had to say, 'Yes.' But she hadn't seen Myles since the funeral. They exchanged weekly messages about the weather and the news and what their children were doing; it hardly constituted an affair, perfect or otherwise. So, she could tell Andrew that there was no one else, that she wanted to go because she needed to go, that her main ambition was to be alone.

He didn't fight for her to stay and even now, months later, when it's all sorted and they've sold the house in Byron Road to a couple with two small children and a dog, this fact hurts her. In fact, sometimes she misses the house more than she does him. They've settled some of Rose's money on Jodie to help her through university and Andrew's moved back to live with his parents while, as he says, he takes stock of the situation, and the house in Belle Avenue has also been sold, this time to some people from Windsor who wanted an annexe for the woman's mother, a need that the downstairs flat fulfilled exactly. And Eve has taken some of what's left of Rose's estate and bought herself this house where she sits by the window and looks out at the sea and sews and walks along the beach and imagines her and Myles's names etched into the sand stretching out as far as the eye can see. But, despite everything, she knows she's done the right thing and Debs knows it too. They spent New Year's Eve in the Duke of Edinburgh halfway along the bay, drinking shots and getting pissed and telling each other that life was bloody wonderful.

But telling Jodie had been even worse than telling Andrew.

Jodie had come home from Thailand aglow. The boy called Al with whom she'd danced on the beach at sunrise had not forsaken her and they'd promised one another they would survive the whole uni thing and, for Eve, it was, despite everything, for the best for it to have been this way.

This was what she'd most dreaded; the thought she was letting her daughter down. Her promise to her family had been to keep it intact, to give Jodie something that was permanent and, telling her that she was leaving, was carving everything Jodie had ever known down the middle, was like a pain worse than childbirth.

Then the awful words were out of Eve's mouth and the seconds before her daughter spoke were suspended between them, stretching from one side of the kitchen to the other, and it was as though the planet had shifted on its axis. Eve had had to hold on to the counter to steady herself, but the Jodie who had come home from Thailand had been both radiant and forgiving, and she took a step towards Eve, held out her hands and said, 'Mum, it's OK. It really is. All we ever want is for those we love to be happy, that's right, isn't it? So, I'm happy: there's Al and uni and

Dad'll be OK and whatever happens you'll always be my mum and I'll always be . . .'

Eve couldn't let her brave and remarkable daughter finish; it was too much to ask of her to do so. Instead, they held on to one another and Eve inhaled the scent of her daughter's hair; it smelled of coconut shampoo; it was soft as silk.

The bobbin thread's run out and Eve decides to stop for the day. She tidies up a bit and stands at the window while she stretches. She's tired and her back aches. It's one o'clock and she should make some lunch. The early morning clouds have cleared and the sun promises warmth. She makes her way to the kitchen.

As she does so, she thinks of Myles. She has tried very hard not to miss him, but she does. The calls and emails are not enough and when she's standing on the cliffs looking out from the coast towards Ireland she can imagine being lifted across the Atlantic, that the sea winds carry his name and that his voice is like music on the waters.

When he'd called two days ago, his voice had been faint, raspish, half-hidden by the sound of a car's engine. She'd imagined him parked up on the side of a road close to where he lives and somewhere nearby stop lights would hang over the highway and a yellow school bus would pass through the intersection. She hadn't told him about the move or the business, about leaving Andrew and about the nights she's slept with the sea a distant moan outside her window, thinking of him, because she didn't want him to know. He'd made his decision, it wouldn't be fair of her to change the parameters now, although there had been times when her fingers had itched to call him or email him and tell him. 'Come,' she'd say. 'Come here, come now! I'm ready. I've made my choice.' And, so in the call, when he'd asked her where she was, all she'd told him were the facts, nothing more; just that she lived in a small house by the coast in West Wales and that she sewed, that she watched the sun on the sea and heard the waves lap on Newgale Sands.

Now, however, en route to the kitchen she sees Rose's box in between the photographs of Rose's parents and the man with the pale eyes which she's put on the top shelf of the bookcase in the lounge. She makes herself a sandwich and a cup of tea and takes them and the box to her chair by the fire. For the first time in all the years she's known Rose, and for the first time in all the months since she lost her, she opens the box. Why today? She has no idea. It's an instinctive thing, a necessary thing.

Inside she finds a telegram and a newspaper cutting about the launch of a ship called the *Ajax Star*, she finds a bundle of letters tied with ribbon, a piece of notepaper headed 'Hotel Byron, Athens'; she finds a bus ticket dated

1 December 1966 and sheets of exquisitely thin white tissue paper folded neatly into a square.

And at the bottom of the box there is a letter addressed to her. It's from Rose and it's dated the day after they went to the races the December before last. It says:

Dear Eve,

If I can give you one gift it is this. I loved a man called Henry. I made a choice to live without him and then he died, suddenly, tragically and I was never able to say goodbye or to tell him I'd been wrong to make the decision I did. I've spent the rest of my life regretting this and missing him and imagining what life would have been like if we'd taken a chance. I don't want you to know what this has been like, so what I've done in my will is to give you and Myles the chance to make a choice and I hope and pray that whenever you find this letter, you will have done so or will find the strength to. I have loved you dearly, Eve, and always will.

Rose

Eve carefully folds the letter and puts it back in the box with the telegram, letters, newspaper cutting and tissue paper and she clears away her plate and cup and locks the back door. She gathers her coat and boots from the stand in the hall, then picks up her bag and keys and opens the front door. She will, she decides, walk to the end of bay and back and, as she walks, Rose is in her head and her heart.

With her hair streaming out behind her and the wind whipping her face and the wet sands gleaming, Eve weeps and the air is salty and, as she does most days, she whispers a small prayer that today will be the day that Myles will come, today he will find her. But she knows that he won't, that he can't; they are far too far away from one another now.

As she walks past the pub she'd got drunk in with Debs, she sees a car parked in front of it. The car is light green and there's a man standing by it. The sun is woven into his beard. He is watching her. He is waving.

28

Eve can hear him tapping on the keys of his laptop through the ceiling as she sews. There's the occasional pause and then the sound starts up again. Briefly she remembers how he touched her that morning when they woke and that afterwards they'd lain in the bed and she'd curled into his body for warmth. His breath had been sweet on her neck.

Later she goes upstairs and knocks on the door of the room where he's working.

'Brought you a coffee. Hope that's OK?'

'Lovely,' he says, turning round in the chair to smile at her.

'How's it going?' she asks. 'How much do you think you'll get done before you have to go back?'

'Oh a fair, bit I'd say,' he answers.

'Definitely no more Pletheroe, then?' Eve asks.

'No, I've left him and the world he lived in behind.

When I met Tom yesterday, he agreed I should write the story you and I talked about.'

She leans over his shoulder and looks at the screen. 'Where have you got to?'

'The first day, the day at the house in Belle Avenue.'

'Still a lot to do, then,' she says, resting her hand on his arm.

'Yes,' he says. 'I have, but it's OK, it's going OK.'

He is sure it will be. Since being here, the words have rung clearly in his head, no longer is he frozen; once again he's come full circle, but it's a good kind of circle this time.

Myles looks out of the window at the sea; it is slate grey, an almost blue. 'I'll go back,' he says, 'sort it out with Celeste, work out how to carry on seeing the boys and be here, with you. It won't be perfect, but it will be as close to perfect as it can be. Is that OK, Eve? Will that be OK?'

She doesn't answer. Instead she points at the screen and asks, 'Should that be a semi-colon there?'

'Get away with you, woman!' He laughs as he says this and lifts his face to hers.

She kisses him and outside the waves breathe and somewhere far away the other people they love and once loved may be thinking of them, of the sea and of love, or maybe they're not.

ACKNOWLEDGEMENTS

Once again, huge thanks are due to my amazing agent, Teresa Chris, and the wonderful Jo Dickinson; their advice and faith in this novel have been stupendous. Thank you as ever to the team at Quercus for making such a lovely book from my manuscript.

I have dedicated this novel to my late mother, but the inspiration for the story came from outside my family and has no real basis in fact. Instead, the story started with a photograph. I was once shown a picture of a reception celebrating the launch of a Greek ship in 1955 and there was something about the body language of two of the people in the photograph that made me think of hidden passions and unspoken secrets. Following this, I saw how the light shone on a stained-glass window in the front door of a house near to where I live. The rest of it: the characters, the settings, the heartbreak, grew from these small beginnings.

Thanks are also due to Gill Learner for her help with things horticultural; to my cousin, Lin Frith, for her generous advice about sewing and her permission to use the name of her real business, Scribble & Stitch; to the Corporate Research Forum for letting me piggyback on their conference in Athens; to Helen Skipper for information about life in New York, to Nigel Hadleigh for the stuff about running and to my son, Liam, for Myles's playlist.

Lastly, there are many other people to thank: my family, friends and you. For reading my book, you I thank most of all.

READING GROUP QUESTIONS

1 Do you believe Eve and Myles are first attracted to one another because they are dissatisfied with their marriages or because this attraction is instinctive and inevitable?

2 Both Andrew and Celeste seem unaware that their partners are unhappy in their existing relationships. How common do you think this lack of communication is within marriages and what should/could the characters have done to remedy the situation?

3 Neither Eve nor Myles grew up in a loving family. How do you think this has informed their notion of family?

4 Eve and Myles are both obviously conflicted by their notion of family and want to do right by their children. However, what is the right thing in such circumstances?

5 Eve's daughter is on the cusp of leaving home. Myles's

children are much younger, much more dependent. How does this affect Eve and Myles and the choices with which they are faced?

6 Rose's story acts as both foil and relief to Eve's. What are the similarities and differences between the two women's stories? What are the differences between the conventions of the fifties and sixties versus the conventions of now and how are their choices affected by the times in which they live?

7 Was Rose right to encourage Eve's relationship with Myles? What do you think are her motives for doing so?

8 Both women choose to sacrifice their happiness for the sake of others: Rose leaves Henry to look after her mother and Eve does not tell Myles of her move to Wales to protect him from having to make a decision about his own future. Do you think they were right to do these things?

9 Eve's life is one of routine and security; it is not a life of creativity and uncertainty. By contrast, Myles's career as a writer seems to fulfil part of his creative need. However, he too is bored with his writing life and wants to try something new. How does the character of DCI Pletheroe reflect Myles's own artistic and emotional outlook and how aware are you, as a reader, of this?

10 Myles's former relationship with Louisa scarred him and possibly caused him to marry Celeste for the wrong reasons. By contrast Eve has known Andrew since they were at school. What difference do you think these past histories make to Eve's and Myles's attitudes to their marriages and one another?

11 Neither Andrew nor Celeste is inherently bad; they both have some redeeming features but both are unsympathetically drawn by the author. To what extent are they to blame for what happens to them and what, in your opinion, are the things they do that are fundamental in the ultimate breakdown of both their marriages?

12 Do you think the choices Eve and Myles make at the end of the novel are the right ones?

So, this is how the day begins.

A man is running across the concourse at Paddington Station. He is obviously late for something. Maybe he caught the eight sixteen instead of the eight ten from somewhere and so is hurrying towards the steps of the Underground, his suit jacket flapping like wings, his briefcase knocking against his thigh. At the moment he skirts the noticeboard alerting passengers to the fact that skating and cycling are forbidden and that thieves operate in this area, the girl, who is actually an art student from the University of Greenwich trying to earn some extra cash, and who is dressed, much to her distress, like something out of a Thomas Hardy novel, turns abruptly to walk back to the gazebo that bears the name of the company who have decided to give out free yogurts on this March morning, thus bumping into the man, causing the tray she's carrying to crash to the floor, the man to shout, 'Oh!' and Fern Cole to look back over her shoulder, one foot poised at the top of the escalator on her way down to the Circle and District Lines.

It is at this moment, this particular, tiny, breathless, coin-edge moment, that Fern sees the man she used to love standing on the far side of the station under the departure boards, gazing in her direction.

Fern's decision now is whether to lift her foot, turn and walk towards him while conjuring up something debonair and sophisticated to say; something like, 'My goodness, Elliott, how wonderful to see you,' and proffering her cheek in a way she's studied during long afternoons at the hairdressers' flicking through the society pages of magazines, or whether she should carry on down to the Tube, get her train to Victoria, meet Juliet, pretend she hasn't seen him.

Would it be better if she swiped her Oyster card over the sensor at the barrier, strode purposefully along the corridor, pretended to look at the advertisements on the walls? After all, she's managed not to remember him quite successfully over the past twenty-five years, hasn't she?

But she has time to walk across the station to where he is standing; she's not due to meet Jules at Victoria for another hour. It's just how the trains worked out; Fern's from Reading, Jules's from Kent, they planned to take the District Line out to Chiswick. How odd, she thinks, as she looks down at her boots – they're new and still slightly too tight – that the studio changed the date of their pottery class to today. If it had been last Tuesday as planned, she wouldn't be here now like this, in this state of limbo, faced with this decision. On any other day she wouldn't be here now, like this.

It's a decision she doesn't want to have to make. She had woken that morning nestled in the certainties of her life: Jack's steady breathing next to her, the shape he made in their bed, the knowledge that when the alarm sounded he would stretch to turn it off, then reach out and rest his hand lightly on her hip. This was familiar and right. It is what she had chosen.

Later, when he left for work he'd touched her arm as she stood by the sink rinsing out a milk bottle. 'I won't be late tonight, I shouldn't think,' he'd said.

'Oh, OK,' she'd replied, turning quickly to smile at him. She didn't need to study his face; its features were printed on to the back of her eyes.

'Hope you have a good day,' he added, hesitating by the door. She knew he was trying to remember what she was going to do today but that it wouldn't matter if he didn't. She would tell him about it later. They would be OK anyway.

'Thanks,' she called out happily to him as he closed the front door. Waiting in the quiet that followed, she heard him start the car, heard its distant purr and the sound of him reversing it out of the drive. She put the milk bottle on the draining board and dried her hands. She did not feel his absence because he was still everywhere.

Now, at the station, Fern considers what to do. She knows that her sons, whatever they are doing, do not think of her as she does of them and that this is as it should be. They don't seem to carry with them the same kind of inbuilt barometer she has grafted just under her skin; the thing that seems to allow her to sense how they are across the miles that now separate them. It's as though she has a slide show in her head which plays constantly: pictures of them running, the soundtrack of their laughter, the shapes they too make in her life. They wouldn't mind her saying hello to an old friend on her way to meet Jules; it wouldn't mean anything to them. It shouldn't mean anything to her either and it wouldn't matter to Jack. They all had enough together anyway; this would not threaten anything.

So, she unpauses her foot from its position hovering over the top of the escalator and swings around saying, 'I'm sorry,' as she dodges a cross-looking woman in a bright red coat who's bearing down on her. The woman's hair has been badly dyed a shade of stale copper that clashes with her coat and makes her look somewhat bilious.

Crossing the concourse towards where Elliott is standing, Fern feels a bit like an iron filing being pulled towards a magnet . . .

* * *

DO YOU REMEMBER THE MOMENT

YOUR LIFE CHANGED FOREVER?

THE MOMENT

CLAIRE DYER

'Emotional and brilliant' *Sun on Sunday*

'Like a modern-day *Brief Encounter*, this will hit a nerve with anyone who has ever wondered: "What if?"' *Bella*

'Heady, thought-provoking and quietly lovely' *Star*

'A man, a woman, and a "what-if" moment that will give you goosebumps. A genuine contender for the crown of this year's *One Day*' Louise Candlish

'Beautifully written, with perfect form and pace. Fern and Elliott's vivid emotional journey will stay with me' Hilary Boyd, author of *Thursdays in the Park*